I0653932

The Well Within

~The Well Within~

Book 1

Joshua Kern

Contents

Other Books by Joshua Kern

The Well Within

Stand Alone

The Ridden

Duologies & Box Sets

The Game of Gods: Arc 1 Duology Box Set

The Dungeon Alaria: The World of Alaria Arc 1 Duology Box Set

Chapter 1

The imposing form of the old and supposedly haunted building loomed in front of Jack and his friend, Steve. Steve had convinced him that tonight was the night they went on an adventure, never mind that it was a Saturday night or that nothing exciting ever happened in their sleepy little Colorado town. Steve was determined to start something, and he had chosen the old haunted building as the place to start.

It was an old school building that had been abandoned since the late fifties when a fire had broken out on the third floor. Supposedly, three students and a teacher had died in the fire. That was the legend anyway. It was also untrue; Jack had asked around and actually looked through old newspapers on the fire.Only a small part of the story was true. There had indeed been a fire, but no-one had died in it. The fire had been long suspected to be the work of an arsonist, but it had never been proven. The fire had started late at night after everyone had gone home for the night.

None of that meant the building wasn't scary looking and more than a little intimidating. It was. It was also dark and there seemed to be a palpable aura of unease that practically dripped from the building.

There was a crash in the building and the windows on the third floor flared with an unearthly light. Jack stumbled back in fright at the noise and the sight of the briefly glowing windows. There was a noise behind him as rocks ground together, followed by the sound of feet hitting the ground in rapid succession. Steve had run away and left him alone.

What a great friend he was! Jack thought sardonically before focusing his attention back on the building in front of him. His eyes were drawn to the third-floor windows as he thought about the flash of light and the crash of noise. He wondered what could have caused it?

Another crash tore through the night air a split-second before light flared white-hot through the panes of aged glass.

Before he could convince himself it was a bad idea, Jack found his feet already carrying him towards the large imposing doors of the building. They were monstrous things, large and heavy to the extreme. One of them hung slightly open on a busted, twisted hinge. Jack squeezed himself through the small gap between the doors and entered the dark building.

Jack thumbed the back of his flashlight, illuminating the darkened interior with its bright light. Old, faded wallpaper and posters lined the walls, mixed with vast splotches of water damage. Weathered tiles full of holes hung from the ceiling, drooping chaotically. Carpet clung to the edges of the room, everywhere else it had long since been worn down or eaten by rodents leaving unpolished wood in its wake.

Darkened hallways lined either side of the entryway leading into the unknown. A stairwell at the back of the entry-hall dominated his attention as he stepped carefully over the creaking floorboards and onto the first rotted step. He tested each step with care before settling his full weight onto it.

Another crash sounded from above, causing Jack to crouch in fright, with his feet on different stairs. His flashlight swung wildly as his wide eyes looked at the ceiling. Clouds of dust fell in droves around him, coating his face and dark-colored clothes.

Quickly, he stood and rushed up the rest of the stairs, no longer bothering to test each of them before using them. A large, open space greeted him as he crested the top of the stairs.

This particular set of stairs went no higher. To get to the third floor, he would have to find a different set of stairs. Jack swung his flashlight around, trying to decide which way to go. A large classroom stood in front of him, its missing door revealing a black hole into the room. On either side, he could see more classrooms extending down long, dark hallways. The water damage up here was worse, causing the walls to bloat outward in places. Some sort of thin off-white tile had been used to cover the floor instead of the carpeting that had been eaten away on the ground floor.

The thin tiles curved up at their edges, threatening to catch the feet of anyone not paying proper attention to where they walked. The glue that had been holding them down was yellowed, and no longer affixed to the tile in many places. The water had loosened and destroyed its bond over time, warping the tiles and damaging the wood underneath.

Jack looked at the tiles warily. With only the light of the flashlight to see by, he would have to choose his steps very carefully. The tiles didn't look sharp or anything, but he didn't think falling on them would be a pleasant experience either. It would be best to choose a different route for now if he was able. The hallways to the left seemed to have suffered the brunt of the water damage. With nearly all of the tiles, he could see being warped and curled in places. The right while also suffering from the same kind of problem didn't appear to be as bad. There were tiles that way that didn't look warped at all.

To the right then, Jack thought with a weak grin. He hadn't been thinking clearly when he had rushed inside. Now that he had a chance to calm down, he was beginning to regret his hasty actions. There was no telling what he might be walking into. Ghosts or monsters of some kind, or maybe a drug dealer cooking up some kind of drug. The possibilities were endless and the chance of him getting hurt or worse grew with each new one, he thought up.

His feet wavered in indecision as he tried to convince himself that it was nothing dangerous and that he should continue on for just a little longer. Truth be told, while this was not the way he had wanted to explore this building, he had always wanted to do so. He just would have preferred to do it during the day, and not at night, while something kept exploding above him.

He squeezed his eyes shut and gritted his teeth as he fought against himself. The supernatural world did not exist. There was no such thing as ghosts and monsters. Whatever was causing the noise had a logical and probably reasonable explanation, and that wouldn't be drug dealers. The flashes of light were much too conspicuous to be someone like that. They tried to avoid attention, not draw it to them like these flashes of light and noise were doing right now.

Jack felt the knot that had developed in his stomach loosen at these thoughts and felt himself step forward at last. Opening his eyes, he kept his flashlight trained on the floor as he began to carefully weave his way down the long empty hallway. Classrooms that were missing their doors, or just had them hanging open, crept up from the corners of his vision as he tried to ignore them. He might have convinced his feet and stomach that monsters weren't real, but that didn't mean he was going to willingly look into the abyss and tempt it to prove him wrong.

A creak sounded above his head, causing him to stop and point his flashlight at the ceiling. The ceiling was bare and devoid of any covering, instead revealing a mass of wires and old ductwork alongside old, ratty insulation. His eyes caught on some motes of dust slowly falling to the ground from where they had been disturbed. Something or somebody was definitely up there.

More noise began to filter down as he concentrated on his hearing, choosing to close his eyes once more. It sounded like someone was talking, well cursing was more likely from the harsh tone he could hear. It was impossible to understand any of the words; however, it was obvious that whoever was up there was not in a good mood.

Feeling slightly more at ease knowing for certain that it was a person and not a monster, he opened his eyes and continued on down the hall. The sound of someone talking harshly above him continued to filter softly down until he was able to discern that the person talking was female. He still couldn't understand what she was saying, but he was now certain that whoever was up there was female.

The far edge of where his flashlight beam illuminated caught his eye as he saw the end of the hallway. Hopefully, he would find some stairs leading up when he got there. He found himself intensely curious about what kind of girl would be in a place like this so late at night, and he really wanted to know just what she was doing and why she was so mad.

His feet caught on the edge of a linoleum tile in his sudden rush to find the stairs, causing him to stumble forward and onto his knees. His dark jeans protected his knees as he slid onto them and then slightly forward. A particularly loud explosion sounded as he finished his short slide. Light filled the end of the hallway as it filtered down from a stairwell that he couldn't see just yet.

His hands clapped over his ears at the loud noise, dropping the flashlight in his haste to protect his ears. The flashlight spun when it hit the floor, causing the beam of light to illuminate the entire hallway in rapid fashion. All around him, he could see clumps of dust and other heavier things falling to the floor and coating him in yet another layer of dust.

With a disgusted sigh, he pulled a hand from over his ear and raked it through his shaggy hair. The movement dislodged some of the dust and anything else that might have gotten stuck in it. His light brown hair hung over his eyes as he ran his fingers through his hair a second time before pulling it back into position once more. He liked his hair slightly longer than was fashionable. It was only when something got into his hair that he regretted having it longer than necessary.

His other hand finally dropped from his ear as he picked up the flashlight from where it had fallen. He had just finished standing when he heard a noise of a different sort than he had been hearing. It was a deep, long cracking noise that he could feel at the very core of his being. It rumbled through him like a large, deep bass drum.

Spinning in place, he shined the flashlight back down the hallway from where he had come, not seeing anything but falling motes of dust. The deep cracking noise continued pulling his eyes toward the ceiling as he felt a rumble through his feet. There was a crash as a large piece of ductwork fell from the ceiling and rolled across the damaged flooring.

Jack stumbled backward in fright at the noise, catching the heel of his foot on a piece of warped tile and falling hard onto his back. Pain shot through his back as it crushed the sharp edges of tile that had been pointing upward as he fell. The air in his lungs exploded outwards with a gasp as he lay there in shock.

Over his head, he could see an actual crack forming in the ceiling that continued to grow, snaking its way down the hall. His eyes widened in terror as he realized what was about to happen just before it did. Forcing his sore and breathless body into a roll, he hugged the side of the hall as the ceiling began to fall down around him. Curling into a ball, he tried to protect himself during the long moments that seemed to stretch into eternity as the upper floor fell around him. The sound of wood falling around him and the loud crashing of metal filled the air and deafened him momentarily.

Jack kept himself curled up tightly until the wood had finished settling around him. Carefully, he began the long and laborious process of extracting himself from the mess that now surrounded him. Somehow, during everything that had just happened, he had managed to keep his grip on his flashlight. The air was heavy with dust and other particulates that clogged his mouth within seconds. He was forced to cover his mouth with his shirt in an effort to get any air that he could actually breathe.

Right away, he could see just how lucky he had gotten. Where he was had been hit lightest of the rest of the hallway, with most of the floor still holding strong above his head. The rest of the hall, though, was blocked from where the third floor had actually collapsed.

Hopefully, the stairs he was near would allow him to go down as well as up, otherwise, he was going to have a problem. Then he remembered the voice he had heard above him earlier. Whoever had been up there might be buried in the mess in front of him, requiring his help.

Choosing his steps carefully, he made his way to the pile of debris that now blocked the rest of the hall.

"Hello?" He called out before coughing from the thick layer of dust and grime that had clung to his tongue and esophagus. "Hello? Are you alright?" He tried again, calling out after covering his mouth with his shirt.

He remained quiet as he strained his ears to hear through the still-shifting rubble. A low moan reached his ears as he stood there. With a sudden burst of energy, Jack surged towards the top of the pile, his feet slipping and sliding as he struggled to the top. From the top, he could see that only a small portion of the floor above had collapsed into the hallway.

The bottom of the third floor was still a few feet above him, even at the top of the pile. He had been expecting to see much more damage than there was. The sound of everything falling around him as he hugged the wall still filled his head with noise minutes later. Another moan trickled through the air and reached his ears. The noise was slightly muffled and the thick dust that filled the air made everything more than a few feet away, hazy and indistinct.

Choosing his steps carefully, he began his descent from the top of the debris pile and back to the ruined floor. The pile stood just over six feet in height, slightly above the top of his head. Each step needed to be carefully placed, otherwise he would find himself stuck or slipping onto one of the many sharp or pointy pieces of metal and wood.

A shallow cough and groan buried beneath rubble echoed up from beneath his feet. Marking the spot in his mind, he looked forward and leaped from the pile, landing on a warped piece of old aluminum ductwork. It crumpled beneath his feet as he landed cushioning his fall and helped to prevent him from sliding into anything dangerous.

Stopping to catch his breath, he looked back at where he had just jumped from. It was probably a good thing that he had jumped from where he had, everything below that point was covered in a thick layer of chalky dust and pieces of insulation. The chances for him to slip and injure himself would have been too high.

Carefully, he extracted his feet from the crumpled and malformed aluminum, taking care of where he placed his feet. With his flashlight firmly in hand, he studied the edge of the pile, trying to decide where he would most likely find her.

She hadn't been at the top of the pile, so that meant that she had fallen down and then been covered. From where he had heard her coughing, it seemed likely that she was near the edge and had been further covered when everything had settled.

A rasping cough came from the floor near his feet.

"Hello?" He called out, crouching near where he thought it had come from.

"Is someone there?" A raspy voice asked weakly.

"Are you alright? I'm going to try and get you out. Just hang on!" Jack found himself calling out as he began to panic at the thought of the person being hurt. He had no medical training, he had no idea what needed to be done for anything serious.

"I... I think I'm fine, but everything is pressing on my stomach, so I can't breathe properly." The raspy voice forced out in a weak rush.

"Hold on, I'm going to get you out of there!" Jack said as he began pulling pieces of wood from the pile and throwing them behind him. If the speaker was having trouble breathing, then he needed to work as quickly as possible.

With that thought in mind, he began talking aloud, letting his voice fill the air as he continued moving the pile of debris.

"I came here tonight on a mutual dare from my friend. We thought it would be interesting, maybe even a small adventure. The rumors about this building have everything from ghosts to monsters living here. I even heard one once about a fire-ax wielding psychopath. I don't think anyone takes them seriously anymore, but no-one is allowed in the building normally and we hadn't heard of anyone exploring it either, so we decided that we were going to." Jack stopped talking for a moment as he grunted under the weight of the wood he was moving.

"Anyway, we get here and practically right away we see lights flashing on the top floor and this loud crashing sound. He ends up running away in fright, while I stupidly decide to come inside by myself. For all I know, you really are an ax-wielding psychopath who is going to eat my face as soon as you're free!" Jack paused at that thought. "You're not, are you? I mean, you're not some crazy person that is going to kill me as soon as you're free, right?"

The bubble of laughter that sounded forth from the pile was clearer than before. He must be nearly there.

"No, I'm not going to eat your face or kill you!" The now clearly female voice laughingly said.

"Humph never can be too careful." Jack sniffed as he resumed moving the pile. "Can you breathe easier yet? I'm not entirely sure where you are."

"Yes, there isn't as much weight on me now as there was before. I can feel everything shifting above me." The words came out as he moved another large piece of flooring from the pile.

With how much had ended up on top of her, he was amazed that she was still alive. He shuddered to think what would have happened to him if he had been the one to have this much weight fall on him. She must have gotten supremely lucky to have survived, or maybe she was just tougher than him. It wouldn't be that hard. He may have been six feet tall, but he was fairly scrawny.

He was built more for speed than for strength, and he was, fast, that is. He had been on the track team since middle school, running in all the events. Speed is all he had, however. He had tried cross-country once, and it had nearly killed him, he was not built for that kind of endurance either. No matter how hard he tried to push himself, that had never changed.

With one last heave, he managed to shift another large piece of smashed ductwork to the side, revealing a lightly tanned hand with bright purple, almost lavender painted fingernails. Before he could stop himself, Jack found himself reaching for the newly revealed hand, praying that it belonged to whoever he had been speaking to and not to someone else.

The skin was warm, and the fingers wrapped around his own, and then everything went white as he felt his body being thrown backward with an impossible force. He felt his back impact a wall and then something hit his stomach, stealing the remainder of his breath from his battered body.

Flashes of white suffused his vision as he struggled for breath. He had lost his grip on his flashlight and saw it laying on the ground, its beam of light pointing away from him. His eyes caught on the figure standing before the pile of rubble.

She was glorious looking in her pair of smudged tan cargo pants and tight black top, revealing tight muscled arms. Long dark blonde hair clung to her face and fell in waves down her back, a layer of dust and grime caked her face except where sweat had run through it. She was beautiful, and she was sparking with electricity.

Jack felt his breath hitch in his throat as there was a sharp pain from deep in his stomach. Glancing down, he saw a long piece of metal sticking from his stomach, blood dripping down its length.

"I thought you said you weren't going to kill me!" He managed to gasp out as he felt gravity begin to pull heavily at his eyes. The pain was there distantly in his mind, but the sudden cold he felt throughout his entire body was managing to keep it at bay. His eyes flickered open one last time, and he saw the girl from before running towards him in slow motion.

Silly, he thought, if she was just going to move that slowly towards him, then why even bother. He should have stayed home, he could have been in his bed asleep and warm right now. Instead, he had a hole in his stomach and was colder than he had ever been in his life. A shiver swept through his body, causing his stomach to spasm around the metal sticking through it, tearing the wound open more.

Jack felt his eyes close as everything began to grow dim, and then he knew nothing more.

Chapter 2

Jack felt little pain in his stomach as he slowly returned to consciousness. He could feel something wrapped tightly around his midsection, slightly constricting his chest from the pressure. He breathed in deeply as his eyes flickered open, surprised that there was still only a little bit of pain.

He could vividly remember being thrown backward and having a sharp piece of metal pierce him. The feeling of cold coming over him as his blood dripped from his body. The beautiful young woman that he had helped free. He could remember all of it, but none of it even so much as hinted at where he was. He should be dead or in a serious amount of pain. Instead, he was lying in a comfortable bed, alive, and in very little pain.

His hands roved over his stomach as his eyes took in his dim surroundings. Wherever he was, there was very little light in the room itself. A closed door in the corner had light spilling in from the crack underneath it, lending the space the little illumination it possessed.

Jack looked down at his chest as his hand felt the rough edges of the bandage that was wrapped around him. For the first time, he realized that he was barely clothed. His shirt was missing, as were his shoes and socks. Luckily, whoever had bandaged him and taken his clothes had left him his pants.

Pulling the blanket that covered his legs to the side, he carefully swung his legs over the edge of the bed and onto the floor. Making sure his feet were flat on the ground, he struggled to stand and then promptly crumpled to the floor with a groan and a thud. He had pulled at the wound in his stomach when he had stood; the resulting flash of pain was off though. It wasn't a sharp pain like he would have expected for such a fresh wound, but instead, it had felt more like he was pulling at stitches or partially knitted together skin. It had been a dull pain that pulled at the core of his stomach.

Carefully, he hauled himself to his knees and began pulling at the edges of the bandage. He needed to see what had been done to him.

The door to the room swung open with a slam, startling him and drawing his eyes to the person that was rushing to him.

"What are you doing? Get your hand out of the bandage, RIGHT NOW!" She yelled at him as she roughly pulled his hand away from his stomach.

"Who? Who are you?" He asked as she pulled him to his feet, ignoring his pained wince. She quickly let go and hid her hand behind her back.

Light from the now open door flooded the room, forcing his eyes to adjust painfully. Everything gradually swam into focus and he was able to see that it was the same girl that he had pulled from the rubble.

"You!" He said stupidly, not quite comprehending what was going on.

The light from the doorway cut off as it was blocked by a large form before she could respond.

The sudden lack of light drew his eyes to the door and the imposing backlit form that stood there.

"How is the boy?" A deep gravelly voice asked.

The girl jumped back from him, her eyes wide and slightly frantic looking. He pulled his eyes away from her with some difficulty and to the man at the door.

"Who are you, people?" Jack asked carefully, backing away from them until he felt the edge of the bed pressed against the back of his legs.

"He seems to be intact, although he was just about to do something stupid like pull at his bandages." She announced, her eyes crinkling at the edges as she smirked.

"Good, give him a shirt to wear and then bring him out to the living room. There is a lot that we need to talk about." He said firmly before walking away, letting light flow into the room once more.

"Yes, father, we'll be out in just a minute." The smirk had faded from her face, only to be replaced by annoyance. She stood there for a few more seconds, looking at him with a queer look in her eye, like she was trying to figure out a problem or what something meant.

Jack cleared his throat as he crossed his arms in front of his chest, drawing her eyes to his tanned chest and the bandage peeking out from behind his arms. "There was talk of getting me a shirt?" He said with a smirk of his own and a raised brow.

"Right, a shirt. Give me a moment to get it. I ran your shirt through the wash while you were out. It should be dry by now. Leave your hands off the bandage while I go get it." She hurried out the door, leaving him alone as he slowly sank onto the bed.

What was going on here? There had been a piece of metal sticking through his chest, and now he was doing fine? How did any of this make sense? He should be dead right now, not sitting on a bed like nothing was wrong.

More than anything else though he wanted to know who these people were! What had the girl been doing up there so late at night that would cause part of the floor to collapse? There was something about her though that was drawing him in, and it was more than just her looks. She was beautiful there was no denying that, but it was a pull of another kind. Something almost otherworldly.

His hand moved to the bandages around his chest as he thought. There was something going on that was far outside the realm of normal, that was all he knew for sure. The girl hurried back into the room; her steps quick and sure as they touched the soft carpet in rapid fashion. She held out his clean and still warm from the dryer long sleeve dark blue shirt.

"Thank you…" He began as he took the shirt from her hands and began threading his arms into the sleeves. "Sorry, I don't know your name yet."

"Kaitlyn, my name is Kaitlyn LaCouture." She said softly as he pulled the shirt over his head and onto his body, hiding the bandage from view.

"Nice to meet you, Kaitlyn. My name is Jack." He told her, leaving off his last name. He hated introducing himself to people, primarily because of his stupid last name. It was such a ridiculous last name he had been teased mercilessly about it as a child. So, he avoided even thinking about the name whenever he could. "How am I not dead? I distinctly remember a rather sharp piece of metal plunging into my body! Now I haven't seen the wound because you won't let me remove the bandage, but I know it doesn't feel like I was just on death's door!"

She winced slightly at his question drawing his eyes to hers; they were electric blue and filled with uncertainty. "I think it is best if we go to the living room now. My father can explain everything to you. I'm sure he has a number of questions that he would like to ask you as well." Her eyes cleared slightly as she spoke.

"Fine, lead the way!" Jack managed to bite off as he waited for her to move. He wanted answers, and while he was thankful that they had somehow managed to save him, but he knew something else was going on. It was the unknown that was making him nervous and putting him more than a little on edge.

Kaitlyn stepped back as her eyes widened for a second before narrowing into angry slits that obscured the brilliant blue of her eyes. Spinning on her heel, she turned her back to him and stomped from the room, her anger palpable as it filled the air between them.

Jack followed behind her, careful to not make any more noise than needed or to attract her attention. He did not need to make her anymore annoyed or angry with him than he already had. It wasn't her fault that he had no idea what was going on, actually no, he took that back. It was her fault, since she had decided not to tell him anything but her name. He sighed softly as he walked behind her and into a large room filled with couches and comfortable looking overstuffed chairs.

Her father was sitting in one such chair, clearly waiting for them to join him.

Jack dragged his feet behind her as he entered the room. Where, for the first time, he was able to get a good look at her father. What he saw terrified him. The man was a mountain. Even sitting down, it was obvious that he was tall. His arms bulged at the sleeves of his shirt, letting the sharply defined muscles show through the sleeves. His short brown hair and his sharp steel-colored eyes gave him a dangerous look that mixed well with the straight line of his mouth.

"Jack," Kaitlyn began, stopping in front of her father. "This is my father Jon, dad, this is Jack."

Jack remained behind her when her father made no move to stand or try to shake his hand.

Kaitlyn reached for his hand, stopping at the last second. Pointing, she guided him to the couch across from her father. He took the far end of the couch, positioning himself on the opposite end from her and away from her father. He managed to sit down on the couch with only a small wince of discomfort from his stomach.

Her father, Jon, raised his brow as he watched them get seated before clearing his throat. "What exactly happened tonight?" He asked, fixing his eyes on Jack and speaking in a surprisingly gentle voice. "My daughter has already explained some of what happened from her perspective. Now I want to hear it from you!"

Jack flicked his eyes from father to daughter and back again, trying to mentally catch-up with everything. "Wait, wait, wait!" He practically yelled, thrusting his hands outward. "I think there are a few things that need to be cleared up before any of that! I want to know what the hell happened tonight?! And before any of that, I want to know why I'm in barely any pain? What is going on?"

To his side, Kaitlyn lowered her eyes, clearly unsure of what she should say to him.

In front of them, Jon sighed and stood from his chair as he walked over to a clear window that showed the moon hanging low in the sky. "I promise we'll explain everything afterward, but please tell us what happened first."

Jack sat drumming his fingers on his leg for a few seconds as he deliberated about what he should do. With a short nod of his head, he let his hand fall by his side and began talking while trying to keep his eyes on both of them at the same time.

Running his hand through his long hair, he dragged it from over his face and began. "It all started with my ex-best friend Steve, and him abandoning me at the first sign of something weird going on." Step by step he walked them through everything that had happened, the noises, the flashes of light and then the ceiling collapsing around him.As he spoke, Jack found his nerves calming and his voice evening out. To his side, he noticed Kaitlyn beginning to blush in embarrassment the farther along he got in his story. "After the ceiling collapsed, I managed to find where Kaitlyn was buried after I heard her making some noise. I dug her out as quickly as I could, then when I touched her hand everything went white and the next thing I know I'm flying through the air with a piece of metal sticking through my stomach."

Jack stopped speaking as he quickly ran through everything in his head. "That's everything as I remember it. Now explain to me what happened, and how is it that I seem to be mostly healed already?"

Jon visibly perked up as Jack came to the end of his tale, his eyes fixed on his daughter with a shrewd and hard look. Kaitlyn sank into the couch and curled up slightly as if she was trying to diminish her presence. Her cheeks grew redder at the look her father gave her and she averted her eyes, refusing to look at anyone.

"So, everything went white after you touched her hand? Interesting. It seems like my daughter forgot to mention that little tidbit when she was telling me everything earlier." His eyes darkened and thinned as he spoke. His hands drummed against his crossed arms as he looked at his daughter, who refused to meet his eyes.

Jack kept his mouth shut as he looked at the two of them. The temperature in the room had plummeted with the overall mood. A shiver wracked his body as he noticed that the temperature in the room truly had plummeted as his breath fogged in front of him. Wrapping his arms around himself, he shivered again as the silence continued to reign. Finally, he'd had enough and loudly cleared his throat after making sure that he had their attention, he exhaled a long foggy breath.

Seeing the fog, Jon sighed and closed his eyes, running a quick hand over them. "Sorry about that. I believe you wanted answers, and this seems as good as any of a reason to start such a conversation." As he spoke, the air in the room warmed until Jack was no longer shivering.

Moving back towards them, Jon sat once more and leaned back in his chair with his long legs outstretched, nearly touching the couch they sat on.

On the far side of the couch, Kaitlyn quietly sighed and straightened before meeting her father's eyes. "It was magic. I was doing magic up there." The words were spoken softly, but still loud enough for Jack to hear clearly.

The serious look on her and her father's faces kept him from making an overly snarky remark. "Uh, right?" He began hesitantly. He might not be able to say it aloud at the present time, but he was suddenly rather uncomfortable.

"She's not joking," Jon told him, clearly reading the disbelief and sudden apprehension on Jack's face.

"Oh no, I know she's not. That's part of the problem!" He said as he edged as far away from the girl as possible until the side of the couch was jamming into his side.

Jon looked at him for a second before extending his hand palm up. An orb of blue-white light came into being hovering six inches over his hand, pulsing in time with Jack's heart. With each beat of his heart and the resulting pulse, the orb grew slightly larger and brighter until it hurt to look at.

Jack felt his jaw grow loose and drop slightly at the casual display of power and magic. His eyes shot from the dad to the daughter as Jon closed his fist and extinguished the light, leaving dancing spots of light in his eyes.

Kaitlyn's lips curled upwards on one side of her mouth at Jack's reaction and his resulting inability to speak. "Do you believe me now?" She asked, her smirk growing with each second.

"My healing?" He asked uncertainly.

"That was my wife's doing," Jon answered, his grey eyes seemingly beginning to dance at the thought of his wife.

"It isn't a full healing," Kaitlyn interjected, drawing their attention back to her. Her face was still slightly red as she spoke. "All it does is accelerate the body's natural healing speed. That is probably why it feels like your skin has already knitted together but is still a little sore."

Jack's hand fell to his stomach as he felt at the bandages that covered it. He wanted to accept what they were saying, but part of him just couldn't, even with what he had just seen. It was just too far removed from the reality that he had grown up knowing. It was a fantastical concept that had no place for him in it and knowing that was sadder than not knowing magic existed at all.

"Where is she? I feel like I should thank her or something!" He asked, softly forcing the words out.

"She's asleep right now. Healing you took a lot out of her," Jon answered seriously.

"Why, why did you save me to begin with?"

"You helped my daughter. It was only natural. Besides, she was screaming her head off when she called. Helping you was the only thing that calmed her down." Jon was looking at the two of them closely as he spoke. "Putting everything else aside for the moment, there is something I need to confirm with you and I need you to answer me honestly and seriously."

Jack tilted his head to one side in confusion as he pulled his hand away from his shirt and the bandages underneath it. "Alright, what is it you want to know?"

"Is what you told me true? That when you touched my daughter's hand, everything went white and then exploded outwards!" On the far side of the couch, Kaitlyn seemed to shrink in on herself as her father spoke.

The confusion was obvious on Jack's face as he answered. "Yes, that is what happened. Why does it mean something in particular?"

"It might, and if what I am thinking is correct, then it explains why my wife was so tired after healing you." He began only to be interrupted by Kaitlyn.

"Dad don't! Don't do this! If you do, you'll be changing his life forever! He, no, we won't be able to go back after this. You can't do that to someone we know nothing about!"

Jon's face grew stony as she spoke to him. "Quiet, this is happening regardless. If it isn't us, then it will be someone else! He has been 'touched' now! Others will be able to find him. He either joins with us, or he is forced to join another. The choice was made the instant the two of you made contact!" The volume of his voice continued to rise as he spoke.

Jack felt his confusion grow as the two of them spoke, he knew that they were talking about him, but there was a large piece of the puzzle that he seemed to be missing.

Chapter 3

The sound of shuffling steps drew everyone's attention to the doorway they had entered from previously. A woman with dark brown hair and deep blue eyes was leaning against the side of the entrance with her eyes focused on Kaitlyn. This must be her mother. The resemblance between the two of them was uncanny.

"He's right, dear," She spoke gently, her voice soft and melodious. "When the two of you touched, it brought him into our world. If we don't take him and protect him, then someone else will come along and force him into doing whatever they want. His kind are far too valuable to be left alone!"

Kaitlyn's face smoothed and her eyes grew hard at her mother's words, hiding her emotions behind a mask of her own creation. She kept her eyes off of Jack as she stood from the couch and walked away, moving towards her mother and the hallway beyond.

Her mother reached out and grabbed her arm, pulling Kaitlyn to her side before she could walk past her. Holding her close, she whispered something too softly for anyone else to hear and then released her daughter, letting her walk past.

"We haven't been introduced yet," She said, focusing on Jack as she left the doorway and began walking towards them. "You were almost dead when I saw you earlier. I'm glad to see that you're doing so much better now. My name is Shantell LaCouture. You've already met my husband and daughter. I was the one who healed you, as I'm sure they already told you." She moved to the chair next to her husband and sat down, keeping her eyes on Jack the entire time.

"Uh, thank you for that. I appreciate not dying." Jack began lightly. "Is Kaitlyn okay? I didn't really understand what you all were talking about just now, but it seemed to upset her."

Shantell looked first at her husband and then back to Jack before sighing. "I'm sure you at least caught on that we were talking about you." She stopped talking as he nodded in agreement. "Let us start at the beginning. You are what we call a *'Potere Generantis'*, or in more modern terms, a 'Power Generator'.

"Generators can't use magic directly except in exceedingly rare cases, but they produce an incredible amount of it that they can then share with others. They are fairly rare, however, because their abilities remain inactive until they interact with someone who uses magic. In your case, it was touching Kaitlyn's hand."

Jack lifted the hand that had touched Kaitlyn's in the hallway and looked at it closely. Everything seemed normal. There were no marks on it that he could see. Both adults chuckled as they watched him, causing him to flush in embarrassment and drop his hand to focus on them once more.

"It doesn't cause a visible change in you, but all people who use magic can feel it if they look for it. I felt it when I was healing you. That is partly the reason I was able to heal you as much as I did and also the reason I was so tired. Each person normally produces a certain amount of magical power that they can use each day. The amount can change with time, allowing for more or less, depending.

"Either way, using more than you have produced affects the body in various ways, most often causing sickness and death. When using power from a generator, it merely makes us tired instead of risking worse. Do you understand what I'm saying so far?" She asked gently, watching his eyes to make sure he understood everything.

He nodded hesitantly, understanding what she was saying was easy. However, believing everything and wrapping his head around it all was another matter entirely.

"All right, now that I've covered what you are, let me explain what that means for your future." She moved on, though she doubted that he fully understood what this meant for him. His eyes were clear and firm, which was good enough for now. "In our society, *generators* are a rare and precious thing, something that can push a mage to their absolute limits, helping them grow faster and stronger than they otherwise would have. As such, *generators* are treated more like property, with their owners ensuring that they never bond."

"Hold up. What do you mean, property or bonding?" Jack cut in, not liking where the conversation was headed. "No one owns me but me!"

"If you had never run into mages, then that would be true. Unfortunately, that is no longer the case. The fact of the matter is that in our society, you are too valuable to be allowed to be free. Your life is no longer your own. I admit that you could walk out of this house right now, and for a while, you would be fine, but then someone would find you and then your freedom would be over. It is a matter of time, not an *if* it would happen, but a *when*. It is a guaranteed certainty."

"So, what exactly are you suggesting? That I hand the reins of my life over to you, people that I know nothing about?" The heat in his voice was obvious as he began to lose his temper.

"No, nothing quite as bad as that. What I am suggesting is that you join our family. Kaitlyn will be transferring into your class at school on Monday. Spend time with her and get to know her. She will protect you while you are there." Jon's eyebrows were raised, and his eyes narrowed at his wife's words.

"What do you mean join your family? And you didn't explain what bonding is?" Jack felt his head beginning to hurt at everything he was being told. He no longer knew what was going on. His understanding of the situation had long since disappeared.

"A bond changes your powers. It is a link between you and a single other person. Usually, people who bond are best friends or lovers. In other words, they are people that are committed to one another in some way. When you become bonded, only the other person in the bond has access to your powers, and in return, you gain access to a portion of their powers. You would become a limited and untrained mage at that point, eventually able to use magic to some extent. Your strength as a duo would be second to only the other bonded and alone you would be able to at least defend yourself." She elbowed her husband repeatedly as she spoke until his narrowed eyes were focused on her alone.

"Who exactly did you have in mind for this bond?"

"I thought it was obvious! I was thinking our daughter Kaitlyn would be perfect for you!" Her lips were tight as she spoke, preventing him from understanding her mood.

Jack sat, stunned. His mind going in a hundred different directions. "I'm not saying yes or no. There is a lot that I need to think about, but before any of that. I need to know what you would get out of any of this! More than that, I need to know how she feels regarding any of this!" His voice raised as he continued talking.

"I'm fine with it." A small voice said softly behind him when he had finished.

Jack twisted his hips and looked over the back of the couch to where Kaitlyn was standing. Her face was pointed at the ground with her hands crossed at the wrists and her body leaning heavily against the wall. Her long, dark blonde hair hung over her face, preventing anyone from seeing her eyes. Everything about her posture was screaming at the vulnerability and uncertainty that she must have been feeling.

"Look, I still don't really know what is going on," He began as he stood from the couch and moved to stand in front of Kaitlyn. "But it is obvious that whatever it is, is not something that she really wants. I think it's time that I leave. There are obviously some things that the three of you need to talk about and figure out." Jack held his hand out to the suddenly shy and withdrawn girl.

"We shouldn't," She said quietly, shaking her head. "I would lose control again if I touched you at all right now."

"I understand. Thanks for pulling the metal from my chest and getting me help. It was... interesting meeting you." He said to her softly before stepping back.

"Thanks for healing me and everything, but I don't belong to the same world as the three of you, so I am just going to excuse myself now." Through an open door on the side of the room, he could see a darkened hall that he hoped would lead to the front door. Not that he even knew where they were, he could only hope that they were still in town somewhere. He had been injured at the time, so it stood to reason that they hadn't taken him far.

He backed away from them before they could respond and hurried through the door he had seen. At the end, he spotted another door and a bunch of shoes in front of it, including his boots. He heard raised voices behind him as he ran towards the door. Without stopping, he twisted the handle on the door with one hand and picked up his boots with the other. Pushing through the open door, he launched into a sprint as he ran over the soft green grass, a remnant left over from the fading summer.

The moon hung low in the sky and the distant horizon had started lightening with the still distant coming rays of morning. The stars in the sky had faded to mere dots with the coming light, leaving the night dark and impenetrable where the streetlights didn't shine.

The town water tower rose into the inky night in the distance, providing him with some idea of where he was and where he needed to go. He was miles away from the abandoned building where he had begun the night, at this point he was closer to his own home than where he had left his bicycle. His parents couldn't afford even a beater of a car for him, so he was stuck riding his bicycle everywhere. He had his license, just no vehicle.

The wind ruffled the trees lightly as he passed; the leaves rubbing against each other in the otherwise still night. His pounding bare feet hit the pavement in an off-beat rhythm as he ran away from the LaCouture house. His eyes were fixed on the dark strip of ground that was the road, using it to guide his rushing feet.

Three streets away from their house, he left the safety of the road and slipped behind a tall hedge, slowing to a walk before stopping to catch his breath. He tied his boots together and draped them over his neck. There was no way he was going to wear them without socks. Sweat dripped from his brow as his still-healing body sucked the energy from him. His shirt was wet and sticky where blood had seeped through the bandages. His knitting skin ripping apart painfully in spots as his muscles moved beneath his skin.

Pushing his hand under his shirt, he felt at the damp bandages and the previously torn skin beneath them. His shoulder hit a metal light pole that was dark from a broken bulb. The sweat on his brow grew cold as he shivered in the cold night, pushing on farther down the street to where he could see a working light pole.

His back was sweaty as he stumbled along, determined to reach the pole of light before stopping to rest. His breath came in short gasps as his expanding chest fought against the restricting bandages. Above him, the streetlamp buzzed softly, offering a comfortable background to the dark and otherwise silent night.

A sharp crack shot through the air, startling him at the sudden loud noise that came from the dark. His eyes had adjusted to the soft light from the lamp and couldn't pierce through the veil of night that obscured everything.

His skin prickled as the wind moved gently through the trees, making their tips sway against the background of the waning pearlescent moon. Taking in one last pain filled breath, he pushed away from the pole and looked around wearily, the hairs on his arms standing straight up. His hand ran over his arm, smoothing down the hairs, as he looked nervously into the trees.

Something felt different tonight. Maybe it was just the knowledge that magic existed, or maybe it had something to do with him supposedly being valuable. All he knew was that there seemed to be a perceptible charge in the air that he was only now becoming aware of.

He felt his eyes adjust to the dim lighting as he set off at a run, the flesh of his feet beating a steady rhythm into the pavement. His breathing evened out and was steady as he kept his eyes on the ground in front of him.

From behind him, a new noise reached his ears. The soft pounding of padded feet taking up pursuit forced him to look back, his breath hitching at the sight. Three large beings cloaked in shadow held his eyes in place as he stumbled over the unseen ground. They had odd loping gaits that at times sounded like they were running on four legs and at other times on two. Their glowing red eyes belonged to nothing he had seen before, foreign to both animal and human.

He stumbled, his feet catching as his eyes remained on the beings behind him. His head swiveled around, his hands touching down on the rough pavement as he fought for his balance. Digging in deep, he pushed himself to run faster, holding his sprint as long as he could, his boots smacking wildly against his chest. The muscles in his legs burned from the strain. Sweat poured down his face and into his eyes, stinging as he gasped for breath, his stomach frantically trying to expand against the bandages.

The wind kicked up as he pounded down the street, cooling the sweat against his chilled skin. The leaves rustled in the trees before being torn off and flung into the sky. The dead leaves on the ground skittered and lifted into the air, scattering as the wind pulled them along.

Behind him, he could hear the loud breathing and grunts from the things chasing after him. He could feel them drawing closer with each step, his vision tunneling to just the road in front of him. All thought fled his mind as he concentrated on just running as fast as possible. Nothing existed but the next step, the next breath.

Blood pounding hotly in his ears, the sounds of the world around him faded under the pressure. Spots began to appear in his vision as he continued pushing himself. A stitch in his side caused a flash of pain to roll through him, making his legs go weak as all strength left them.

Jack found it impossible to lift his legs as his arms flailed wildly. Forward momentum kept his upper body moving as he face-planted onto the ground, his chin digging into the pavement. He felt the skin being torn from his face as it ran over the rough ground. The skin on his stomach, under the dressing, ripped open, undoing all the healing that had managed to occur. Blood flowed from the reopened wound coating the bandages and the ground beneath him in a slick coating of sticky red liquid.

The sound of padded feet hitting the ground behind him stuttered and then stopped as he sprawled across the ground. An odd huffing laughter replaced their earlier growls as they drew closer to his helpless form. His eyes screwed shut at the sudden influx of pain that shot through his stomach and face. Their laughter grew harsher as they crept closer, a rank, sweaty smell filling the air around him.

In the distance, Jack heard the roar of a powerful engine scream through the night as a pair of headlights flashed around a corner farther down the road. He forced his eyes open as he felt the headlight beams hit his face, illuminating the red behind his eyelids.

Above him, he saw the teary water blurred forms of the monster's spin and look at the oncoming car. Rage filled snarls replaced their huffing laughter as they saw the car speeding towards them. Each of them glanced back at him in turn before casting their glowing red eyes to the approaching car and then running to the side of the road and vanishing into the darkness.

Jack closed his eyes as another wave of pain rolled through his body. Tears leaked from his eyes as he tried to block out everything that was happening. The screech of tires only dimly registered in his overly shocked mind.

"Mom, help me get him in the car! He's covered in blood again!" Kaitlyn's voice echoed inside his head as she leaped from the car and to his side.

His eyes opened weakly as she approached. "Hi, thanks for the save!" His bloody face stretched into a painful smile as he rolled onto his back.

Kaitlyn sighed heavily as she saw how bloody his face and stomach truly were. "We wouldn't have had to save you if you hadn't run away in the first place!" She said in exasperation as her mother joined her outside the car.

Her mother's eyes seemed to glow with a blue light as she stood above him with a severe frown stretched across her face. "I hope you know that this is your fault this time! If you had just stayed and talked with us, then none of this would have happened! There are many new things in the world you have entered and because you refused to listen, you nearly died for the second time tonight! I will heal you, and then we will drop you off at your house. Let us know when you feel like listening properly, your life will depend on it, so don't take too long."

She gripped him by his armpits as Kaitlyn grabbed his boots from where they had fallen. Dragging him, she unceremoniously lifted him into the car and onto the backseat. Kaitlyn hopped into the driver's seat while her mom climbed in beside him and grabbed his hand. He felt something intangible shift and quiver inside him as she reached for his power. Her grip tightened and a deep blue-green glow encased her hand. This was the first time he was seeing her use her magic as a warmth began to spread through his body. The warm feeling grew hot around his chin and the reopened wound on his stomach.

Chapter 4

"**D**o you need my address?" Jack asked haltingly as a spasm went through his body.

"I already have it," Kaitlyn said confidently from the driver's seat. "Dad looked through your wallet while you were out. Nice last name, by the way!"

The mocking tone in her voice was nothing new. Truth be told, he hated his last name. It had never caused anything but issues. For as long as he could remember, people had been making fun of his last name, and him by extension. Jack Rage, son of Jason and Elinor Rage, with a younger sister by the name of Penelope. His entire family was a joke of tear-inducing proportions. He felt bad for his younger sister especially, it was bad enough for him, with her name the nicknames 'Pen Rage' or 'Penny Rage' were just waiting to happen.

Jack opened his mouth to respond but couldn't say anything as his back arched, fiery pain sweeping through his body. The light emanating from Shantell's healing hand grew brighter as he felt something shift within him again, then begin to rush out. She was drawing heavily on whatever power he had in order to heal him as quickly as possible. She was forcing the healing to such a degree that it was causing the healing heat to turn evermore painful.

His whimpers filled the car as his back arched at an unnatural angle. Above him, he saw her smirk slightly before she forced more power into her healing. His eyes shot wide open as he began to scream. The car jerked to the side as the loud noise shocked Kaitlyn. The light provided by Shantell's healing magic lit up her face enough for him to see the harsh, malicious smirk that had spread across her face. A shiver rolled through his mind as he saw the almost evil glint in her eye. She knew that she was hurting him while also healing him at the same time, and she was enjoying it.

In the front seat, away from the prying eyes of her slightly sadistic mother, Kaitlyn's face tightened into a white mask as the blood left her face. The whimpers and screams that filled the car behind her seat shocking her as she floored the accelerator, wanting this over as fast as possible.

The burning heat that flowed through his body was concentrated on his wounded stomach and chin, gradually fell away. The healing was already nearly complete, leaving him feeling empty and exhausted in its wake. He had never had someone pull so heavily on his power before and was unused to what the loss of magical power felt like. It felt like he had just sprinted an entire mile at full bore without breathing the entire time.

His screams ceased as his hoarse and raspy whimpers replaced them. The pain was quickly fading, but the memory of it all was still there. If that was how she healed someone, then he never wanted to be in a position where he needed to be healed by her ever again. Unless he was dying, the pain was just not worth it.

He felt the rumbles of the engine smooth out as the car slowed and then stop as they arrived in front of his house. Kaitlyn climbed out of the driver's seat and opened the rear door next to Jack's head before helping him out. He leaned heavily against her, feeling weak all over after that intense and painful healing. His boots were placed around his neck by her mother at the last second.

Holding most of his weight, she pulled him from the car and onto his family's front lawn. Closing the door to the car behind him, she gripped him tightly as they moved away from the soft growls of the engine. It was a good thing her mother had drained all of his energy. He didn't feel like getting flung across the yard from simply touching her right now.

"I'm sorry about that. My mom has a somewhat sadistic streak whenever she gets annoyed!" She whispered softly to him as they walked across the dew-soaked grass.

"I annoyed her?" He whispered back hoarsely.

A snort of amusement rocked her body at his question. "You ran out of our house when they were trying to explain everything! Then right afterward we had to rescue you and she had to heal you all over again. Yeah, I'd say you did a good job of annoying her!" He could see her smirking from the corner of his eye, most of his attention focused on walking.

"Right, I might have to apologize to her." He said with a wince.

"Not right away. I'd give her time to calm down." She helped him up the steps and to his front door before continuing. "I'll see you again on Monday when I am transferred into your classes at school. After school is over for the day, you'll come over to our house once again. We'll explain everything to you in detail then. It might be a good idea to apologize to her then."

He weakly lifted his head to look at her as he opened the door and leaned heavily against the doorjamb. "Alright, I guess I'll see you then." The full import of her words and their meaning, escaping him as exhaustion settled heavily into his weary bones.

Letting go of his shoulders, she released him and stepped back. "I'll talk to you more on Monday. There are... a few things we should discuss before you see my parents again!" Her voice was soft but firm as she backed away from him and ran back to her waiting car.

Jack waited for her to climb into the driver's seat, her mom watching him with a small smirk from the backseat. Kaitlyn closed her door without looking back and then shifted the car into gear, leaving only a roar from the powerful engine and a thick pall of exhaust in their wake.

Pulling himself away from the door, he closed it with a soft 'snick' and locked it in his wake. Stumbling down the hallway, he dimly registered that there were no lights on in the house. He had gotten lucky that his parents hadn't awakened sometime in the night and found him missing. With that thought bouncing comfortingly in his mind, he opened the door to his room and shuffled inside. Closing the door behind him, he slipped his boots from his neck. His eyes were fixed on the bed, feeling an almost perceptible call from it. Falling into its sweet embrace, still fully clothed, his mind said goodnight to the world.

***

The dryness of his raw throat is what eventually pulled Jack from his slumber. His throat was so dry he had trouble swallowing. The breath catching in his esophagus causing him to cough violently, as the still tender muscles of his stomach clenched.

Sitting up in his bed, Jack reached weakly for the bottle of water that always sat next to his bed on the nightstand. Unscrewing the cap, he tipped the warm bottle of tepid water into his mouth, enjoying the feeling of the liquid flowing over the dry desert of his tongue. Each swallow hurt, his throat swollen and tender.

The events of the night before had left him weak and exhausted. It had all been too much! Monsters were real. Magic was real! Not only that, apparently, he had some special kind of magic as well. One that made him a target.

Everything was different now. Overnight, the very fabric of his world had changed. Things that he thought he knew had been proven to be untrue.

Just thinking of the adjustment he would have to mentally go through was exhausting.

The warm beams of sunlight coming through the window above the desk in the corner of his room attested to how long he had been asleep. The streams of light stretched far into the room, bathing everything in a golden glow.

A knock on the closed door to his room encouraged him to swing his dirty, scratched and bare feet from his bed and onto the floor. Loud popping cracks echoed throughout his body as he stood and then stretched. A groan bubbling up as his sore muscles protested at the sudden abuse. Bare feet were not made for running on hard rough surfaces, and that is exactly what he had done with them last night. No, he hadn't been running but sprinting. Going all out for minutes at a time while in an injured state. Just how much healing had occurred in the backseat of that car?

Another knock came from the door, this one slightly louder and more insistent.

Hurrying over to it, he flung the door open without thinking about his appearance.

His younger sister stood there with her arm raised to knock again, her wide chocolate brown eyes lightening noticeably in his presence. Whenever she was near him, the color of her eyes had a tendency of turning into a molten caramel color.

A scream ripped forth from her adolescent lungs as she stared at him with tears filling her eyes.

The pounding of feet echoed through the house as his father yelled out, "Jack! What did you do to your sister?"

"I didn't do anything! I just opened my door!" He yelled back as his sister continued to scream.

The pounding of feet drew closer as the diminutive form of his furious mother cleared the corner at a run. Hurrying to her daughter's side, her strawberry blonde hair trailed along in her wake. At ten years old, her daughter Penelope was quickly catching up to their mother, Elinor's height of 5'2.

Elinor's hazel eyes almost always had a honey-like coloring to them from her long hair.

Currently, those warm honey-colored eyes were flashing dangerously as she looked at her daughter's tear lined screaming face. Her long hair flipped into Penelope's face as she spun to glare at her son.

Jack had stepped back into his room in shock when his sister had started to scream. Her reaction was entirely unexpected, and more than a little disturbing, she seemed to be genuinely afraid of him. Then there was his mother, her glaring eyes widened as she stared at him. Behind her, Penelope finally stopped screaming as she brushed her mother's hair away from her face.

"Jack, are you alright?" His mother asked in a wavering voice as she reached out for him.

Stepping further back into his room, he avoided her questing finger. "What are you talking about?" He asked as he looked down at his chest where her finger had been reaching for. Seeing the torn and filthy remains of his shirt made everything click together in his head.

He had been so tired when they'd dropped him off that he had fallen asleep without changing. The clothes he was wearing looked like they belonged on a slasher victim in a horror movie. His pants were covered in dirt and grime and more from where his blood had fallen on them. His shirt was torn and discolored with stained blood and dirt from his various accidents during the course of the night. There was no telling what his face looked like, but he was sure it was also covered in dirt and dried blood.

"Is this related to whatever you were doing last night, young man?" Elinor stepped away from her daughter and crowded into her son's space. "I know what time you got in this morning and don't think for a second that we aren't going to talk about you being out all night!" Her voice had dropped in volume, so it wouldn't reach her daughters' ears.

"Uh yeah, I was with Steve last night. We went to explore the old, abandoned school building on the other side of town." He began hesitantly, not daring to step away from her.

"What. Were. You. Doing. Out. There?" Her eyes started to flash dangerously as she enunciated each word carefully. "I have told you before that you are not allowed inside that building! And what does any of that have to do with the condition of your clothes? You're absolutely covered in blood, but you appear unharmed. So, what exactly happened?" Her eyes narrowed to tiny slits as she studied his face.

His chin may have been healed, but all the blood from it was still smeared across his face and neck. There was no way he could explain to her what had happened the night before. She would never believe him! Heck, he barely believed any of it and he had been there! He would have to tell her a small portion of it and hope that did the trick.

"Alright, I'll tell you, geez calm down mom. I'm unharmed and intact, see?" He began moving his arms like noodles, trying to break some of the tension that had gathered in his room.

His mother stepped back and turned to Penelope, who was still standing in the hall with wide eyes. "Honey, go get a wet towel, so your brother can wipe the make-up off his face. It seems he is already practicing for Halloween." Her voice was even and sweet as she spoke to her daughter, while Jack was mentally palming his face. It was only the middle of September. Why would he have been practicing doing make-up for Halloween already?

"Alright mom," the relief in her voice that it was nothing more serious was obvious. Her brother was alright, and in the end that was all that mattered!

"Now you; talk fast and explain what happened last night!" Her voice dropped again as the air around him seemed to become charged with electricity. "And tell me, who unlocked your powers?" A shiver ran through him as his mother's eyes began to glow. She knew about his powers, she knew what he was! She had powers of her own!

Jack felt his mouth drop open in shock as he saw the change come over his mother. He licked his lips, closing his mouth as it began to dry out again. His heart was beating fast as he tried to form an answer.

"What, what do you know?" Was all he managed to squeeze out in a dry, hoarse voice before his sister ran back into the room with a slightly damp dark blue towel.

She still seemed somewhat apprehensive of him as she passed the towel to their mother. "Thanks, why don't you go eat lunch while I talk to your brother?" She asked sweetly, keeping her glowing eyes fixed on Jack.

"Alright mom, do you want me to make anything for the two of you as well?" Her voice was melodious as she walked back into the hall, heading for the kitchen.

"No, I think your brother and I will be heading out for a while." Her voice had taken on an almost imperceptible edge that her daughter completely missed. "Don't forget that you still have some homework you need to finish, and I want you to clean your room as well!"

Behind his mother's back, he saw Penelope stick her tongue out at her before replying with a sigh. "I know, I was waiting for dad, so he could help me with my math problems." She skipped down the hall and disappeared.

Taking a step back, Elinor thrust the damp towel into Jack's hand before turning to leave as well. Her eyes had stopped glowing before his sister had left for the kitchen. Talking to her daughter seemed to have calmed her for the moment.

"Clean yourself up and get changed! Make sure you're presentable, depending on what you tell me, we may need to go see some people." She leaned against the wall near the door with her eyes closed. The frustration she was feeling at the moment could clearly be seen on her face. I've been trying to protect you from this for so long! Whatever happened last night, just undid over seventeen years worth of effort!"

Opening her eyes, he could see them glinting with a hint of tears in the bright light. "Just get changed, and then we'll leave." Her voice was sad as she left his room. All the anger she had felt earlier had left her completely, leaving only feelings of sadness and exhaustion in their wake.

Stripping his torn and filthy shirt off, he looked down at his chest and tossed the towel to the side. He was going to need more than that to clean himself properly. Grabbing some clean clothes, he hurried from his room and into the bathroom.

Turning the water on hot enough to create steam, he stripped the rest of the way down and hopped into the shower. Letting the water stream over him, he let it soak his hair and run over his muscles, feeling them loosen from the heat. He hadn't even realized how tense he had been until just that moment. Unconsciously, his fingers trailed over the smooth skin where he had been pierced the night before.

Soaping himself down thoroughly, he quickly scrubbed himself clean and turned the water off. Grabbing his towel, he noted the wisps of steam running over his skin as he began drying himself.

Pulling on the clothes he had set out, Jack rushed from the bathroom and retrieved a pair of shoes. Slipping them on, he ran through the house, waving to his sister as he went through the kitchen. Through the window over the sink, he could see his father working in the backyard. He found his mother already waiting for him at the front door. She was dressed in a pair of tight jeans, worn brown leather knee-high boots, and a closed black fleece jacket.

She said nothing as she looked him over before opening the door and walking out of the house. Jack closed the door behind them as she walked over to her car and slid into the driver's seat. He couldn't tell if his mother was mad or just preoccupied. She wasn't saying anything, and her face was carefully blank.

For the first time ever, he was aware of an almost imperceptible air of power hanging around his mother. It was the same kind of feeling he had felt last night around Kaitlyn and her parents. It gave the air in the car an almost electric charge that, while new to him, felt familiar.

Her eyes were glinting in the sunlight as she focused on the road, driving them through the town he had lived in all his life but suddenly no longer recognized. Last night had changed everything. It had introduced him to a world where monsters and magic existed. The bright deep blue sky was cloudless and the air outside the car held the bite of fall in it.

When he could hold it in no longer, he sighed in frustration and twisted in his seat to face his mother.

Shaking her head, she cut him off before he could say anything. "Just wait, we're almost there and then we can talk!" Next to her, Jack grunted in agreement and twisted back around to look out the window as the car sped outside the town limits and picked up speed.

Chapter 5

Outside of town was an old building that had been refurbished into a steakhouse a few years before. It was next to the highway and was full each night. During the day, however, it was usually empty and ran a skeleton shift during the lunch hours. Elinor pulled into a parking spot near the front of the restaurant and hopped out while Jack was still working on his seatbelt. He hurried after her and together they entered the nearly empty restaurant as her car locked with a beep behind them.

"We want an empty booth away from everyone else!" She said calmly to the hostess waiting just inside the doors.

Behind them, Jack choked back a laugh at his mother's words. Did she even realize what that sounded like? Or more likely, did she just not care? In front of her, the hostess's eyes widened slightly, and a small smirk appeared as she turned around and led them to an isolated corner of the restaurant.

"This is our darkest and most private booth at this time of day. Your waiter will be by in just a moment, enjoy your meal!" The hidden meaning behind her words was splashed across her face as she spoke.

His mother exhaled in annoyance as she caught the look on the younger girl's face. "He's my son. We need to have an unpleasant discussion and there are too many people at home for us to do it there."

"Oh, that's too bad! What I was imagining was much more interesting than that!" The hostess spun on her heel in a huff and left them alone, all her interest in them apparently having vanished with his mother's admission.

"Silly girl," She said as she took the seat on the far side of the table and motioned for Jack to sit across from her. "Letting her imagination run away like that!"

"To be fair, the way you were talking did kind of make it sound like something else." He said as he sat down in the booth across from her. "Now mom, what are we doing here? And why couldn't we just talk at home?"

"Your father doesn't know what you are. I never told him!" Her voice was firm as she spoke softly.

"Does he know what you are, at least?" He asked, trying to understand what she was saying.

"Yes, of course he does. It would have been stupid to hide something like that from your father. It's even part of how we met. Your father has always known what I was, and supported my decision to hide the truth from you and your sister. Besides, the last time I was truly and visibly active in that world was before you were born."

She took a glance around before continuing. "Jack, I'm the one who cast the spell on you when you were born that kept you hidden and your powers sealed. I knew what would happen to you if you were ever found and discovered. My spell hid you from being found and kept your powers sealed as well. However, when I cast the spell, it also took most of my magical ability to maintain. So, I made the decision that it would be best if I remained hidden as well, and dropped out of sight except for what my position demanded of me.

"I could still accomplish those tasks with what remained inside my well. By never casting any more spells than necessary, I hoped no one would suspect anything was amiss with me. It worked too, better than I thought it would in fact. I was prepared for everything to fall apart years ago. Instead, the world continued to turn, and I grew complacent, thinking that we were safe. Now, before I tell you anymore, tell me, what happened last night?" The emotions that had filled her voice were varied and complex as she spoke.

"Have you decided what you would like to order?" The waiter asked, appearing next to the table. She was dressed in clean black slacks with a spotless white blouse.

They both ordered hamburgers with everything, fries, and ice water to drink.

Elinor waited for the waitress to leave before focusing back on her son with a soft sigh of annoyance. "Let's wait until after we have our food. That way, we aren't disturbed during our conversation."

Jack nodded as he looked at the mostly empty tables. "So, dad doesn't know what I am then?"

"No," She sighed, shaking her head. "I never told him. All I ever said was that I wished to live as normal a life as possible after you were born. Which is what I have tried to do!"

"What about Penelope?" He asked, wondering about his sister.

"What about her?" Across from him, he noticed his mother stiffening when he mentioned his sister.

"Is she like me, or is she normal?"

She squinted at him, trying to decide what to say as her nails began tapping against the table. "She's not like you, thankfully. I didn't have enough power to protect both of you in that manner. However, she is also not normal. She's a mage, like me, but also something more. Thankfully, I don't think she has realized any of this yet. "Soon, I will have to tell her everything and begin her training. In a way it is good that this has happened to you when it did. With my abilities restricted like they were I wouldn't have been able to teach your sister and would have had to send her away for her training. Now, I can do it myself."

The waiter appeared through some doors at the back, carrying their drinks. "I'll have your food out in just a moment!" She told them happily as she set the glasses of water in front of them.

Jack nodded gratefully to her before looking at his mother once more as their waitress hurried off. "Why did we come to this restaurant? Surely there is another reason for us coming here than simply you not wanting to have this discussion inside the house! I mean, surely you're going to tell dad about me eventually, anyway."

His mother winced slightly at the mention of her husband. She was not looking forward to having that conversation with him. The use of magic had never bothered him. Hiding information about their son since his birth though, was another matter.

He would be furious, and rightfully so.

She was sure that eventually, he would understand why she had done it. He was rather smart, after all. Until that time, however, things between them would be rather strained. Not only that, but she also had to tell him about their daughter!

"I am not looking forward to having that conversation with your father. When he finds out I was hiding something like this from him. It is not going to be pretty!" She took a few deep breaths as she calmed herself and refocused on their conversation.

"As for why we came here, in particular, yes, there is indeed a reason. This place actually used to belong to a coven of witches that lived out here years ago. They were already long gone by the time we moved out here ourselves, but the protections and runes they laid across the building are still active and very strong. They prevent scrying and listening in remotely to private conversations, among other things.

"It is a good place to have this discussion without being heard by anyone else. The house would have been better, but it doesn't have quite the same level of protection. Besides, it would have been hard to keep your father and sister from inadvertently hearing something they shouldn't before we were ready."

His eyes widened as she nonchalantly described the magic and what the building used to be. The knowledge that magic was real was still new enough to him that hearing about some of its uses was surprising.

The appearance of their waiter with the food put their conversation on hold as she began setting the twin orders down on the table.

"Enjoy your meal and be sure to let me know if there is anything else you need!" There was a wide smile on her face as she walked away.

"She is way too happy to be working here." Jack heard his mother mutter softly before biting into her hamburger.

He began to pick up his hamburger as well when he noticed her glaring at him. "Alright fine, I'll tell you everything before I start eating. Is that what you want?" He asked sarcastically, bringing the glass of water to his lips instead.

Seeing his mother's serious nod made him pause in annoyance before he rolled his eyes at her and began explaining everything that had happened the night before.

"Sit up straight and raise your shirt!" His mother commanded him when he got to the part where Kaitlyn's mother had healed him a second time. "Let me see the spot she healed!"

Looking around the dim restaurant, he raised his shirt and pointed to the spot on his stomach where the metal had plunged in. The skin was smooth and just a touch lighter than the rest of the tanned skin surrounding it.

"Amazing, she did a superb job healing you as well as she did in such a limited time. Sit down and eat. That kind of healing uses your own body's reserves as well." Her fingers tapped the table rhythmically as she watched him devour the hamburger and fries.

"What?" He asked curiously after he had finished eating. She had been staring at him the entire time without talking.

"Did they happen to mention what their names were?"

Jack nodded. "Yeah, but I don't remember it. I wasn't really listening right then. I was more worried about why Kaitlyn had walked out."

"I need to meet these people. I was not informed that any new magic users had moved into the area. I may be out of practice, but strictly speaking, I still should have been notified when they arrived! I want to meet the daughter as well. The idea of having you bond with her is not a bad one." She was mostly talking to herself at this point and ignored him when his eyebrows shot up at the mention of her being alright with him bonding to someone they didn't even know.

"I said I want to meet them first, but the idea is not a bad one in and of itself." She said correctly, guessing what he was surprised about. "This family, whoever they are, seems to have some ability. Also, they went out on a limb when they let you go and didn't immediately notify the council about you. Now that your power has been unlocked and is in the open, it will only be a matter of time until you are discovered. I can't do the spell a second time. You're too old now. It wouldn't take hold again, and it was showing signs of failing anyway.

"At this point, it is a race against time to have you ready. If this family is willing to help get you there and defend you, then I am more than willing to join with them if I think they are decent people. More than that, once you are bonded to someone, the actions the council can readily take against you will be limited. I'm not saying that you will be safe, but they will have to operate outside their laws." She sighed and ran her hands over her face, rubbing the palms of her hands into her closed eyes.

"I guess," Jack paused as he tried to find the right words. "I guess I just don't understand what a bond truly is. At times, it sounds like you're all talking about some type of intimate relationship and at other times... it is more like a business arrangement."

Across the table, his mother bit into her hamburger and looked at him with a thoughtful look on her face. "Is she cute?" She asked after swallowing.

Jack fought to keep his face neutral at the question.

She smirked as his face went carefully blank. "So, she is, huh?" Her eyes were wide in mock surprise as she laughed at her son.

He didn't respond as he shoved a fistful of her fries into his mouth.

She rolled her eyes at his childish behavior. "To answer your question, it can be either. It just depends on the people involved and what they decide they want. The bond itself is something intangible that binds the two people together for the rest of their lives. For some people, it is easier to do this through a purely unemotional business relationship. For a select ever decreasing few, they can make a relationship work."

"Why do you say it like that?" He choked out around the mouthful of fries.

"Because people are immature and self-centered, they think only of themselves. In a proper relationship, you can't do that. It seems like more and more people do not understand that." She paused as she took a drink of water.

"In a relationship with your bonded, it becomes even more important to not think of yourself. A relationship with that person is for life. It's not like a marriage where you can get divorced for whatever reason. If one of you screws up, it affects both you, and in the magical community, that usually ends with both of you dead or severely injured. If you go down that route, then you had both better be sure that you're prepared to make it work!"

Jack was silent as he carefully worked through what she had said. "I think I need some time to think about all of this. It could all be pointless anyway; you might meet them and decide that they are terrible people." He sounded almost hopeful to her.

"Do you actually think that will be the case?" She asked, pinning him with her gaze.

"No, they seemed like alright people. Outside of the mom, she was slightly sadistic." He said with a sigh.

"That's what I thought." She waved the waiter over to them and asked for the bill. "You said she was going to see you again on Monday and take you to their house?"

He nodded as he finished off the last of his fries.

"Good, I'll meet with them then as well. Send me the address after school and I'll meet you at their house. There are several things I need to speak to them about outside of your issues. Them being here, without me being notified, is more than a little off. I need to find out why!"

"Alright, I'll try to get the info from her when I see her tomorrow."

"Also," She stopped speaking as the waitress appeared and hurried off with her credit card. "If I think that these people are able and willing, then I will let them be in charge of your training. If they can handle your training, then I can focus on Penelope's right away." She sighed and accepted her card back as she signed the receipt. "Let's go. I need to explain some things to your father! There's no sense in putting it off any longer."

Jack followed her from the table, noticing that her mood had fallen at the thought of what she needed to do. It was odd seeing his mother act this way; he had never really seen her apprehensive before.She was rarely one to show any emotion besides happiness. She would laugh and enjoy the time she had with her family, emotions that took away from that she kept private from her kids. She had wanted her kids to enjoy their lives, without letting the real-world influence them in a negative way.For the most part, she had even succeeded. Little things had crept into their own lives, but none of it came from their parents.

Wordlessly, she tossed the keys to her son and waited as he opened the passenger side door for her. From the corner of his eye, he saw her put on her seatbelt and then lean her head against the window.

"Take us home," He heard her say quietly. Starting the car, he backed out of the parking spot and pulled back onto the road. He wanted to say something to her, but he couldn't think of anything. Everything she had done had been for him, in an effort to keep him safe!

Reaching across the car, he grabbed her hand and squeezed it reassuringly. "It will be alright mom, once you explain everything to him, I'm sure he will understand why you did it!"

The smile she gave him was sad. "I'm not worried about him understanding. I know he will. Your father is a good man, and smarter than people think. I'm worried that regardless of his understanding that he will still feel betrayed. He and I have been through a lot. I'm afraid that someday it will be too much!" He squeezed her hand one more time before releasing it, ignoring the tears he saw in her eyes.

"Don't be silly, mom. He's not that kind of person and you should know that. I realize that you're scared right now, but you shouldn't let that affect what you know to be true. Dad may feel betrayed, he may even be angry, but he will never stop loving you!"

"I know, believe me, I know that! I'm still afraid though!" Hearing her talk like that was making him curious about what they had been through together? He had always thought his parents were just normal college sweethearts. He only now knew that was not even close to being the truth. It made him wonder what the truth really was. For the first time that he could remember, he wanted to learn more about his parents. After his mother spoke with Penelope, he would have to talk it over with her. Hopefully, between the two of them, they would be able to learn something.

Speeding through town, the drab buildings that lined the main thoroughfare blurred past the windows. Inside the car was a near stifling silence that only grew more intense the closer they got to their house. It was only when he had parked the car in front of the house that the silence was finally broken by his mother.

"I want you to take Penelope into town for a while, take her for ice-cream or something. Just make sure you keep her away while I talk to your father!" She told him while pulling some cash from her purse.

With a silent nod, he took the money, unsure of how to respond as they climbed out of the car.

"Penelope!" He called out as soon as he walked through the front door. In front of him, his mother hurried through the house, looking for her husband. It was obvious that she wanted to get through this as quickly as possible.

"What?" The slightly shrill voice of his younger sister called out from somewhere in the house.

The door to her room was open as he poked his head inside. "Mom told me to take you out of the house for a while. She needs to talk to dad and doesn't want either of us around while she does."

Uncertainty and fear took root in her face as her eyes widened at his words. "Is everything alright? Are they getting a divorce?" She asked rapidly as her lower lip began to tremble.

"Yeah, I mean no, they're fine. It's nothing like that. Don't worry!" He winced slightly as he continued, "It's something about me."

Her eyes narrowed as she grabbed her jacket from the back of her desk chair. "What did you do? This has something to do with the way you looked this morning, doesn't it?"

He said nothing as he walked back through the house and out the front door with her on his heels. Sometimes his sister was entirely too perceptive. Someone her age should not see things that clearly.

"I knew there was something different about you this morning! I could feel it. I've never told you this, but I've always felt a kind of energy whenever I'm near you. This morning and right now I can feel that energy stronger than ever before. Something happened last night, and mom knows what it is!" His steps faltered as he neared the car, surprised at what she was saying.

Chapter 6

He looked at her as she walked around the car to the passenger side door. "What do you mean when you say energy?"

She climbed into the car before responding. "Exactly that. It's part of the reason I've always liked being around you. That energy was always reassuring and warm!" She bounced lightly on the seat as she put on her seatbelt, before scrunching up her nose and continuing. "Now though, it's more like a sugar rush or like I'm drinking a bunch of mom's coffee. It's different. It still feels like you, but stronger, more intense. I don't know what to think!" As she spoke, he noticed her eyes changing color and streaks of fire engine red spreading through her hair.

"Penelope, look into the mirror." He said quietly as he started the car and backed down the driveway.

She tilted her head at him in confusion and then lowered the vanity mirror and gasped.

"What is happening to me?" She screeched, her eyes fixated on her changing hair. Her eyes had changed from molten caramel to a golden honey during the time she had been in the car. Her hands scrabbled at the door handle as Jack pressed on the brake, not wanting her hurt for what she was about to do.

She flung the passenger side door open and ripped off her seat-belt with a cry. Penny tripped and rolled as she ran back towards the house, her feet pounding up the paved driveway. Behind her, Jack threw the car into park and yanked the key out of the ignition as he followed after his panicking sister.

"MOM!!!" Penelope screamed out as soon as the door was open. "MOM!" She called out again as she ran into the house.

Elinor came rushing out of the office at the back of the house with her husband in tow. Her eyes were wide with panic at her daughter's frantic yells.

Clearing the corner, she stopped as she saw her daughter's nearly luminescent eyes and the bright red streaks that now ran through her hair. For a heartbeat, the color seemed to fade, only to surge brighter as Jack ran into the house behind her. His eyes sought out his mother's, unsure of what to say or even do under the circumstances.

Jason stood behind his wife and heard her curse softly under her breath. "I... I... what is going on here?" He asked in exasperation. Elinor had just told him that she had been keeping a big secret about their son from him. Something that was both life-changing and incredibly dangerous. Now he was finding out she was also keeping a secret about their daughter as well.

"I was going to tell you!" she whispered quietly before pulling her daughter into her pale and lightly freckled shaking arms.

Jack saw how close his father was to freaking out and knew he needed to take control of the situation. Slamming the front door closed, he grabbed everyone's attention. "EVERYONE, calm down!" He said forcibly. "I'm sorry mom, we got into the car and this happened." He told her as he pointed to Penelope's hair. "I pointed it out to her without thinking! I'm sorry I couldn't give you the time you needed to talk through everything." He apologized with a wince, realizing just how badly he had screwed up.

The look on his father's face was raw and painful. This might be too much at one time, blindsiding him without giving him the time he needed to work through his feelings properly.

Jack swallowed heavily as he saw his father take a step back from his mother and sister, his tortured face going carefully blank. It was not something he had ever seen his father do, shuttering his emotions like that, hiding them away from his family. That single action scared him more than everything else that had happened within the last day.

"I, I think I need a few minutes," Jason said, finally brushing past everyone and opening the front door. With a barely stifled cry, Elinor sank to the ground, still clutching to her confused and scared daughter. Jack hurried forward and clutched at his mother and sister, unsure of what he could do to reassure them that everything would be alright.

The front door closed with an ominous click and what little control his mother had managed to cling to disappeared. Jack could only watch as she buried her face in her daughter's ever redder hair and began to cry piteously.

"Sorry! I did not handle that well." Refusing to let go of his sister and mother, Jack twisted his neck and saw his father facing the now closed door with a bowed head. "Please Elinor, stop crying, you know what that does to me." He said softly, stepping away from the door and turning to face them.

Nudging his son to the side, he carefully unwound his wife's arms from around their daughter and pulled her into an all-encompassing embrace. Jack reached for his sister and wrapped an arm around her as they watched their parents.

Penelope's eyes were still wide, but he could see that the panic that had been in them before had vanished. Seeing their mother lose control like that had temporarily made her forget about her own problem.

"Come on, let's leave them for now. They have a lot that they need to talk about, and it would be better if we weren't here for it." He whispered into her ear, noticing that as he did so, the hair there had turned red.

"Alright," She agreed, pushing him from the room. Her eyes remained fixed on her parents, who had yet to move.

Jack let her push him from the room and towards the back of the house as her finger began to jab into him painfully. He arched his back and took a hurried step forward, twisting around until he could see her.

"Ow, what was that for?" He took a step back as the look on her face unsettled him. No, it wasn't the look on her face, it was her eyes. In the dim, windowless hallway, it was easy to see the glow that suffused them. The angry squint of her eyes mixed with the thin white line of her lips would normally have had him laughing at her. She was too young to be able to pull off that kind of look properly. Right now, was anything but ordinary.

She looked dangerous. The stance of her body told him how close she was to losing it! Her curled fingers with short but sharp nails promising pain. Her slightly bent legs and forward lean hinting at her intentions.

Raising his hands, he stepped back from her and tried to calm her down. "Calm down Penelope, I'll explain what I can, but I only know what mom told me this morning! We can't be loud either. If we make too much noise, we'll distract mom and dad from talking everything out! Do you want that?"

At the mention of their parents, she seemed to deflate as her body sagged and lost the tension that had kept it coiled. The glow of her eyes remained, but the dangerous gleam had left them. It left her looking like what she was, a young girl who was scared of so many things. At the corners of her eyes, he could see the flicker of moisture as she sniffed and rubbed at her suddenly runny nose with the back of her hand.

"Into my room," He said quietly. He wanted to comfort her, but he knew that if he so much as reached for her, she would start crying. He hated seeing his sister like this, but he hated seeing her cry even more. She was such a happy girl that her crying always felt wrong to him.

She hurried into his room and perched herself on the bed while he sat at his desk. One of his pillows was gripped tightly in her arms with her legs crossed beneath it. He had closed the door behind them, so they didn't have to speak so softly.

"How bad is it? How badly did mom mess up?" Penelope's voice was soft and barely carried to his ears as she buried her face into his pillow.

"I don't know. I think pretty bad though. I know she was worried about how dad would take it. I've never seen her that scared to talk to dad before!"

"What did she do?" She asked, peaking her eyes out from within the pillow.

"She's been hiding the truth about me and apparently you, from him since our births!" He said with a sigh.

"What truth? Why would she do that? Did she have an affair?" She spit out in rapid fashion.

"No, she did not have an affair!" He shot out, shutting down that line of thought right away. He did not want his little sister thinking about their mother like that. "I'm talking about the truth of what we are, what mom is."

Penelope absentmindedly pulled a lock of her newly red-streaked hair into her mouth as she waited for him to continue. Seeing that he had her full attention, he relaxed into the chair and told her everything his mother had told him at the restaurant.

She was silent while he spoke, sucking on her hair in disbelief. It was only when he had finished speaking that she said anything. "I'm not sure what to say right now. Magic is supposed to be fake, not real!" She stood and spit the lock of hair from her mouth as she wound herself into a fit. "How could mom keep something like this from us? Especially me? I can at least somewhat understand her keeping it from you, considering everything that would entail. But it is an entirely different situation when it comes to me!"

Jack couldn't help but roll his eyes at her reaction. Of course, she would be willing to accept such an outlandish story as truth right away and then make it about herself. It wasn't that she was self-centered or anything, at least no more than anyone else her age. It was just that she was seeing how it affected her, with her eyes and her hair. Actually, he wasn't sure if she had even noticed her eyes yet. In the car, her hair had been more noticeable than the shifting color of her eyes.

"Right and I'm sure that is exactly what mom was concerned about all these years!" He said dryly as she began to pace in front of his bed.

She paused to glare at him for a second and then went back to her pacing.

"I want to talk to mom! How much time do you think they need?" She whined to him as her feet beat out a rhythm on the carpet.

"I don't know, but I imagine more time than we have given them at this point. There is a lot that they need to discuss and work through. You saw how close dad was to walking out earlier!" At the mention of what had almost happened, he saw her tense before sinking back onto the bed. He could only imagine just how confused she was feeling right now.

Jack stood from the chair and crouched in front of his sister, pulling her into a hug. He could feel her trembling against his chest as she struggled to keep everything inside. "It's alright, just let it go. I'm here for you, and I'm not going anywhere!" He whispered to her softly as he stroked her hair.

The sound of her sobbing into his chest reached his ears as he felt her tears begin to soak through his shirt. Through it all, he held his little sister close, trying to reassure her that everything would be alright with his presence. Sometime during the midst of her crying, she had slipped from the bed and onto the floor with him.

She was quiet and her body still when the door to his room finally opened and his mother peeked her head inside. "How is she doing?" She asked quietly when she saw Penelope curled into his chest.

He beckoned her inside with a wave of his head before answering. "I told her what you told me, but honestly, it's a lot to take in. Then there was the thing with dad and her hair changing colors, plus her eyes now glowing. Although I'm not sure if she knows about that one yet..."

"Honey, slow down." She interrupted her son from his rambling.

"Right." He took in a deep breath and released it slowly. "I think that you need to start whatever training you were going to do with her right away. She needs to feel like she has some control, and you need to talk to her!"

Elinor tilted her head as she looked at him. "That... that sounds like an incredibly mature response, and not at all like something you would normally say."

"This is something important, something that is going to affect her entire life. I can't afford to be flippant about something like that." He said as he squeezed his sister tighter, his eyes growing slightly moist. "How's everything with dad? Were you able to explain everything to him properly?"

She winced as she sat on the floor next to her kids. "He is not happy with me, and I understand why, just like he understands why I did what I did. He holed himself in his office a few minutes ago after we finished talking. He thought that part of my life was mostly contained to just my work, and now to have it thrust back at him like this, I think really blindsided him. "Not to mention me hiding everything about you from him for all these years has him questioning what else I might have been concealing from him." She sighed and seemed to deflate into herself. "It's going to be a long road before he fully trusts me again, but at least he isn't leaving."

The air around them had taken on a heavy dreary quality as she had been speaking, fitting the mood that now filled the small bedroom.

"Mom," Jack finally began, looking her in the eye. "What were those monsters last night? I've never seen anything like that around here before." His hand kept stroking his sister's increasingly red hair as she breathed deeply into his chest, asleep and blissfully unaware of the world around her.

"I have a few ideas, but I can't be certain without seeing them in person. The description you gave me is worrying. I thought I had removed all the monsters, nightwalkers, and other such beings from this area years ago. There are many monsters in the world that regular people have forgotten about through the years, or just plain never knew existed. Many have been hunted into extinction, but something new always appears to take their place."

She sighed and leaned heavily against him. "I haven't been following parts of the world of magic and monsters as closely as I should have been these last few years. Some of the things I knew and the things I thought I knew are woefully outdated at this point."

Jack could almost feel the despair emanating from his mother as she spoke. "It'll be alright mom, all of it. Dad will come around, and I'm sure Penelope will find it exciting as soon as she stops freaking out. And me, I'll meet up with Kaitlyn and her family and start learning about my abilities. Everything is going to be fine. You just wait and see." He wasn't entirely convinced that it would work out like that at all, but it sounded good and he could feel his mother relaxing next to him at his words.

"I hope so." He heard her whisper softly next to him before straightening and climbing to her feet. "Give me your sister. I'll take her to her room and talk to her there. She and I have several things that we need to talk about, but I'm going to let her sleep for now."

Jack readjusted his grip on his sister as he stood next to his mother. The light-weight of her sleeping body stirred gently in his arms.

His mother took her from his arms and walked out of his room. Leaving him alone and with his emotions in flux. Wordlessly, he sank onto his bed and curled into a ball, waiting for sleep to come over him. He had gotten only a couple of hours of sleep that morning, and it had been an emotional roller coaster ever since he had woken.

Jack woke with a groan as the alarm on his phone blared hatefully next to his head. It was light outside his window, with the dawning sun hanging just above the horizon.

"I need more sleep!" He said into his pillow, closing his eyes again.It was Monday, which meant he had school. It also meant that he would see Kaitlyn and her family again. Worse, he had fallen asleep so early yesterday that he had never had a chance to talk to his father or mother again! He only knew what she had told him, which admittedly was something. If she hadn't ended up being some kind of witch or magic-user or whatever, then he would be going into this situation even more blind. Regardless, it didn't exactly help him to feel at ease.

Punching his pillow, he pushed off his bed and grabbed some clothes before stumbling into the bathroom for a shower. The hot water and steam helped to wake him up as the chilly air of the bathroom receded for a few moments.

He hurriedly pulled on his clothes and ran back to his room for shoes. Penelope would be wanting the shower next if it wasn't already too late.

Jack burst into his room and shoved his feet into his shoes as he grabbed blindly for his wallet and phone. Pulling his bag off his desk, he rushed from his room and stopped in shock when he ran into the kitchen. Sitting calmly at the table was Kaitlyn, talking to his mother.

"Huh, what? What is going on here?" He managed to ask in a barely coherent manner.

Looking away from the guest sitting in front of her, his mother answered. "I woke up early to drive you to school. You mentioned yesterday that you had ridden your bike Saturday night, it was left behind during everything. I thought I would pick it up after dropping you off. Kaitlyn here, apparently, was thinking something similar."

"Uh, okay." He had completely forgotten about not having his bike. It was how he got everywhere, including to and from school.

"This is my family's address. I'll see you there after school. It seems that we have more to discuss than we thought." Kaitlyn said somewhat stiffly, as she slipped a piece of paper across the table to Elinor.

"I'll meet you both there then." She said, taking the proffered paper.

Chapter 7

Kaitlyn pushed away from the table and stood, her back ramrod straight. "We should be going. I believe I have a meeting with the headmaster before classes start."

"Principal, they're referred to as principles here, not headmasters," Elinor told her without missing a beat.

Jack saw Kaitlyn's cheeks color slightly as she nodded her head in thanks before turning to him. Her brow cocked as she looked him over once and then walked out of the room without waiting for him.

His mother's sigh drew his attention back to her before he could follow her out.

"Be careful Jack, I think things just became more complicated than I thought. Just know this, if her mother and father are who I think they are, then you need to bond with her no matter what." Her eyes held a degree of helplessness mixed with anger in them that he wasn't accustomed to seeing in his mother.

"Alright," He said hesitantly, not knowing enough about what was going on to say anything else. "I'll see you at her place after school."

His mind was spinning as he walked through the house and out the door to where Kaitlyn was waiting beside the same car as before. "Get in. I don't want to be late!" Her voice was cold and distant as she ordered him into the car.

Jack didn't respond as he climbed into the passenger seat next to her and buckled up. Kaitlyn's slender fingers were beating an impressive tattoo on the leather steering wheel as she drove away from his house.

"Your mom is a magic user!" Kaitlyn growled at him as she turned onto the main road.

"Apparently," He replied simply. He hadn't even known until the day before. There was nothing he could really say on the matter.

"There were not supposed to be any users in this area! That is why my father chose to move us here, and then there is YOU!" She was getting worked up and starting to spiral, he could tell.

"Don't bring me into this. I didn't even know magic was real until I met you. I have nothing to do with this." He told her, trying to remain calm.

"I have nothing to do with this." She repeated in a high-pitched nasal voice, mocking him. "That right there is the problem. You have everything to do with this! And you don't even know it."

"Then enlighten me!" Jack roared at her, losing his cool, everything from the last couple of days bubbling up as he yelled at her. "Nobody has told me anything. You grew up in this world of magic.

"I grew up in a world where magic is make-believe and fairy tales. How can I understand anything that is going on around me when no one will tell me what is going on? So, I can generate magic, whoop-de freaking do, that means nothing to me! I don't know how everyone else works. Hell, I apparently don't even know how I work! There is no baseline for me to go off of!"

The car was quiet except for his heavy breathing when he finished yelling. Neither of them said anything for the remainder of the drive as Jack stared out the window and Kaitlyn gripped the steering wheel with everything she had.

Kaitlyn exhaled shakily before responding with a tight, anger laced voice. "Fine, I guess I know what one of the first things that we need to talk about tonight is. For now, though, you need to be aware of one thing."

"And that would be what?" Jack asked in annoyance, keeping his head turned towards the window.

She sighed softly and loosened her grip as she turned into the school parking lot. "Never mind, just wait for me outside the principal's office and you can show me around the campus afterward." She finished as she parked in an open spot.

"Do you even know what classes you are signed up for yet?" Jack asked as he opened his door and slung his backpack over his shoulder.

"Yes and no," She said somewhat hesitantly.

"Uh, what exactly does that mean?" He asked, looking at her and letting the last of the anger and annoyance he had felt in the car drain away.

Her cheeks took on a rosy pink color. "It means that up till Saturday night I was homeschooled. The only reason I am coming to the high school now is because of you. So, I know that I am registered in all the same classes as you. I just don't know what they are yet!" She refused to look at him as she hurried to the front doors of the building.

"I was wondering why I had never seen you around the school before. I just figured you barely moved here or something." He said, hurrying to open the doors for her.

She smiled slightly at him as she entered the building. "My family moved here this summer, but the reason you haven't seen me around is because of the homeschooling."

Jack stopped as he looked at her quizzically. "If you were homeschooled, then you weren't going to enroll in school here. How did you manage to enroll and get into the same classes as me over the weekend?"

A cloudy, guarded look flashed across her face before vanishing just as quickly. "My parents have connections. Getting into a public school like this is nothing."

"Oh..." Was all he said as he skipped past her and led her to the principal's office.

The principles secretary was a stern-faced, no-nonsense type of lady. She said exactly two words to them when they ran up. "You're late!" Okay, so maybe it wasn't exactly two words, depending on how you counted, but it was close enough.

The next thing Jack knew, he was sitting in an uncomfortable chair looking at the wrinkles that lined her face while Kaitlyn went in to see the principal. Thankfully, whatever it was that they had to talk about couldn't take very long, since he could see people filling the halls rapidly. The noise that accompanies a hoard of teenagers was impressive, and not something Jack had ever noticed until then. Sitting there in that uncomfortable chair while trying to hear something from inside the room proved impossible once they showed up.

The door opened, and Kaitlyn calmly stepped out with the principal hot on her tail, saying pointless platitudes. She grabbed Jack's hand and pulled him from the office, ignoring the principal's words. "Come on, show me where my locker is. I was told it was right next to yours."

Jack sighed, because of course her locker was next to his. He wasn't going to get a single second to himself from this point on; she was always going to be right next to him. He might as well get used to it.

The halls were crowded, almost packed, but everyone moved out of Kaitlyn's way without ever touching her or even acknowledging what they were doing. With every step she took, people shuffled to the side and then back into position as soon as she had passed. Leaving him scrambling to keep up with her, which was odd considering he was supposed to be showing her where their lockers were.

Hurrying through the crowd, he got in front of her and showed her to her locker, which was indeed next to his. She looked at the combination lock for a second, and then at the slip of paper in her hand before tapping it with her finger. The lock spun and clicked, allowing her to pull the door open a second later, revealing the empty metallic insides of the locker.

Jack looked from her to the lock and back again before shaking his head and opening his own. Shoving some of his books inside, he kept his bag and closed the door to focus on Kaitlyn. "Did they tell you what classes you have?"

"I already told you, I am in all of your classes!" Her tone was short and clipped, like talking to him was a chore.

"Sorry," He said, backing away with his hands raised. "I just wanted to make sure."

Kaitlyn watched him push through the throngs of people filling the hallway for a second before slamming her locker closed and hurrying after him. She was annoyed at him, at herself and at this entire situation! There was a reason they had moved here. They had wanted to get away from the politics and the constant jockeying for power. Now she found herself in a situation where as soon as it became known would thrust her and her parents right back into the life they had all hated!

Jack pushed through the packed bodies, ignoring the sound of slamming lockers and the constant dull roar of chatter. He didn't feel like talking to anyone that morning, and frankly, he was still rather annoyed with Steve for abandoning him on Saturday. As far as he was concerned, everything that was currently wrong with his life could be traced back to Steve!

He stepped into the classroom, no longer caring if Kaitlyn had followed him, and chose a desk at the back. Since the bell hadn't rung yet, there were only a few other kids in the room and the teacher hadn't even arrived yet.Jack pulled a book from his bag and set it on the desk as he watched Kaitlyn glide into the room. Her long legs were encased in a pair of tight jeans with black leather boots that had one-inch heels. She had taken off the jacket she had been wearing earlier to reveal a olive-green long-sleeve blouse.

The students in the room all stopped what they were doing and stared at her as she walked gracefully to the back and sat at the desk next to him. "Why is everyone staring at me?" She whispered to him softly.

Jack snorted and rolled his eyes. "Because you are pretty, and they have never seen you before. You're a shiny new toy that they know nothing about."

Kaitlyn glared lightly at him, "What a delightful way of putting it! I wish they would stop; their stares are making me slightly uncomfortable." She said softly, turning her head away from them.

"You could just ignore them or tell them to stop looking at you!" He said, looking at her curiously. He had not expected her to be shy like this. Nothing he had seen of her thus far had even hinted at a shy personality.

"Can I do that?" Kaitlyn wondered next to him.

"How long have you been homeschooled?" He asked, wondering if that might be part of the problem.

"About a month and a half. It's a fairly new thing that my mom wanted to do when we got here." She looked at him with an eyebrow raised. "Are you hinting at me having no social skills?"

Jack flushed in embarrassment at being called out on his thoughts. "I might have been wondering about something along those lines."

She gave a short bark of laughter. "No, it's nothing like that. My last school was just different from this is all."

Jack recalled part of the conversation he had heard that morning between her and his mother. "That's right, you went to some kind of fancy prep school, didn't you?"

Her face became carefully blank at his question. "Something like that." She turned away from him and faced the front of the classroom.

Jack made a note of her reaction. It seemed she didn't like talking about her family's past. He wondered if it had something to do with what his mother suspected?

The teacher trundled in a few moments later; the classroom having filled around them while they were talking. The teacher looked around the room for a second before spotting Kaitlyn. "It seems that we have had a student transfer into our class mid-semester. If you would please stand and introduce yourself before we begin?"

Kaitlyn stood somewhat stiffly and introduced herself to the class before sitting back down with a small sigh of relief. That was how each of their classes happened that day. Kaitlyn would stand and introduce herself while being stared at by the entire class. She never spoke to anyone, she barely even spoke to Jack again.

She vanished during their lunch hour but was by his side again as soon as he finished eating, and when he asked where she had been, she ignored him.

The end of school for the day approached and Jack was almost certain that she hadn't spoken to anyone but him the entire day. She ignored everyone after she introduced herself; it didn't matter if they were male or female, popular or not. She ignored them all equally.

As they were walking to her car, Jack felt that he had to say something to her. "You're going to have to talk to them, eventually. It wouldn't be a bad idea to become friends with some of them."

She whirled on him. "And what about you? I didn't see you talking to your friend from Saturday night!"

It was true that he hadn't talked to Steve at all, but that was because he hadn't been in school that day, not an entirely uncommon occurrence for him. "He wasn't here today." He answered simply as he stopped walking and focused on her. "Why don't you want to talk to any of them?"

"Because they are unimportant! They exist in a separate world than ours. There is no need to mix the two worlds and associate with them beyond what is needed!" Kaitlyn replied angrily.

"You don't actually believe that crap, do you?" Jack asked in disbelief, stepping away from her. "From what I understand so far, we still live beside them and probably work beside them as well! Separating yourself like this from everyone you meet is beyond stupid! Who cares whether or not they can't use magic? They're still people!"

"But they're not our people!" She said forcefully, though her eyes were fixed on the ground.

"They may not be yours, but they are mine! Don't forget, my dad is one of those people, and I grew up believing I was just like them for the last seventeen years!" He brushed past her and hurried to her car, he was done discussing this with her.

Kaitlyn didn't say anything as she unlocked the car and slid into the driver's seat. She waited just long enough for him to sit down and close the door before speeding out of the parking lot.

Jack clicked his seatbelt into place and glared at her from the corner of his eye. "You couldn't have waited five seconds?"

She growled softly but remained silent with her eyes fixed on the road.

The drive to her house was only a few minutes long, but the stifling silence between them made it feel far longer.

Pulling his phone from his pocket, Jack shot a quick message to his mother, letting her know that they were on their way to Kaitlyn's house.

Pulling into her driveway, Jack saw that his mother's car was already there, and that she was still sitting in the driver's seat.

Kaitlyn pulled her car in beside and then in front of his mother's before shifting into park and shutting the engine off. Jack hopped from the car and saw his mother walking towards them, having exited her own car as soon as they passed her.

Jack hurried over to her and gave her a hug and a soft hello.

"Do not tell them anything about your sister just yet!" Elinor whispered into her son's ear as she hugged him back.

Jack gave a quick nod as he pulled away and fell into step beside her as they marched towards the front door where Kaitlyn was waiting for them.

"We're here!" Kaitlyn called out in a flat, emotionless voice as she opened the front door.

Jack and his mother entered the house behind her and closed the door with a soft click as they waited for her parents to join them in the entryway. Kaitlyn shrugged out of her jacket as she stood there waiting, her eyes were fixed on the end of the hall.

Jack and Elinor exchanged glances as they saw how oddly Kaitlyn was acting. She had been polite for the most part, but now she was acting distinctly aloof and distant.

From the end of the hall, her parents Jon and Shantell LaCouture appeared. They had walked through the same doorway that he had fled from Saturday night. Jack shook his head, dispelling those thoughts, and focused on his mother. She had stepped slightly behind him, so she wouldn't be seen right away and had gone stiff.

"Jack, it's good to see you again! Have you made a decision?" Jon asked calmly as he drew near.

"About that. It seems there is a problem," Kaitlyn said as Elinor stepped out from behind her son.

"Hello Jon, Shantell, it's been a while. I must say when my son described the sadistic woman who had healed him, I thought of you! It wasn't until I saw your daughter though, that I knew for sure." She said with more than a hint of derision in her voice. "Why have you moved into my territory without informing me? And before you think of lying, know that I already checked with the state council. There are no records of anyone moving here. Which means you did this without their approval!"

Jack saw Kaitlyn stiffen when his mother had first begun speaking. By the time she was finished, she was leaning against the wall and pale.

"What are you doing here?" Shantell screeched.

"This is my territory!" Elinor thundered. "If you had bothered to notify the council, they would have told you that!"

Jon had surreptitiously stepped away from his wife as she began screaming. "How do you even have a territory? Those are never given out!"

Jack stepped over to Kaitlyn, where he wouldn't be in the way of the screaming ladies. Jon motioned for them both to join him and walked back down the hall.

"Did you know they knew each other?" Jon asked as he closed the door to the sitting room behind them, blocking out the screaming.

Chapter 8

"Hah, you're joking, right? I didn't know about any of this before you told me!" Jack said as he sat heavily on a couch. "My mom knew that my power had been unlocked yesterday morning. That is when she explained some of her history to me. There is still a lot I don't know," He paused, regrettably. "Really, I don't know anything!"

"I found out she was a magic user like us this morning, but I didn't think it was anything major," Kaitlyn said softly as she sat on the couch across from Jack. "Why didn't you tell me we moved here illegally? I know we moved because of me, but why would we do this?"

"Honey, you have got to stop saying that we moved because of you!" Her father told her firmly.

"But we did, it's because..." Her eyes flickered over to Jack and she abruptly stopped speaking and withdrew back into herself.

Jon ran his hand over his face, taking the time to massage his closed eyes with his fingers. "Kids are cruel and malicious creatures." He said in a soft and sad rasp.

Jack felt his eyes fix on Kaitlyn at the exchange, watching the various emotions flicker across her face.

"To answer your question, it's because that is what your mother wanted. She wanted us to fly under the radar, to get away from everything. She thought this would be the perfect area. It's been quiet for years, and there are very few users in the area." Jon smirked as he spoke. "I guess now we know why!" His chin tilted to point at Jack.

"I don't really understand what this talk of territories and needing permission is all about," Jack said, speaking up. "I understand that my mom is in charge of this territory, but other than that, none of what you have been saying makes any sense."

Jon scratched at the light dusting of stubble on his chin before answering. "Think of it in terms of how kingdoms used to work. You had the King, and then directly beneath him, you had Dukes, Viscount's, etcetera. The duke is in charge of numerous areas, while a baron is in charge of a single area.

"The baron is responsible for the upkeep and wellbeing of their holding. As such, any time someone of power moves into an area that is under a baron's supervision, they are required to announce themselves. In this example, your mother is the baron. This section of Colorado is her territory, and we are the people of power that should have announced ourselves on our arrival."

Jack sat up straighter on the comfortable couch. "Okay, so far it makes sense. I still have questions like how my mother came to be in charge of the area, but we can get back to that. More importantly, why didn't you or your wife want to announce yourselves when you moved here?"

"That would be because of me," Kaitlyn said somewhat timidly.

"I just told you…"

"Do not say anymore!" Shantell said loudly from the now open doorway of the room. None of them had noticed that the yelling had stopped. Jack's mother, Elinor, was standing behind her with a harsh, unhappy expression on her face and fisted hands on her hips.

"Jack, we are leaving now!" Elinor said imperiously. "I will not have your training conducted by this, this…" She seemed at a loss for words. "This venomous viper of a woman!"

Jack was slow to respond in the wake of his mother's anger. He had never seen her so mad before at one person. Elinor spun on her heel and stalked away when she saw him stand and begin walking towards her.

"Bye, I guess. I'll see you tomorrow at school." Jack whispered to Kaitlyn as he walked by.

Shantell stood in the doorway, blocking his way as she glared at him with pinched, angry eyes.

Her blonde hair was ruffled and looked like she had been pulling at it angrily. She met his gaze, letting her flashing eyes bore into his. "I don't know what you and your mother are up to, but I don't like it!" Her mouth barely moved as she whispered harshly at him before moving to the side and allowing him to pass.

Jack said nothing as he brushed past her and joined his mother. She was quiet as she started up her car and backed down the driveway.

"I picked up your bike earlier. It seems you'll be needing it tomorrow morning." She finally ground out angrily.

"Mom," Jack began tentatively. "What happened between you and Kaitlyn's mom?"

Elinor breathed in sharply and held it for a few seconds before releasing it. Her hands were tight on the steering wheel. "Let's just say that we have a history and leave it at that. First, I need to talk to your father and then I need to decide if I am going to report them!"

"Don't!" Jack said suddenly. "I still don't really understand what they did wrong, but from what they told me, they did it for Kaitlyn. If you report them, it will negatively affect her. I still feel like I owe her for saving my life."

Jack could hear his mother grinding her teeth as she processed his words. "If you owe her, then I guess I owe Shantell for healing you as well. Fine, I won't report them, but that doesn't mean I'm happy with whatever they are doing here!"

"Thanks, mom, I appreciate it," Jack told her, giving her a shoulder a squeeze.

"This does complicate things though, I can't train both you and your sister at the same time. The two of you will need completely different styles of training!" She said in exasperation.

"Speaking of Penelope, why didn't you want me to mention her to them? I get the feeling that she isn't exactly normal either. Is she?" Jack asked as they pulled into the driveway of their house.

Elinor was quiet as she exited the car and waited for her son to stand next to her. "No, she isn't, but remember to be careful what you talk about when you aren't at home."

Jack looked around before they entered the house. "Do you really think people are listening to us?"

"No, I don't, not yet anyway. The information about you is still too new, but I want you to start being careful now so that it isn't an issue when it really matters!"

Jack closed the front door and leaned against it. "What about Penelope? Is there anything I can do to help her?"

Elinor sighed sadly as she turned and looked at her son. "You can stay away from her for now. Her hair still hasn't changed back. Thankfully, her eyes have stopped glowing, but next time they might not. You being near her is what is causing these changes in her. Until she has some control over her powers, I think it would be best if you didn't spend too much time with her."

Jack's face fell at her words. "Mom, she's my sister, she's my friend and we live in the same house, we eat at the same table! How do you expect me to not spend time with her?"

Elinor stepped forward and hugged her son tightly. "I don't know, honey, that's just one of the many things I need to discuss with your father when he gets home tonight."

"I, I understand. I think I'm going to go to my room and take a nap," Jack said as he lightly pushed his mother away and hurried to his room.

He needed to talk to Kaitlyn, maybe she could help him regardless of her mother. Everything had become so complicated over the last couple of days! Jack knew it wasn't really her fault, but he needed to blame someone right now. Getting her to help him was key right now, and if she felt like it was her fault, then that would make it that much easier to convince her.

Jack closed the door to his room and dropped his backpack on his bed, then hurrying over to his window, he opened it and climbed out. His bike was leaning against the side of the garage where his mother had left it after fetching it for him earlier.

He had some time before anyone would know he was missing. Penelope usually barged into his room after she got home from school, wanting his help with her homework or just to hang out and play. She had something going on after school this week though, and he was fairly sure his mother would stop her from seeing him anyway.

The wheels of his mountain bike sped over the sun-warmed pavement. The air was clear, and the sun was only just starting its descent. The strain on his muscles felt good after sitting in school all day, and the exercise was helping to clear his mind.

Jack swung his bike off the road and onto a dirt path. His breath came in short gasps that forced all extra thought from his mind. The small shocks on the mountain bike depressed and extended over the rough terrain. The frustration he had been feeling slowly ebbed away, leaving his mind clear and his emotions stable.

Jack firmed his grip on his handlebars and jumped the bike from the dirt path and back onto the paved road. The road he needed to turn on to get to Kaitlyn's house was directly ahead of him. He skidded to a stop before he could turn onto her street, the wheels on his bike locking up under the pressure of his brakes.

Kaitlyn was walking away from her house towards him. Her head was down, and she had her hands shoved into the pockets of her fleece jacket. Her long hair was bound into a ponytail that draped down her back.

She seemed angry with each step she took, looking like she wanted to kick something.

"Kaitlyn!" Jack called out as she neared him without having looked up.

The smile she gave him when she saw who had called her was tremulous at best. "What are you doing here? I thought your mom took you home?"

"She did, but I needed to talk to you, so I came back," Jack informed her as he pulled the bike alongside her and started walking with her. "Why do you seem so angry right now?"

Kaitlyn looked at him like he was an idiot. "Why do you think? My mom laid down the law after the two of you left! I am not to speak with or see you again. She was going to try to pull me out of school, but dad stopped her from doing that thankfully. He told her that it would look suspicious and would draw unwanted attention. Also, apparently your mom, and by extension, you, are the spawn of the devil who only lives to cause her grief!"

Jack stopped walking and leaned on the bike as he began laughing. "Do you have any idea what their deal is? My mom wouldn't tell me anything more than that they have a history!"

Kaitlyn stepped off the sidewalk and onto the grass before flopping to the ground and looking at the sky. "I have absolutely no idea. Mom doesn't talk about the past all that often. I wouldn't even be surprised if my dad doesn't know either."

"Nothing? You don't know if they went to school together, or if they picked on each other? Not even if they were bitter rivals or something?" Jack asked, sinking to the ground beside her.

"Nope, nothing. All I know is that something happened in my mom's past that she's ashamed of and it's related to her parents, my grandparents." It was hard to miss the disdain with which she spoke those familial words. "Everything, before she married my dad, is just a blank. She rarely talks about it. Don't get me wrong, she's a great mother and I love her. I just don't know anything about her past." Kaitlyn's eyes were closed as she spoke.

"Weird." Jack let the matter drop and looked up at the orange-streaked sky. "Are you going to be able to help me still, or is that no longer an option?"

Kaitlyn's ponytail lay on the grass next to her head as she turned to look at him. "Why can't your mom train you?"

"Promise not to say anything to your mom or anyone else?" He said, twisting his head to look her in the eye.

Her eyes narrowed as she blinked at him. "If it's something about your family, I can keep it to myself."

Jack held his breath as she answered, trying to decide if he really wanted to go against what his mother had said. "She needs to focus on my younger sister. I can't be around her right now. Releasing my power, or whatever, is affecting her as well! My mom told me to keep it a secret, but I need help!"

"I'm not going to lie to you Jack, I'm not really qualified to train you by myself. I was going to help, but my parents were going to be in charge, especially in the beginning." She took a deep breath and looked back up at the slowly darkening sky. "That said, I do have some idea on what we would need to do. If you want, then we could start tomorrow, either right after school or later in the night? We could meet up at the abandoned school building without anyone being the wiser."

"That should work fine." Jack stood and brushed off the back of his jeans. "I guess I'll see you at school tomorrow. Have a good night!"

Kaitlyn sat up as he straddled his bike. "No, I'll still come to pick you up tomorrow morning. It's my mom that has the issue with training. If I can talk to your mom, she may be able to give me some ideas for the training."

Jack smiled weakly at her. "Sounds good. I'll see you in the morning, then."

***

Dinner was a quiet and strained affair that night. Jack hadn't had a chance to talk to his mother again since he got back from his bike ride. He also hadn't had a chance to talk to Penelope.

The red in her hair was still there and had settled into streaks, but her eyes had settled down into a soft caramel color. The table was quiet with each person lost in their own separate thoughts.

Jack pushed back from the table and picked up his dishes and stuck in the sink as he walked past. "Mom, I need to talk to you when you're done."

Elinor nodded in acknowledgment before returning to her plate of food.

Jack was sitting at the desk in his room finishing the last of his homework when his mother walked in.

"What do you need Jack?" She asked as she sat on the edge of his bed.

He turned to look at her. "I spoke with Kaitlyn earlier, and she is still willing to train me regardless of what her mother wants. She is going to pick me up in the morning for school, and she wanted to talk to you then. She needs to know the best way to train me, she said she has some ideas but isn't sure of the best way to go about it."

His mother took in a deep breath as he spoke looking like she might interrupt him. "I'll speak to her in the morning, I have some questions that she needs to answer first. When I spoke to her this morning, she seemed like a nice girl, but I only spoke to her for a couple of minutes. I'll need to lay down some ground rules and make sure she understands that her mother is not to be involved in any way without speaking with me first."

Jack's eyes narrowed in speculation. "That was a lot easier than I thought it would be, why? What are you thinking?"

Elinor gave a short bark of laughter. "Hasn't anyone ever told you not to ask stupid questions when you get what you want?" Her tone gentled as she continued. "Look I know how much being around Penelope means to you, I also know that I can't train and teach both of you at the same time. Allowing Kaitlyn and possibly her family to help is really the only option."

"Is the training going to be hard?"

"For you? Not really, it is more a matter of getting you used to the feel of magic and being able to control it on your end. It will be mentally exhausting but that is really it. If you are able to use magic once you bond then it gets truly difficult, magic for people in a bond changes and becomes different. It becomes more powerful, more innate, more everything. Control is everything for people in that type of bond, so you need to learn as much control as you can now."

"Why, there's no guarantee that I'll be able to use magic when I bond with her?" In his mind, Kaitlyn was still the person he was going to bond with. The thought had gotten under his skin in a significant way in the last few days.

His mother smiled somewhat sadly as she stood and faced him. "You will need control to be around your sister, as for the matter of you being able to use magic once you have bonded. There is no doubt in my mind that you will be able to, especially if you bond with her. Don't forget I know her mother!"

"What does that mean? What does her mother have to do with this?" Jack asked as his mother walked away.

She paused next to his door, "I'll talk to Kaitlyn in the morning, get your rest now. You're going to need it!"

Chapter 9

J ack found himself twisting and turning in his bed for most of the night. Images of monsters and the uncertain future held sway over his waking thoughts. When he finally drifted off into a fitful slumber, the dreams were even worse. Fears he hadn't even fully acknowledged held influence during that nightmarish time.

When the alarm blared next to his head in the morning, it was tired glazed eyes that opened to the morning sun peeking through his windows. His hands had a slight tremble to them as he threw off his blanket and sat up.

Grabbing some clothes, he hurried into the bathroom for a quick shower, letting the hot water calm his battered nerves. Jack's hands had steadied by the time he was dressed in fresh clothes.

A dark blue jacket and his backpack in hand, Jack hurried down the hall and into the kitchen. The sound of two people talking reached his ears a moment before he stepped into the bright sunlit kitchen. His mother was sitting at the table talking to Kaitlyn, similar to the way he had seen them talking the day before. This time, his mother was notably more relaxed as she spoke with the tall blonde-haired girl.

"Where do you intend to conduct his training?" Elinor asked the slightly off-put young woman.

"In the building, he found me in on Saturday, just not on the top floor this time," Kaitlyn answered quickly, trying to regain her mental footing.

She had not expected Jack's mother to be so intense! They had been talking for over five minutes already and the questions had been coming non-stop. Thankfully, she had explained some more on how she should go about training him as well. That had been very enlightening!

It wasn't something that was truly difficult, so much as it was time-consuming and somewhat awkward. The first step was simply getting him used to having magic flowing through his system. The easiest way to do that was to hold his hand while she cast a simple spell or circulated her magic continuously and drew on his reserves.

"Have you gotten everything figured out?" Jack asked, stepping into the room. His eyes tracking across Kaitlyn's flushed face.

Elinor raised a brow as she turned to face her son. "I think it is safe to say that we understand each other."

"Err, okay, I guess," Jack replied, somewhat confused.

"She explained things to me clearly. Now come on, I think we are ready to go!" Kaitlyn said, quickly pushing back her chair.

Jack cocked his head slightly as he stepped past the table and looked at his mother.

"It's nothing dear. I just wanted to make sure she understood her position. Have a good day at school and be careful during your training. I'll be working with your sister by the time you get back, so I'll need you to get dinner ready, please?" Elinor told him as she pushed away from the table and stood as well.

"Sure-thing mom just leave the recipe for whatever you want me to make on the counter. I'll see you later. Have a good day and tell Penelope to work hard!" Jack said as he used his bag to gently push Kaitlyn out of the kitchen and down the hall.

"You know how to cook?" Kaitlyn asked softly as they walked out of the house.

Jack shrugged before responding. "I know how to follow a recipe. It's not hard. The directions are all printed out and in order, as long as you follow that you can't mess it up."

Kaitlyn was quiet as she unlocked her car and slid into the driver's seat. "Can you show me how to cook sometime?"

Jack clicked his seatbelt in place before looking at her. "Your mom or dad don't cook?"

"No, we used to have someone that cooked for us before we moved here. Since we have lived here though, we've been mostly eating takeout or frozen pizzas." Kaitlyn explained as she looked over her shoulder to back down the short driveway. "I don't think my mom knows how and my dad is always pretty busy with work."

Jack wasn't sure how to respond to that information and lightly scratched at his cheek before responding. "I don't mind showing you how. Like I said, it's not hard. Why don't you just come over after we are done today, and you can help me make dinner? We'll make a double portion of it and you can bring the second portion home with you." He offered, deciding to not address what she had said about her parents.

"I'd like that, thanks!" Kaitlyn said excitedly, both of them momentarily forgetting that what they were doing was a secret from her parents.

***

School that day was much like the day before. Kaitlyn spoke to no-one but him. Keeping herself aloof and detached from the rest of the student body. As a result, more people ended up speaking to Jack, wanting to know what her deal was and why she wouldn't talk to anyone. He tried to answer as truthfully as possible, but the truth of the matter was that he just didn't know why. He wasn't sure if it had something to do with her prejudices that they had argued over the day before or if it was something else entirely. In all honesty, he still didn't really know anything about her. She might just be painfully shy and not like talking to people she didn't know.

Jack decided that he was going to get more out of her during their training later. He wanted to know why she wasn't interacting with anyone else at school. He was fine with being her friend, but he didn't want to be her only friend! She needed to have a life of her own with friends of her own!

"Why don't you talk to anyone at school?" Jack asked as soon as they had left the school parking lot behind them.

"I see no reason to get to know those people." She answered simply, not looking away from the road.

"Is this more of that we belong to separate worlds crap from yesterday?" He asked hotly.

Kaitlyn smirked as she replied. "No, well, not entirely." She was quiet as she struggled for the right words. "I know you think my words yesterday were stupid, but you have to understand that is the world I am from! All my friends and the people that I have gone to school with up to this point have belonged to that world. I know nothing of the regular world, so I have nothing in common with those people! What would I talk about with them?"

Jack twisted his body in the passenger seat so he could fully face her. "I'm going to call BS on that. Even if everyone you used to know could use magic, you still lived in the regular world. Surely you must have talked about other things besides magic, like music or movies or something? Right?"

Kaitlyn's fingers tapped on the steering wheel as she thought. "Magic was always the most interesting topic around. What did we care about movies when our own abilities were more entertaining? What did we care about boys or models when most of us were destined for arranged marriages?"

"Wait!" Jack stopped her. "What do you mean arranged marriages?"

"Your mother running off to marry someone without magic is outside the norm. It's so far out there, in fact, that she is the first person that I have heard of doing that in recent years. The magic community spans the world, so it's not exactly small." Kaitlyn said, trying to justify it.

"Still, why is it so bad to marry someone without magic? It obviously worked out fine with my sister and me."

Kaitlyn gave a short, harsh laugh. "No, it didn't. You are an aberration that would normally have been hunted down and forced to work for the council or someone with power. And from what you told me yesterday, your sister is no better. She might not be the same as you, but she is still different. Trust me when I say that in our society, if it was known that the two of you existed, both of you would be hunted down and forced to serve someone else. Your sister is simply lucky enough to pass as a regular magic user, unlike you."

Jack swallowed and licked his suddenly dry lips. "What about you then? Are you destined for an arranged marriage as well?" He asked, trying to wrap his mind about what she had just said before addressing it.

"No, not for lack of trying on others' part, but my father didn't want me to enter into that kind of relationship. I think that might be part of why he jumped at the idea of me bonding with you. It was an out for me, one that would allow me to choose my own path and not be forced."

Jack took a deep, calming breath and asked his next question. "Would my sister and I really be tracked down and enslaved if we were discovered?"

Kaitlyn stopped the car and shut off the engine before replying. "For you, most definitely! For her, I don't know enough to say for certain, but if she actually is different, then something would happen for sure. I just couldn't say what."

Stepping out of the vehicle, Jack closed his eyes and breathed in the smell of fallen leaves and wood that filled the fall air. "Let's do this then. I can't let anything happen to Penelope!"

"Right, and don't forget I'm coming over to your place afterward for cooking practice." Kaitlyn reminded him as she led him up the worn concrete steps and into the building.

"So, why exactly did you choose this place for practice, anyway?" Jack asked as he hurried after her.

"It just seemed like a good idea at the time. We can't do it at either of our houses, and I don't really know any other places in town. Since my family moved here, I've spent most days training at this building. Ever since I first saw it, it has seemed like the perfect location." Kaitlyn explained as she slipped through the broken door. "Of course, now that the third floor is broken, I can't train up there, so I figured we could just use the ground floor." Her voice echoed strangely in the abandoned building.

"Why were you using the top floor for your training?" Jack asked as he pushed the door open a little more.

She turned to look at him, the dim light of the moldy interior leaving her face in shadow. "The way I figured it is that even if someone came into the building while I was practicing, they weren't likely to go to the top floor and find me."

Jack started laughing at what she said. Bending at the hips, he fought for breath as he continued laughing. "You do realize that it was your practicing up there that caused me to go up that far. The noise from whatever you were doing is what made the rumors that the place is haunted start back up."

Kaitlyn's face fell as the full import of his words rocked her world. That meant everything that had happened with him was her fault! She was responsible for the danger that he now found himself in!

Jack nudged her with his shoulder before walking past her, still chuckling lightly. "Where do you want to start?"

"Let's stay on this floor, just in case," Kaitlyn said absently, her mind still caught up in reviewing the many ways she had messed up his life.

Jack walked past the old, decrepit staircase that he had climbed Saturday night and into the old hallway he had ignored before. The ceiling panels were warped and yellow, and more than a couple were on the ground crumbling. The paint on the walls had faded long ago and was covered in moldering watermarks that had discolored the walls.

The first classroom he came across had the wooden door missing from the hinges. Peeking his head inside the room, he saw the door leaning against the wall inside the room. The room was empty of everything, but the door and the wooden flooring had been laid bare by the elements. A light spot on one of the walls showed where a chalkboard had hung years before.

"This room is empty. What do you think?" Jack asked Kaitlyn, withdrawing his head from the room.

"Any room will work; we'll just be sitting for this first part anyway," Kaitlyn said as she brushed past him into the room.

Jack settled onto the dusty ground, ignoring how dirty his clothes were getting. Kaitlyn sat directly in front of him and grabbed his hands. Her fingers intertwined with his as she closed her eyes and focused on her breathing.

"For this first part, I want you to close your eyes and try to feel the movement of the magic within you." Her voice was slightly strained as she spoke. "I'm going to circulate the magic from my body into yours and back into mine. Don't distract me though, it's a struggle to keep my magic under control while touching you."

Jack closed his eyes and matched his breathing with hers.

"Alright let's begin," Kaitlyn said as her hands tightened around his.

Jack focused his mind, straining to feel everything. The beat of his heart pounded in his ears as his senses turned inwards. This wasn't like when Kaitlyn's mom had healed him. Then she had taken his power, ripping it mercilessly from his body. It had been easy to feel then. The sheer magnitude of how much was being taken ensured that. What Kaitlyn was doing was merely moving it, not taking it.

Every once in a while, her hands would grip his tighter before slowly relaxing. Seconds turned into minutes as they sat there on the dusty floor. Shadows lengthened and still, they continued on, pushing themselves harder.

Sweat was dripping from Kaitlyn's face, falling onto her drenched blouse and hands as she struggled to keep herself under control. Power of this magnitude was new to her and controlling it was not something that she was used to. Her own well of power was tiny in comparison. It always had been. That was why she was practicing constantly. She had done everything that she and her parents could think of to expand her well, and still, it had refused to grow as it should. Her control though, her control had gotten better, her spells used only the magic they needed and nothing more. There was not any extra to be wasted.

Holding Jack's hands like this and feeling the well of power that was begging to be released fought against her control, threatening to overwhelm her like it had on Saturday night. She didn't want to hurt him though, and that was exactly what would happen if her control slipped.

Gradually, she began letting more power circulate through them. If he hadn't been able to detect the flow before, then soon he would be able to. A river of energy circulated through their bodies in a continuous stream. There was no beginning and no end. It was a perfect circle linking her small puddle of a well to his vast lake.

Jack stiffened as he began to feel something coursing through his body. It grew larger and larger until it was easy to feel. He focused on the feeling of it coursing through his veins and let his mind sink into something vast and powerful, but just out of reach.

With a cry of pain, Kaitlyn released his hands and scooted backward before falling to her back. Her breath came in deep gasps with her hands clenched at her sides.

Jack moved to her side, and only just barely held back a gasp. Her eyes were closed, but he could still see a blue glow shining through her eyelids, highlighting the individual veins in them.

Kaitlyn's face twisted into a painful grimace as her hands began to clench and unclench. "Do not touch me!" She barely managed to grind out. "I'm only just keeping in control."

Jack backed away quickly, his hand falling to his side. "What can I do?"

"Just give me a few minutes!" Kaitlyn's voice was strained as she fought for control.

"Alright," Jack said softly as he settled in the far corner of the room.

Sitting there, he watched as her body would slowly relax, only to tighten again as her eyes would flare brighter beneath the closed lids. Long minutes later, when the sun had fallen beneath the horizon, Kaitlyn relaxed for the final time. Stiffly, she sat up and opened her no-longer glowing eyes.

"That is probably going to happen every time we practice." She said weakly, just sitting there letting the strength come back into her limbs.

"What happened? I thought you said you had good control?" Jack asked as he climbed to his feet.

Kaitlyn raised her hand, stopping him from getting closer. "I do have good control for the power that I have access to. The problem is that I have always had a rather small magical well, so even if I brought all my power out at once, it still isn't that much. You, on the other hand, are like a vast ocean in comparison. Just touching you forces a veritable tsunami of power to flood my being. I was able to keep it mostly under control while I was circulating it through our bodies, but it built up." She grinned weakly as she struggled to her feet. "At least I didn't blast you across the room this time!"

Jack stood there, unsure how he should react to that revelation. "Err, do you still want to come over and help with dinner, or do you need to go home?"

Kaitlyn swayed gently on her feet as she cocked an eyebrow at him. "Do I look that tired?"

"Yeah, honestly you do. I'm not even sure I should let you drive home right now." Jack said as he plunged his hands into his pockets. The urge to reach out and steady her was nearly overwhelming. That would be the worst thing he could do right now though.

Closing her eyes, she reached out to the wall and steadied herself. "I should be fine. Having that much energy circulating through me and building up like that though, is tiring. Tomorrow, we'll need to set an alarm or take breaks. Pacing ourselves will be key."

Jack said nothing as he watched her slowly retract her hand from the wall and stand tall. "So, you never answered my question. Are you coming over or going home?"

Kaitlyn stepped next to him with a wry smile. "I think it would be better if I went home for the night. This took more out of me than I thought it would."

"That, and there is your mother you need to deal with!" Jack said as he followed her into the nearly dark hallway.

"She's not usually that bad," Kaitlyn said with a short laugh. "There's something about you and your mother that seems to rub her the wrong way."

"Yes, I can see how me running from your house and then nearly getting attacked by monsters might have that effect on someone." He replied sarcastically.

Dimly, Jack was aware of Kaitlyn spinning around to look at him. "Yes, you certainly do seem to attract trouble."

"I never used to. I can assure you, all of this is an entirely new thing for me!" Jack wasn't even sure why he was protesting. What she was saying was true, even if only recently. "Speaking of monsters, do I need to be worried about seeing them more often? Mom wouldn't really say anything on the matter."

Chapter 10

They stepped into the foyer, and Jack could see Kaitlyn worrying at her lower lip. "I don't know. Don't forget, my family has only been here for a short while ourselves. I will say this though, during that time I have not encountered any monsters in the area. The night you ran into them was the first time I even so much as saw them in the area!"

Yellow light from the lamps on the sidewalk shone into the room through the partially open door as they hurried out of the building.

"Why did they attack me then?" Jack asked as he breathed in the crisp fresh air outside the building for the first time in hours.

Kaitlyn didn't look at him as she responded. "Did you know that monsters tend to only attack those with magic? The magic that flows through us is like a beacon to them, illuminating our location and telling them how good we are going to taste." Her voice was slightly sardonic as she continued. "With my small well, I've never had to worry about being attacked. I didn't have enough magic flowing through me for them to even bother.

"I'm nothing more than an appetizer, hardly worth going out of their way for. You, on the other hand, have more magic flowing through you than ten powerful magic users combined. That is why they attacked you, and yes, I imagine it will happen again. So be careful at night, when the sun falls, they come out!"

Jack looked at the sky and the last fading light of day. "Uh, maybe we should be careful when we end our training then."

Kaitlyn laughed at his ignorance. "They don't come out right away! There is a grace period of sorts, during which they are waking up and then moving into position."

"Right, of course, there is. It only makes sense when you actually think about it! Why wouldn't monsters require time to get ready after waking up just like everyone else?" Jack said sarcastically as he followed after her to the car.

"There are many different kinds of monsters." Kaitlyn smirked at him but said nothing more as she started the car. The drive to his house was short and filled with a comfortable silence.

"Good luck with your mom. Hopefully, she'll be understanding!" Jack said as she parked the car in his driveway.

"She won't be. Whatever history our moms have with each other is influencing her thinking in this matter. No, I am going to try hiding the truth of the matter for as long as I can." Kaitlyn told him with a hollow laugh.

"Whatever, be careful on your way home and I'll see you tomorrow!" Jack said as he opened his door and climbed out of the car.

"Bright and early, I'll be here! There are a few more things I want to talk to your mom about in the morning."

Jack waved and watched as she backed out of the driveway and sped off. Slumping slightly, he let out a breath and opened the front door.

The training he had gone through with her had been mentally exhausting! Sitting there holding her hands, not feeling anything, he had begun to think that they were there more for her than him. Then she had done something, and he had begun to feel it moving through him. Focusing on that feeling, trying to grasp it and hold on with just his mind, had been strenuous.

What made it worse though, was knowing that she was doing all the work. If he was exhausted just doing this much, then how tired must she be?

Leaning heavily against the door, he rested for a moment before heading towards the kitchen. He had been holding it together for her, not wanting to show her just how much of a wimp he was! The result though, was that he was now even more wrung out than when they had finished.

Jack's hands moved slowly as he focused on cutting up the vegetables and putting them in a pan to cook. Thankfully, what he was making for dinner was something that he and his mother had made many times in the past. Otherwise, it wouldn't have been edible. His focus was just too far gone for him to properly focus on cooking right now. His hands were operating on their own, going through the motions without any mental input.

No one was home yet when dinner was finished, and after eating by himself, Jack pulled himself into his bedroom and onto the bed. Still clothed and with no thought towards his homework, he drifted off to sleep.

Jack's body was sluggish and sore when he woke the next morning, his muscles protesting to the slightest movements. The hot water from his shower helped to loosen some of the muscles, but the ache in his body was deep and in places the heat couldn't hope to reach.

There was a knock on the door, followed by his mother's voice. "Hurry up. Kaitlyn is here already!"

Pulling himself from underneath the spray of water, he quickly toweled off and pulled on the clothes he had brought in with him. Grabbing his jacket and backpack, Jack slipped on his shoes and hurried into the kitchen.

His mother eyed him as he grabbed an apple and a bagel for breakfast. "Hmm, the power in you is moving much more smoothly already. That's good, if we can bring it under enough control, then passing magic users might not notice you. Were you able to feel its movements yesterday?"

"Feel it yes, touch it or control it, no," Jack told her as he waved to Kaitlyn, who was sitting at the table with his mother.

His mother's eyes widened as she listened to what he had said. "Don't try to do too much too fast. The fact that you could even feel it moving inside of you is already impressive. It usually takes a week or two of solid practice before people can feel it moving in them!"

Kaitlyn coughed lightly and explained to her. "He was able to feel it because of how much power he has. I was circulating a lot of power through him when he finally felt it. Today I'm going to dial it back. He needs to be able to feel even the slightest fluctuations. He won't be able to control his power from leaking out until he can feel that small amount."

Jack flushed slightly as he remembered his little sister and why he was doing this. His mother wrapped her arms around him and whispered in his ear.

"Your sister says hi, and that she is doing her best and that you need to as well!"

"I will, mom, don't worry!"

Her arms tightened before loosening and falling to her sides. "Don't push yourself too hard. Injuring yourself is not something I will allow!"

"Don't worry, Mrs. Rage, I won't let him do anything that foolish," Kaitlyn said as she pushed back from the table.

His mother stepped back with her eye's closed and nodded to them. "You should go now. Penelope will be waking up soon. It would be better if you were already gone when she gets up."

His stomach twisted at her words as he followed Kaitlyn out of the house. Hearing his mother say that made him feel like he was doing something wrong in even being near his sister. It felt like they were blaming him and that he shouldn't even want to see her.

Jack shook his head and cleared the lingering thoughts from his mind as he entered the car and sat next to Kaitlyn. "How did your mother react last night when you told her where you had been?"

Kaitlyn snorted softly and started the car. "She didn't talk to me all night; I didn't even need to tell her. Apparently, when I got home, my eyes still had a slight glow to them. She saw that and stormed right out of the house! When she got back, she wouldn't say anything to me at all."

"Why are you doing this for me?" Jack began. "I don't want to be the reason things between you and your mom sour."

"This is more important," Kaitlyn said quietly, looking away from him.

Jack turned his head to look at her and waited.

"You know about the small size of my well?" She began, staring straight ahead at the stop sign in front of them.

"You've mentioned it," Jack said, cocking his eyebrow.

"The reason my parents originally wanted me to help you is because it might change that. Circulating your power through me like we were doing yesterday increases the pressure on my well, forcing it to expand."

"Wait, so why can't you just do that with anyone?" Jack asked, interrupting her.

"It requires a vast amount of power. It only works when the other person has an ocean's worth of energy like you!" Her hand tapped rhythmically on the steering wheel as she pressed on the accelerator.

"Hmm, so you are getting something out of helping me then," Jack said, facing the front thoughtfully.

"Yes, I am." Kaitlyn agreed with him. "The reason I am willing to go against my mother is because this is a once in a lifetime opportunity for me!"

"Is it really that important?" Jack asked ignorantly.

Kaitlyn's lips quirked in a self-deprecating smile. "Yes, it is. It's why we needed to move this summer. Somehow, people discovered how inferior the size of my well really is." Her voice grew pained and small as she continued. "The other people our age made my life a living hell. That one simple thing was enough to convince them that I wasn't worth anything! Friends I'd had since I was little all turned their backs on me, all because of how small it is."

Jack watched as a tear slid down her cheek. "It's their loss. If they are stupid enough to let their perceptions color their opinion of you, then you are better off without them!"

Brushing the lone tear with the back of her hand, Kaitlyn smiled sadly. "Thanks for saying that, but it doesn't hold any bearing in the real world."

Wracking his mind, Jack struggled for the appropriate thing to say. "Well, you're here now, and I won't treat you like that!"

Kaitlyn snorted as she steered the car into a free parking spot in front of the school. "Thanks, that makes everything better!" She said sarcastically.

Jack grunted in annoyance as he opened the door and hopped from the car, leaving her behind. He was just trying to help her feel better, and in return, she gets all whatever that was on him.

"Jack, wait!" Kaitlyn yelled after him as he pushed through the doors into the building.

Ignoring her, Jack pushed through the crowd of people that were milling through the hallway. The low roar of their chattering made it easy to ignore her calling after him. People that he had known for years surrounded him, but for the life of him, he couldn't bring himself to say hello to them. It was like a veil of some kind separated them now. Each of them belonged to a world that he was now gradually being removed from. He had only stepped his toe into this new world and already he was finding it hard to associate with people like before. Suddenly everything Kaitlyn had told him yesterday made a sort of twisted sense!

Jack frowned as he hurried to his locker and stored his bag, remembering what he had told Kaitlyn. He didn't want to seem like a hypocrite, but certain things were making more sense now. The world he was preparing to face, the one that he would be forced to live in. It held no sympathy for people that were weak, and that is exactly what it seemed normal non-magic using people were. Weak.

That was the truth of his life now. It was no longer his own! When the truth of what he was trickled out, he would become someone that was owned. He would no longer be his own person, and the only way to prevent that was by working with his mother and Kaitlyn.

Looking at the other students around him, Jack couldn't help but wonder why he didn't know more of their names? Had he been holding himself apart from these people without even realizing it, or was his memory just that bad?

A hand clasped onto his shoulder as he closed his locker. "What the heck man, it was only meant to be a joke! Why have you been avoiding me?" The voice of his ex-friend Steve asked from behind him.

Jack held in a sigh as he turned around and looked Steve in the eye. "Man, I'm not mad at you for running like a little girl and leaving me there alone! I've just been busy."

"Oh yeah, I know what you've been busy with! I've seen you and the hot new girl hanging around each other!" Jack cocked an eyebrow at him as he saw Kaitlyn appear behind him, close enough to hear what he had said.

"Is that true Jack? Am I the hot new girl?" Kaitlyn asked with a cold smile on her face.

Steve froze and closed his eyes before turning to face her, his hand falling from Jack's shoulder to hang limply at his side. "Uh, those are, or rather were, my words, not Jack's! I promise he wasn't bad-mouthing you or saying anything wrong!" He explained, trying to prevent a misunderstanding.

Jack mentally upgraded Steve back into friend status as he watched them interact. There was a slight smile on his face as he listened to them talk. He needn't have worried. He had friends, maybe not a lot of them, but he had them. The cloud that had hung over his head since entering the school building vanished as quickly as it had appeared.

Kaitlyn stepped close to Jack as the bell rang. "He seems like a nice enough fellow. He even made sure I knew you had done nothing wrong!"

"Yeah, he's certainly something," Jack replied as they hurried to their first class of the day.

***

Steve sat with them during lunch but seemed content to just watch them talk and interact without saying anything. It was only when lunch was over that he said anything at all. "I don't get it? It doesn't seem like the two of you are dating after all! The way you interact with each other is all wrong for people that are dating!" Steve told them, showing a rare moment of social brilliance.

Kaitlyn looked at Jack for a moment before responding. "That's because we're not dating. Where did you hear that we were?"

Steve took a step back from them. "Uh, it's what everyone is saying. Jack is the only one you talk to, and the two of you are always together."

Sighing in annoyance, Kaitlyn relaxed across from Jack. "Well, I guess it doesn't actually matter. It might not be true now, but it is one of the eventual goals."

Steve coughed, looking at her weirdly. "Wait, so you have an eventual goal of dating each other instead of just dating? What are you, stupid?"

Jack waved away his comment. "There is some family drama involved between our mothers, so, for now, we are just getting to know each other properly."

Shaking his head, Steve looked away from them. "I don't understand, but whatever! I need to get to my next class." Hopping to his feet, he clapped Jack on the back. "Don't spend all your time with her, or you'll get sick of each other!"

"I think your friend might be an idiot!" Kaitlyn said dryly as they watched Steve scurry off.

"Nah, he's just lonely," Jack said with a laugh as he pushed away from the table and stood.

"Are you sure about that?" She asked as they walked towards their next class.

"Yeah, Steve is kind of an odd guy. He gets along with everyone, but as soon as he gets interested in someone, he gets all weird around them. It varies from not being able to talk to them to not even being able to be in the same room as them."

They stopped outside the classroom door as Kaitlyn asked her last question. "So, what you're saying is that he is hopeless?"

Jack sighed and hung his head. "Yeah, more or less. To make it worse, I don't even know what he likes. It seems to change from day to day. One day it'll be girls, the next guys, the day after that plants! I don't even know if he likes any of them sexually or if he just finds those people interesting for some reason."

Kaitlyn laughed as she opened the door into the room. "I can't tell if you're joking or being serious."

"That's Steve for you!" Jack finished as they slid into their seats and quieted down.

The teacher walked in and they didn't have a chance to talk for the rest of their time at school that day.

"Is there anything we should do about those rumors, or do you not even care?" Kaitlyn asked as they walked to her car after school had ended for the day.

Jack shrugged next to her. "I don't particularly care. There aren't any other girls I'm interested in dating, so no worries on that front. Like you said, it is the eventual goal in any case." He paused as they opened their doors and slid into the car. "While it may be true, I currently have no special feelings like that. I am open to the possibility. So far, I haven't seen anything that would convince me otherwise. Your mom is a problem, but I wouldn't be surprised if you think the same about my mom."

"No, I actually don't. I think your mom is pretty nice. I agree with you that my mom is the problem in that regard!" Kaitlyn said, interrupting him without a second thought.

"Well, putting that aside, I have no experience with being in a relationship."

"What's that supposed to mean?" Kaitlyn asked, focusing on the road in front of them.

Jack scratched at his cheek before replying. "Uh, it means that I have no idea what it means to be in a romantic relationship. I've never fought over differing opinions with a girl I'm interested in, I've never had to make a relationship work before. I have certain preconceived ideas about what being in a relationship is like, but nothing more."

Kaitlyn's face was closed off as she replied to his confession. "I'm no better Jack. I could never risk allowing someone to get close enough to learn how small my well was before. Then, when people did learn, I was scorned and made fun of. If we are serious about doing this, then I think we both need to agree that not only is this not going to be easy, but it is also going to require constant work!"

Jack nodded in agreement, content to let the conversation end with that. There would be time for many more conversations later. For now, they needed to focus. The old abandoned school building stood in the distance as Kaitlyn pulled over and they got out of the car.

Walking quickly, they settled into the same room as before and sat down. Stretching out his hands, Jack reached for Kaitlyn as she sat in front of him. Their hands intertwined as he closed his eyes and waited for her to begin.

Chapter 11

Kaitlyn settled into position, breathing in and out deeply several times before gripping his fingers tightly and beginning. Almost immediately, her hands closed even tighter around his in an involuntary spasm as his power coursed through and filled her. Without delay, she began circulating the power through her well and back into him.

Jack remained still as he felt her exercise control and recognized the subtle movements in his body from the day before. Settling in for the time being, he tried to relax and follow what was happening as she focused on his training.

The light outside dimmed as the sun fell below the horizon. It was only when the alarm they had set on their phones went off that they separated.

Kaitlyn handled the pressure that his power created within her better than the day before. That said, when they separated, she was still covered in a fine sheen of sweat and panting. Her eyes were glowing brightly as she shuffled back away from Jack and flexed her hands as blue arcs of electricity began to flow from one finger to the next.

Jack didn't dare to move as the arcs moved faster and faster until they created a ring around her palms that slowly grew in size. He watched as

Kaitlyn's brow furrowed in concentration and the ring began to change shape. With a grunt of exertion, she forced the change until the glowing bolts collapsed into a ball that floated above her hand. He could hear the sharp crackle and pop of air igniting along with the smell of burnt ozone. The hairs on their heads sprang to attention as static electricity filled the air around them.

Jack felt unable to move as he watched her exercise her power for the first time. With every second that she held the blue ball of compressed energy in her hand, the glow in her eyes faded a little more until the glow had disappeared completely. Finally, she closed her eyes and cut the connection to the well of energy inside her. With a loud pop, the ball of lightning ceased to exist, and the room was plunged into darkness.

She cursed as he heard her climb to her feet. "We stayed out too late. We need to hurry!" The panic in her voice was enough to remind Jack of the monsters that had chased him the night he met her.

Fumbling with his pocket for a second, he withdrew his phone and turned on the screen, illuminating the darkened classroom. Their shadows elongated and twisted in the dim light, setting their nerves on edge as they scrambled to collect their belongings.

A distant howl filled the air and made them pause with wide, terror-filled eyes. Both filled with the fear of knowing that monsters lived in the darkness.

"We need to hurry," Kaitlyn said as she pushed him from the room. "If we can make it to the car, then we'll be fine." She informed him, even though both knew they would be out in the open for several minutes. She never parked the car near the abandoned building, opting to have them walk a few minutes each day for secrecy purposes. She didn't want a cop stopping to check on the building because they had gotten reports that a vehicle was parked near it.

Jack's hand was warm as he firmly and unthinkingly took hold of hers and pulled her along at a faster pace. With every step they took, and every second they remained touching, the glow in her eyes grew stronger and brighter.

Another howl came, this time from multiple directions as they stepped from the building and into the open air. The sound of gravel being crushed drifted across the open space, reaching their ears as they stilled in fright.

A harsh laugh that sounded off echoed in the suddenly frozen air, the breeze itself stilling at the sound.

Kaitlyn buried her head into Jack's back as she whispered to him. "No matter what happens, do not let go of my hand and do not let them see my eyes." She shivered in fear and pulled him back a step, so she was once more hidden inside the building.

Jack could feel electricity fill the air around them, making his clothes cling to him uncomfortably as she began to prepare for their visitors.

The furred face and elongated muzzle of a monster stepped into view. One of its eyes was red, while the other was completely black. With every step it took, saliva that hissed like acid bubbled from its misshapen maw and fell onto the pavement. Each splash leaving small smoking craters in its wake.

"You smell delicious!" It growled at them, its scarred tongue making the words almost impossible to decipher. "We've been waiting for you to come out to play again."

"We didn't get to taste you last time!" A hard-growling voice came from the side as another monster stepped into view. Jack somehow knew it was one of the two from last time, but he found himself unable to deal with the shock that these monsters could talk.

He found it hard to believe that a living, breathing being that could think and speak wanted to eat a human. Behind him, Kaitlyn could feel him stiffen in shock as they spoke and guessed what he was thinking.

"To them, we are nothing more than cows and pigs. They aren't human even if they can speak right now, and regardless of how they look during the day. Our energy helps to extend their lives and make them stronger. Something about the way our power works makes us taste different from regular humans. Apparently, they can't stand the taste of non-magical people." She told him, as she remained hidden, waiting for the right time.

"You should listen to her," A third voice spoke up as it also stepped into view, letting them know that all three directions in front of them were now blocked. "To us, you are nothing more than the most delicious piece of meat we will ever eat. The best part is that we don't even need to cook or smother you with spices before we eat. You are both perfect just the way you are."

Kaitlyn was suddenly shoved into Jack's back as a fourth monster appeared, this time behind them. "You might as well just give up, little girl. We've seen you practicing with your little flashes of electricity and they won't do you any good against us."

Kaitlyn gasped as Jack lost his balance and fell to his knees. The arcs of blue-white electricity she had been gathering disappeared from her hand as she lost her concentration. Both of them were tired from training and the process, which normally took an instant, was taking longer right now.

A wet warm nose sniffed at her neck before she felt a long slimy tongue lick the sensitive flesh. "You smell different from before." The presence that they had yet to see pulled back and yelled to the other monsters. "I think she's gotten stronger; she might even be worth eating now!"

Jack felt the bottom of his stomach fall into oblivion as the reality of their situation became clear. With reckless abandon, he grasped for the energy inside him, feeling it twist and writhe as it flowed through him. Time seemed to stop as he focused even harder on the ocean like well of power inside him, unaware of the blood that flowed freely from his nose and eyes. After what felt like forever but was only seconds in real-time, he managed to grasp a thin tendril of power and forced it into Kaitlyn in a sudden rush of power. "Do it now!" He ordered her, unaware that his own eyes had begun to glow for the first time and that a thick coating of magic covered his words, carrying them to her ears alone.

Thick bright white sparks as wide and long as her legs flashed into being. Each bolt of energy radiating out from her entire body. She was letting the power run rampant through her body instead of focusing and controlling it as she would normally. Her hair floated into the air as the electricity filled the space around them. Arcs of plasma shot from her body, attacking everything indiscriminately. Only she and Jack were safe from the effects of her power.

The air screamed as it ignited and burst, creating constant booms of localized thunder. Jack felt his consciousness dim as Kaitlyn's breath became labored and she pressed against his back, giving everything to the electrical storm she had created around them. The last thing he remembered feeling before passing out was her collapsing on top of him, while the heat of an inferno roared somewhere behind them.

***

Jack felt wrung out when he finally came to. It felt as though someone had reached into his body and twisted some unseen part of him that he hadn't even been aware existed.

"Don't move yet," His mother's voice whispered to him as he stirred with a groan.

"Kaitlyn?" He asked through a thick dry mouth and swollen tongue.

"She's going to be fine. She's still unconscious though." She told him as she dribbled water into his mouth.

He swallowed thirstily and let it fill the inside of his mouth, relieving the desert-like dryness. The water was pulled away from his mouth and sprinkled onto his eyes as she ran a cloth over his lids, freeing them from whatever held them shut.

Jack's eyes fluttered open as she pulled away a small blood-soaked hand towel from his face. "Is that blood?" He asked softly, his mouth quickly drying out again.

His mother's tear-swollen eyes appeared above him. "What were you thinking using that much power? It could have killed you!" She shrieked, forgetting that they weren't alone.

"It wasn't that much; it was only a little stream." He tried to defend himself from her wrath.

"You just barely learned about it. Anything more than a drop at this point is a lot! I should never have let her be the one to train you. The two of you almost got yourself killed tonight because you were careless."

"That's not what happened. It was monsters." He muttered, trying to defend their actions weakly.

"There were no monsters there when we arrived!" The sharp voice of Kaitlyn's mother shot across the room to them.

"I guess we were successful then," He muttered wryly as the last of the moisture was wicked from his mouth. It took everything he had in him to twist his head and look across the room to where Kaitlyn was laying limp and pale.

There was a soft, disbelieving snort from Kaitlyn's mom before Kaitlyn herself interjected with a whisper-soft, raspy voice. "He's right. There were monsters there, four of them."

Shantell's mouth snapped closed with a click as her daughter confirmed what he had said. Her eyes shot to Elinor's with a glare. "I thought this area was supposed to be safe!" She hissed angrily.

Elinor slumped down onto the bed next to her son as she thought about what had happened. "It was safe until you moved here. We hadn't had an attack in years before you arrived."

"Water?" Jack asked hoarsely as the bed shifted beneath him.

Absently, his mother held a glass of the clear refreshing liquid to his lips. "We need to do something. Either way, this marks the second attack within a week." Her eyes drifted down to her son. "I have a feeling that the attacks are only going to become more frequent and intense now that the seal on him has been broken."

Jack pushed the glass away from his mouth. "How is Kaitlyn?" His voice was a little stronger and clearer than a minute before.

Shantell looked down at her daughter with warm, concerned eyes. "She just barely avoided being seriously hurt. When you sent your power into her, she didn't have a chance to circulate it properly and instead sent it out without having it touch her well. That is the only reason she isn't in worse condition; it will be a few days before she can use magic again, however.

"The connection to her well has weakened because of her actions and the channels throughout her body have frayed from the pressure. She'll need to re-establish and strengthen that connection so that it doesn't happen again. I can heal the channels, make them stronger, but it will cause her a lot of pain."

She sighed and looked over to Elinor. "On the other hand, the very fact that she didn't burn herself out from the sudden influx of power proves that they are suitable to be bonded. If they weren't, his power would have burned her from the inside out. I remember how it felt when I was using his power to heal his body. I don't think I would be able to withstand the pressure for very long."

Above him, his mother stilled as she glared at Shantell. "I'm fine with your daughter. She is not the issue. It's you and your parents and the kind of people you are that is the problem!"

Jack barely held back his sigh as he looked over at Kaitlyn, who rolled her eyes at the conversation going on above them. Once again, their mothers had gotten carried away with their talk of bonding without asking for their input.

Elinor sent one last glare at Shantell before focusing on the bedridden teenagers. "The real issue here is how late the two of you stayed out. I know you chose that spot to stay out of your mother's sight," She couldn't resist the subtle dig implying this was all Shantell's fault. "But you need to be more conscious of the world around you. Before you start training again, we need to find a better place for you to train, somewhere where you will be safe regardless of the time."

Jack struggled to sit up before collapsing weakly back onto the bed. "I don't suppose the two of you can do this somewhere else? Kaitlyn and I need to get our rest if we're going to go to school tomorrow."

"School?" His mother screeched, "After draining yourself like that, you are not going to school tomorrow. You are going to stay home and get your energy back."

Jack struggled to keep his face straight at his mother's predictable reaction. They didn't have to worry about school now. Across from him, Kaitlyn smiled softly, feeling the same way as him about not having to attend school.

Although the rumors about the two of them would be out of control when neither of them showed up to school.

The mothers stood from their respective places and stomped from the room, glaring at each other. Elinor flung open the door and impatiently tapped her foot on the carpeted floor as she waited for Shantell to walk through first.

The door closed behind them with a resounding click, that had both teenagers sagging back into their beds in relief. "They really don't like each other," Kaitlyn muttered from across the room, looking up at the ceiling.

Jack felt his stomach clench suddenly as he realized he was alone with her. Everything was different now, for him at least. He had realized it as he felt her hugging his back before they had passed out. He trusted her; he cared for her, and more than that, he was attracted to her. Okay, that last one wasn't exactly new; he had always known how attractive she was. It had simply been secondary up to this point, however, and now, with his realization, it was at the forefront of his mind.

Did she like him back? If she did, was it in a boyfriend way or just as a friend? Should he ask her? Was he willing to throw away the time they had together if she said no, and what if she said no, but they still had to keep up his training? That would be so awkward.

He had only known her for a few days, but so much had already happened to them both.

Jack breathed in deep and slowly let out the captured air. "Where are we going to train from now on?" He asked her, chickening out on saying anything regarding his growing feelings.

"I don't know. It sounded like they were going to find a place for us anyway," Kaitlyn said while stretching her hand to the ceiling. "I can barely feel the magic in my body now," Her voice was soft as her eyes filled with tears. "I'm nothing without my magic. It's why we came here in the first place! I was almost nothing with it, and now I might lose it altogether if my mother can't heal the channels in my body."

Jack squeezed his eyes shut, desperately wishing he knew what to say to her. "Your mom said it would be painful but that she could fix them." He turned to face her. "Kaitlyn," He waited for her to turn and look at him, his heart clenching painfully at the sight of her tears. "We need to change up our training from here on out. I don't want you to get hurt again. We need to start working on getting your abilities and channels stronger as well. We can't focus solely on your well. You have to be strong enough to use my power without getting hurt."

Kaitlyn sucked in her lips before releasing them with a sniffle, "You're right. I have to become stronger than I am. If I can't safely use your power, then there is no way we can ever be fully bonded."

"Is that what you want?" Jack asked, before clarifying his question. "To be fully bonded with me?"

She kept her eyes on him as she swallowed thickly, "I don't know, but I don't hate the idea as much as I should."

The raised voices of their mothers in the hall arguing ended their chances of saying anything more.

Elinor's face was livid, and Jack could swear he saw a portion of her power beginning to peak through her eyes. "Jack get up we are leaving, NOW!" She turned from him to Kaitlyn. "Kaitlyn I'll be expecting you at dinner tomorrow night, make sure to leave your wrinkled old hag of a mother at home."

Kaitlyn's eyebrows rose as her mother screeched from the doorway. "Wrinkled old hag? We're the same age!" Her shrill voice echoed through the small room painfully.

Jack struggled to sit up as his body protested him moving.

"I've got him, I'll carry him out to your car. Both of you shut up or go somewhere else." Jon's voice cut past his wife, her mouth shutting with a snap as she turned to glare at her much taller husband.

"Thanks, Dad," Kaitlyn whispered weakly before either mother could start up again. "And don't worry I'll be there Mrs. Rage. I've been wanting to meet Penelope, anyway."

Jon gently pushed Elinor to the side and pushed his arms under Jack, lifting the teenager without difficulty.

"I'll see you tomorrow, Kaitlyn," He managed to get out before he was carried from the room.

Jon's head swiveled to look behind them for a quick second, "I need to thank you for trying to keep my little girl safe today. That said, you almost did more harm than good to her. If the two of you are going to continue training together in the future, then you need to be more careful and more aware of the world around you. Do you understand?"

Jack could only nod dumbly as he was carried from the house like a princess, once more reminded of how close he had come to screwing up. "I'll do better." He promised quietly to himself and to Kaitlyn's father.

Chapter 12

E linor glanced back at her son as she climbed into her car and took a deep breath. "I'm going to show you something first, and then we are going to have a very long, very direct conversation with each other. Do you understand me?"

"Yes," Jack answered, not daring to look his mother in the eyes. He was sitting up weakly, the seatbelt being the only thing that was keeping him upright.

His mother was quiet as she drove them down the road. He could practically feel the waves of anger and worry coming off of her as her mind went through what she knew. He had yet to tell her everything that had happened in detail and was debating if it would do more harm than good when she stopped the car and pointed.

Past the flashing lights of police cars and fire trucks were the still-smoldering remains of the abandoned school building they had been training in. "This is what happens when you act irresponsibly and without control." She took in a deep breath, her entire body shaking with anger, before turning to face him. "I had to work with... that... that woman to control the damage you two caused. And apparently, you risked injury for nothing, since we didn't find any bodies in the area belonging to monsters or otherwise."

"They were there mom, we're not lying. There were four of them, and one of them was there the night I was injured." Jack's voice was still weak as he spoke, his eyes refusing to leave the building they had inadvertently destroyed.

She growled and gave a short nod.

"That is worrying to hear, far more than you know." She said after a moment, her eyes growing lidded with worry. She sighed and ran a hand over her face before turning the car back towards their house. "We'll talk more at home. I want to know exactly what happened today, and what you did to use up so much of your power."

***

Elinor helped her son into the house after making sure her daughter Penelope was already asleep in her room. Her husband held the door open for them, his face grim as he took in the condition of his son and the smoky smell that surrounded them both.

"Wait until we're seated," She ordered her husband before he could open his mouth.

Jack held his arm out, using the wall to remain steady as his mother kept control of his other arm. She steered him into the living room and pushed him onto the couch before seating herself across from him. Jack waited for his father, Jason, to be seated before starting.

"All right, what do you want to know?" His voice was stronger than it had been earlier. He still felt worn out and devoid of energy, but to a lesser degree than even a few minutes before, when he had been in the car.

Jason looked worriedly at his wife, clearly waiting for her to answer.

"Just start at the beginning. You were obviously there for training. Did the attack happen after you were done for the day or during?" Jack settled back into the couch at her words, settling in for what he was sure was going to be a long discussion. One he didn't have the energy to run away from.

"After, we had just finished our training when they found us. It took Kaitlyn a little longer today to get rid of the excess energy her body had accumulated, and by the time she had, it was night outside. When we realized that, we rushed to the exit, and that's when we saw the first monster." His eyes glazed over as he went back to the event that had happened hours earlier.

For the next few minutes, Jack relayed everything that had happened. What the monsters had said, and more importantly to his mother, what he had done.

Elinor was holding tightly to her husband by the time he had finished speaking. "No, this behavior is too far from the norm. Somebody or something must be stirring them up, maybe even guiding them. They rarely attack here, and now all of a sudden they're everywhere and seem to be targeting you specifically.

"No, something else is going on and I need to find out what. This is my territory, and I need to maintain the balance." Her grip on Jason tightened painfully as she spoke, the ire she was feeling obvious to everyone in the room. "Tell me more about what you did to send the energy to Kaitlyn." She demanded after regaining her control.

Jack shrugged, not understanding the significance of what he had managed to do. "I mean, I was desperate at the time. All I remember doing is grabbing hold of it and shoving it into her through our connection."

"That, that right there is the issue! You have only been learning to feel your well for a couple of days, much less being able to touch your magic. People that generate magic like you are supposed to have a hard time touching and controlling their magic. Yet somehow, you, a person with next to no training, were able to touch and control your magic well enough to send it to Kaitlyn. A girl that apparently you already share a connection of some kind with."

She was visibly trying to keep her voice down as she yelled at him. "Bonds are not made that quickly. They take time." She twirled and glared at him. "And then there is your ability to control your magic! If you can control it even once in desperation, then you're already well on your way to being able to use it. Which is another thing that you're not supposed to be able to do without a fully developed bond and years of training."

She sank onto the couch next to her husband and panted, "I don't understand what is going on anymore. This isn't how things are supposed to work at all. They aren't meant to be this easy for someone!"

"Well, I mean, it was a life-or-death situation, and I wouldn't say it was easy." Jack countered, trying to be helpful.

"That doesn't matter. It sets a precedent. If you can do it once, then you can do it again. All you need is the training." She sat up suddenly, her eyes growing hard. "Did you have sex with her? That would explain the connection, the bond that is already powerful enough to accept your energy. Everything."

"What? No!" Jack exclaimed, jumping to his feet and then sinking weakly back into the chair as his vision swam.

"Then I have no idea why your bond with her would be so strong already. If it truly is that strong after only a few days, then the two of you were meant to be bonded."

"What like soul mates?" Jack asked flippantly.

"Yes," Elinor answered, giving up.

He froze and then began to laugh, his wide eyes making the panic he was feeling clear.

His mother stood and pulled her husband up as well. "I'm not saying you absolutely need to marry the girl, no matter what. What I am saying is that the bond between the two of you makes it clear something is pulling you together." She sighed and rubbed her eyes. "I'm tired and am going to sleep. Jack, get some rest and think about what you could have done differently tonight."

Jack watched as his mother pulled his father along behind her. His mother's words spiraled through his head as he remained sitting in the chair for a long while afterward.

Penelope was standing in the doorway of his room when he woke the next morning. "Mom says you are going to be training with us for the next few days, and that you are not to go to school today!" She gave him a happy smile before scurrying off.

He relaxed into the depths of his bed for several more minutes before deciding it was time to fully wake up. He felt better after his shower and was dressed in clean, non-smoke-smelling clothes.

His mother was waiting for him at the kitchen table, a mug of steaming tea sitting in front of her. "Sit, we need to talk," She ordered him without looking up. "I know Penny already told you, but you going to begin training with me today. If I think you can control your powers, then she can be there with us later as well. It's going to take several days for Kaitlyn to heal properly. When she is well enough, then the two of you will begin training with her mother.

"As much as it pains me to say anything nice about that woman, she has done a remarkable job training her daughter. Together, the two of them will make sure you have your abilities under control." She pointed to the full plate of bacon and eggs across from her. "Eat. You're going to need your energy. I'm going to put you through your paces today and do what I should have done before. I'm going to see what your control is like and how much of your energy is being leaked with every touch."

As soon as he was done eating, that was exactly what she did for the rest of the morning. Hour after hour, she tested his limits and control, cycling the magic through their bodies in varying amounts and speeds. Jack could feel the magic coursing through his body, the mana channels that they used stretching and straining to contain the increased pressure. His mother kept pushing him until lunchtime had long since passed.

"We'll stop there for today," She finally said. "I can feel the channels in your body beginning to weaken from the pressure I have put them through. Making them go through this kind of exercise now will help them get stronger in the long run."

Jack pulled his hands back with a groan, his entire body aching from the exercise. His head hurt from the strain of maintaining a connection to his mana for so long. He hadn't even been trying to manipulate it, merely trying to continually sense its movement.

"You're making progress, more than I thought you would, in fact." His mother leaned back in her chair and massaged her temples.

He wasn't sure how to take her words, unsure if she was saying she had originally believed he had no talent or something else.

"You have to understand just how rare people like you are." She had noticed his reaction to her words and correctly guessed what he was thinking. "There are so few of you that most of what the average person knows is little more than hearsay.

"One thing that has been established, however, is that those who generate magic can't control it. Not without a bond and plenty of practice, at least. Yet you can! Granted not well enough to do anything more than control the flow, but even that should be impossible. In time and with enough practice, you may actually be able to do more than that."

"I don't care about being able to use magic. I just want to be able to control it. I can't be near Penelope right now and I keep hurting Kaitlyn." Jack stood and stumbled from the room, every step hurting as his body protested at being forced to move.

"Control will come in time; besides it depends more on your sister's control than yours in her case." His mother explained behind him. "Get some rest, the LaCouture's will be here in a couple of hours for dinner."

He stopped in front of his door as the bottom of his stomach dropped like a rock. "Have you talked to them at all today? How is Kaitlyn doing?"

"I've been with you all day. When would I have had a chance to talk to them?" Elinor asked in exasperation. "Now go into your room. Penelope will be home soon, and you aren't ready to be around her yet. Dinner will be pushing it as it is."

"Wait, why are all of them coming? I thought you only invited Kaitlyn?"

"Officially, I did, but I know Jon won't pass up the opportunity to reconnect and Shantell will want to crash the party, simply because that's the kind of person she is."

"Oh," He had no better response than that. Pushing open the door to his room, he nodded to his mother in acknowledgment and walked inside. His legs were shaking as he made his way over to his bed and collapsed on top of it with a blissful moan.

Burying his head into the pillow, he felt his entire body relax slightly and groaned, this time in relief and pain. His mother truly had pushed his body to the brink. He had no idea if his control had improved at all, but his channels had certainly grown. Every breath he took caused them to pulsate and twinge in pain as they spasmed.

Jack eventually rolled over with a grimace, trying to decide if a hot bath would help at all before deciding he didn't want to move more than necessary. The painful pulses gradually disappeared around the time he heard his little sister get back from school.

There was a soft knock on his door followed by Penny opening it a moment later, without waiting for him to say anything. She hung back in the doorway and looked at him, sprawled on his bed, covered in a layer of pain-induced sweat. Her hands were clenched as she fought to keep her own powers under control. The small distance between them was still enough to start causing problems she hadn't been prepared for.

"How was school?" He croaked; his mouth was almost painfully dry.

Penny's eyes lightened and darkened in turn with each breath, before settling on a molten caramel color that was lighter than normal, but not dangerously so. "People were talking about the fire last night constantly." She opened with. "Training with mom is harder than you thought it would be, right?" She asked, while trying to hide her smile.

"The woman is a demon!" He groaned. "I knew the way Kaitlyn and I were training might not have been the most intensive, for me at least, but the difference is just too extreme."

Penelope nodded and leaned against the frame, her clenched fist relaxing slightly as she practiced her control. "What you are feeling right now is probably similar to what Kaitlyn was feeling last night after you pushed your magic into her."

"Mom told you about that?" He asked, struggling to sit up in his bed. The flashes of pain were mostly gone, leaving only weariness in their wake.

"This morning," She swallowed thickly. "She also told me about the monsters that apparently exist close to our town." She closed her eyes and let her head thump against the door frame. "You need to be careful moving forward! The world is even more dangerous than I thought it was with just humans. Now I have to worry about monsters and people wielding magic. Not to mention when word of you gets out, I'll have to be careful of people that want to use me to get to you."

"I," He stopped. "I hadn't even thought of that possibility."

"Neither had I until mom mentioned it this morning. She said that the bonding between you and Kaitlyn is almost a guaranteed thing and that it will close off the most obvious way of getting close to you."

Seeing his little sister act like this felt as though something precious was being taken from her. She was still too young to be worried about these things. Yet, here she was. It was sad, and it made his heart ache.

Jack swung his legs over the side of the bed and patted his mattress before stopping, remembering that she couldn't be that close to him right now. "I don't know about it being certain, but that is how they were talking about it last night after we woke up. It really just depends on when they find us though. If they learn of me tomorrow, then we're screwed. If it's a few months from now instead? Then we might be fine."

Penelope looked at her brother for another few seconds. "Dinner isn't for a while yet. You should take a bath before then. Regardless of whether you end up bonded to her, you should still at least appear presentable tonight." She sniffed and waved her hand in front of her nose before turning and skipping off with a giggle.

Looking down, he saw his disheveled and salt-lined crusty state at the same time as a rank smell drifted up to his unsuspecting nostrils. Pulling back in disgust, he stood and quickly found a change of clothes and his towel. His sister was right. No matter what he decided, he was not going to appear in front of Kaitlyn and her family smelling like that.

A quick, but thorough shower later and Jack was sitting at his desk dressed in a clean pair of jeans and a blue open button-down over a t-shirt, thinking. Deep thoughts unsuited for someone his age flitted through his mind one after another.

Shaking his head forcefully, he looked around the room and realized that his backpack was not there. He couldn't remember if it had been lost in the fire or if he had simply left it at Kaitlyn's house the night before.

His phone that was sitting on his computer desk, where he had left it to charge all day, began to vibrate. The screen lit up, and Kaitlyn's name appeared across the top. Flicking the screen upwards, he accepted the call and brought the phone to his ear, pulling the charger cable-free as he did so.

"Hello?" He asked, unsure of why she was calling instead of waiting another hour or two to just talk to him in person.

"Jack, sorry, but apparently we're all coming, and we're about to leave for your house." She opened with, her voice not as vibrant as he was used to. "Mom wants to surprise your mother and put her off balance first thing. It's part of whatever petty rivalry that they have going on. Anyway, just make sure your mom knows what to expect, because I have no idea what is going to happen tonight."

"Alright, thanks for warning me. I'll let her know. How are you feeling?" He asked softly, staring out the window next to his bed.

"I'll tell you when we get there." She replied and promptly hung up.

Jack pulled back his arm, tempted to throw the expensive phone against the wall. Taking a deep breath, he relaxed his arm and let the phone drop onto his bed.

"Mom," He called out loudly. "Kaitlyn just called. They're on their way already, and you were right, they're all coming!"

Chapter 13

His mother was muttering angrily as she stomped around the kitchen. "Your father isn't even home yet!" She growled, spotting Jack as he tried to slip past.

Penelope came in from the dining room and grabbed the plates waiting on the counter. "You could help, you know!" She hissed, staying clear of him.

"Is she going to be able to maintain her control the entire dinner?" He asked his mother, as he pulled different items from the fridge.

"We'll make sure you are sitting as far from each other as we can, any more than that is up to her." Elinor explained with a frown, directing him to the waiting pitchers of juice and lemonade.

"How bad will it be if they learn of her as well?" He didn't understand enough to know how different his sister was from normal. Kaitlyn had tried to explain it to him before. Unfortunately, there was simply too much that he didn't know about magic still.

Her hands stopped stirring the sauce as she thought. "It wouldn't be the end of the world or anything, it just wouldn't be ideal. Knowing about you is a bigger deal than knowing about her. It is more a matter of just trusting them with too many secrets at once." She continued stirring without looking at him.

Jack had just placed the pitchers on the table when the front door opened and his father walked through.

"You need to hurry up, dad. Kaitlyn called around ten minutes ago, and she along with her parents are going to be here any second."

Jason frowned and began tugging at the tie, choking his neck. "I'll be out as soon as I can. It's about time I met the family your future bonded belongs to." He continued with a mutter that Jack was not supposed to hear. "Not to mention your mother's oldest frenemy, or is it just enemy now?" He was out of earshot before his son had a chance to fully process what he had said.

Stepping outside, he was in time to see a large SUV drive up and park in front of the house. Poking his head back into the house, "They're here." He called out. Stepping off the porch and onto the lawn, he walked towards the people as they exited the vehicle.

"We weren't expecting all of you, or Kaitlyn until later," He calmly told Shantell as he opened the rear door for Kaitlyn, giving her a quick wink as he helped her out of the car. She looked much better than the night before and was wearing a pair of tall, supple leather over-the-knee boots along with a green wrap dress with three-quarter sleeves and a slight ruffling at the bottom that ended at mid-thigh. There was a small gap of skin visible between the top of the boots and the dress. Jack stared for several seconds before pulling himself back to reality.

"What do you think?" She asked softly.

"You look..." He swallowed and tried again. "You look... good." He finished lamely, unable to tell her the truth.

His mother appeared on the steps of the porch with his father while Penelope hung back and stayed inside the doorway of the house.

"I don't remember inviting you Shantell, not to mention you are here early," Elinor said calmly, looking down at the blonde woman for a moment before acknowledging her husband. "Jon, it's good to see you again. Maybe next time, leave the old-crone at home so we can catch up in peace."

Shantell bristled, her face going a deep red.

Jon sighed and held his wife in place with a firm grip. "Do you have to antagonize each other like that? We get it. You both hate each other. Blame her parents and general teenage stupidity and move on already." He let go of her and stepped towards Jason with an outstretched hand. "It's nice to meet you. I'm Jon, Kaitlyn's father. I've also known Elinor since college, though we were in different specialty programs at the time." His voice was warm and inviting.

"She told me you did a lot for her when Shantell betrayed her," Jason welcomed him with a firm handshake and then pulled him into a hug.

Kaitlyn spun and looked at her mother. Neither she nor Jack knew much about their mother's shared history.

"Yes, well..." Jon trailed off awkwardly.

Elinor held back the desire to sigh and waved everyone inside. "Come on, we might as well eat while the food is still warm. We can pick this discussion up again later, after dinner, if needed."

Jack closed the door behind him as the rest of both families went directly into the dining room.

"This is going to be interesting," Kaitlyn muttered from her spot next to him.

He snorted. "Yeah, in the same way that old Chinese curse is."

She flashed him a quick smile and followed after her parents.

Giant plates of spaghetti sat in the middle of the table, next to an equally large plate of meatballs. A simple salad and a bottle of homemade kiwi dressing sat at the top of the table next to Jason. The rolls that were always present when they ate spaghetti were on the opposite side of the table, next to Elinor and Penelope. The only open spots were next to his father, where he could sit as far away as possible from his younger sister.

Shantell wasted no time in bringing up another subject guaranteed to annoy them all once they were seated. "I'll need to borrow Jack for a short time after dinner. I need his help to finish healing Kaitlyn." It wasn't the request that annoyed them. That was perfectly reasonable and something he would have done anyway. No, it was the way she said it.

Jack sighed as his mother slapped her hand on the table and glared at the other woman. "Be careful of how you talk to us Shantell, don't forget I haven't told the council that you are here yet!" It was an empty threat he knew, she wasn't going to do anything that risked exposing him before they were ready.

A dangerous gleam entered into Shantell's eye as she glanced at Jack. Jon put his hand on her shoulder, stopping her from saying anything more. "I'm sure she didn't intentionally mean it the way it sounded." The exasperation he was feeling clearly pronounced in his tone.

"How are you feeling?" Jack whispered to Kaitlyn.

"Better than I did last night," She responded softly with a thin smile. "Mom was able to heal me some more this morning before she ran out of energy. She did some more earlier before we left, but she hadn't regenerated enough to heal me fully. I think that is why she made us leave when she did. She wants to heal me as quickly as possible."

"Well, she can take as much as she needs. I owe you more than that in any case for what I almost did to you."

She squeezed his thigh tightly. "I appreciate you saying that, but no, you don't. You are the only reason we got away at all."

Jason took hold of the moment of peace and began dishing himself some salad, pushing the large bowl of greens down to Jon at his left. "Can you all worry about who is to blame or has the most dirt on the other person later? Right now, I'm more interested in what you can tell me about the movements of the beings you all keep referring to as monsters?"

He gazed down the table to his wife. "You mentioned before that their recent attacks on the two of them are not normal. Do we have a plan to deal with them outside of just staying inside at night? I assume you're going to have to deal with them the same way as before?"

Elinor paused, her fork halting mid-twirl, and nodded. "Yes, I am. Now that I am no longer... restrained, there are certain things I need to start doing again."

Jack grabbed the spaghetti and piled some on his and Kaitlyn's plate, at her request, before passing the bowl to his father and grabbing the plate of meatballs. "What's wrong with just staying inside? Now that we don't have to worry about looking for a separate place to train, I don't see us being outside at night much."

"No, your dad is right." Jon said, pausing as he took a sip of water. "I have a feeling that there is something forcing them to move now. Our initial thoughts were that you were the cause, with your awakening drawing them here. That worked up until your mother told us how peaceful the area has been since she took over and forced the majority of them out.

"The few remaining monsters, nightwalkers, and other beings wouldn't suddenly risk being exposed and destroyed by the local baron over a meal. Especially when the baron, who in this case is your mother, has a history of forcing them out of her domain. Not unless they are making a power-play for the area, and if it's not that, then someone is driving them to act out."

"Speaking of, how did you become a baron? The council almost never hands out titles or territories." Shantell asked, a strange look of confusion flickering across her face as she looked at Penelope's hair. They were sitting next to each other and were able to see the gradual changes in the color.

"Actually, I have you and your accursed parents to thank for that happening." Elinor smirked with relish at the simple proclamation, knowing how the other woman would take it.

"What?" Was the quickly returned screech.

"Didn't you ever wonder what happened to-" Elinor began coldly.

"Eli-" Shantell began, only to be interrupted by her husband.

"Stop it, Shantell.""Dear, not in front of the children!" Jason's voice was firm even as it was layered with sadness for what she had been forced to go through.

"Right, sorry. That isn't a proper dinner conversation in any case."

Jon cleared his throat and speared a meatball with his fork. "We were surprised at how peaceful it was here. That's actually the main reason we chose the area was because of how quiet it is and how few paranormals and other supernaturals live here."

"I wanted my children to grow up in peace. The first thing I did upon getting the territory was eliminate and force out anything that thought they had the right to do what they wanted." She glanced at her glass of lemonade, wishing it had wine in it. "Apparently, some of those beings have forgotten who rules this area.

"In fact, I think Shantell should start going out on some patrols with me at night. I had been doing them during the day while the kids were in school. Unfortunately, that has left the nightwalkers to their own devices more than I would have liked. Now that Jack and Penelope know the truth, however, me going out at night won't cause any issues." A malicious grin had taken over her face as she mentioned Shantell being left alone with her for hours on end.

Shantell paled and swallowed nervously, "You know, I think it might be best if we let bygones be forgotten, and move forward without looking back at the past."

Jack found the entire situation somewhat amusing, though the talk of other magical beings had him curious. How much of what he had read in books was real? He had only seen one kind of monster so far, and he wasn't even sure what it was supposed to be. Werewolves didn't have acid slobber or glowing red eyes in the books. He made a mental note to ask Kaitlyn about it later.

"Later," Kaitlyn whispered to him when she saw he had questions.

"Oh, I don't know about that. The past is what shapes us and tells us who we can trust." Elinor's eyes flickered to Jon. "And who is a snake." Her eyes were hard as they settled on Shantell.

Jon sighed and turned to Jason. "So, what is it you do for work?"

Jack tuned them out and spread some of the kiwi dressing on his salad. He had never seen the dressing anywhere but at his house, and it was amazing. He glanced up and saw Penelope's hair noticeably more red than when they had started dinner.

"You know what? You were right. You all need to discuss some things without us kids being around. Penelope, Kaitlyn, why don't we go outside and let them talk things over?" He pushed back his chair and stood, after hardly having touched his food.

Penelope understood right away what he was doing, as she had been panicking inside for the exact same reason. "Sure, I've been wanting to talk to my future sister-in-law, anyway."

He groaned at the presumption and offered Kaitlyn his arm, her eyes switching between the two siblings.

"Fine, dad may I have the keys to the car? We might as well go eat somewhere else and give you the privacy you need."

Jack and Penelope quickly left the room. They didn't care where they went, they just wanted to get away before someone noticed her hair.

"Is there more red in her hair than when we sat down?" Shantell asked curiously as they fled the room.

The siblings froze, just out of the sight of the dining parents.

"Don't be silly Shantell, your eyesight must really be going for you to imagine something like that." Elinor took the opportunity to throw another barb at the other woman.

"For the last time, we are the same age!" Her voice shrilled in exasperated anger.

Kaitlyn backed out of the room, keys dangling from her fingers. "Let's go."

It was a good thing they had come as early as they had for dinner. Nighttime was still a ways off. They wouldn't need to be rushed for time.

Penelope stretched and played with her hair, pulling a strand of the red hair to where she could see it. "This is going to take some getting used."

Jack looked closer at her. "Is it fading at all?" He backed away from her, so it wouldn't get worse.

She shrugged. "Mom doesn't know, though she thinks it will fade some once I get my powers under control."

"Do you like it at least?"

"The kids at school thought it was cool looking." She answered after a moment.

"That isn't what I asked. It's your hair. What do you think of the changes?" He asked again, clarifying and pushing for a proper answer.

She hesitated and let go of her hair. "If it's only some of it, I don't mind. I like my current hair color the best though. It matches mom's."

He dared to give his sister a quick hug, backing away just as quickly. "Sorry, probably shouldn't have done that."

"Yeah, being stuck together in a car probably isn't a good idea either." She looked down and scuffed her shoe against the grass.

"No, it probably isn't," Kaitlyn said with some regret. She was standing next to the SUV, waiting for them.

"Why don't you go with Kaitlyn and get to know her? I'll stay here in case they have any questions." He volunteered, wanting them to get to know each other better. For better or worse, their two families were on a course that required them to become much closer. Besides, Kaitlyn had been forced to hone her control as much as possible, something that his sister desperately needed.

Penelope jerked her face up, disappointed that they couldn't spend more time together. She understood why they couldn't though, and she did want to get to know the other girl.

"I'm alright with that if Penelope is?" Kaitlyn was the first to speak. She had heard a lot about the younger girl Jack had spoken about, his younger sister more than once.

156

"Just make sure you come back before it gets dark."

They nodded, and Kaitlyn pushed the unlock button on the keyfob. Both girls climbed into opposite sides of the vehicle and the doors slammed shut behind them.

Turning away from them, Jack sighed and opened the front door. A burst of noise echoed forth from the inside of the house as he hurried to enter and shut the door behind him.

"What do you mean, you told people you were moving here?" His mother screamed. "As soon as people realize I let someone move here, I am going to start getting more requests. Requests mean more visitors and questions being asked when I deny them!" Her voice dropped off at the end. "Do you have any idea what you have done?"

Jack swallowed and stepped into the dining room. "How bad is it going to get?"

Jon looked past him for his daughter.

"She and Penelope left together. I decided to stay behind." He answered the unspoken question, his gaze focused on his mother.

"It depends," She began after a moment's thought. "When did you tell them that you had moved here? If it was a month or two ago, then it will be bad. If it was only a week ago, then we might have more time."

"I only told a couple of people right before we made the move, and don't worry, it truly was only a couple of people. Don't forget, we didn't get permission to move here." Shantell answered calmly.

"It will still get around," Elinor slumped forward in despair. The plans she had put in motion years before were all coming undone one by one because of the woman in front of her. Shantell truly was her nemesis in this life, it seemed.

"Alright, so we just have to work on solidifying my control and completing my bond with Kaitlyn?" It was more of a question than a statement, as he still didn't fully know what went into making the bond. Whatever they were already doing seemed to be working just fine, but he knew there must be faster ways. Otherwise, people wouldn't be able to treat others like him as property.

His mother snorted. "Sure, we can force the bond if you want to be little more than a mindless drone." She clearly knew where his thoughts had been going.

"There is the other method, but I'm not going to allow them to go down that road. Think of me what you will, but I will not sell my daughter's virtue like that!" Shantell was adamant.

"I wasn't asking you to, and neither was he," Elinor growled. "I don't think we need to do anything. If you would simply use your brain, then you would realize that their bond is already far stronger than it should be. They are extremely compatible, bond wise, and it is forming quickly and strongly. What he did last night would have had a very different outcome if that wasn't the case. As long as no one looks too closely, then it should be enough to fake a fully formed connection within another few weeks if it continues at the current pace."

"That will have to be enough." Shantell sighed. "Now tell me about your daughter?"

Chapter 14

The temperature in the room plummeted. "What about my daughter?" Elinor's voice was deathly serious.

Jack winced at the snarl he imagined in his mother's voice, careful not to show any other reaction to the question. Not that it really mattered, since no one was looking at him.

"There is something different about her as well, isn't there? I know I saw her hair changing colors during the short time she was sitting next to me. How strong are her powers?" Shantell did a commendable job of remaining calm in the face of Elinor's rising anger.

"Why would I tell you anything more about my family than I already have?" A viable chill filled the room as she spoke. "We are cooperating with the binding of Kaitlyn and Jack out of mutual necessity. Make no mistake, I still despise you and don't trust you in the slightest."

Jack held his breath, not daring to move as he witnessed a side of his mother that he hadn't known existed before that moment. She was scaring him, and he could feel the magical charge in the air as her control slipped.

Jason jumped from his chair and hurried to his wife's side, the temperature in the room continuing to plummet as she glared at Shantell.

"How are you doing that? Growing up, your main element was fire, not ice. How? No, forget that for the moment. When did you become an ice witch?" Jon held his wife firmly in place as she paled and questioned the furious baron.

Jason glared at her as he knelt in front of Elinor and held her hands in his, whispering softly into her ears. The water on the table had frozen, and the breath of each person in the room misted out in a fog as they shivered from the cold.

Elinor took in a shuddering breath, looking deep into her husband's eyes, using him as an anchor while she regained control. The chill in the air disappeared and the water and juice on the table hissed as they returned to liquid form. She smiled sadly and looked away from her husband to her scared son and then to their guests. "This is also, at least in part, because of you and what I had to go through to survive."

"Are you alright, mom?" Jack whispered, struggling to meet his mother's gaze. He had never been scared of her before, and now he was. He had been afforded a glimpse of the depth of her powers. Powers that overshadowed and smothered the piddling displays that he had seen with Kaitlyn.

Nodding her head, she took a moment to respond. The subtle strain of whatever she had done receding from her youthful face. "Better now."

Pulling out a chair from the table, Jason set it down next to her and sat as close as he could, all the while keeping a steadying hand on his wife's shoulder.

Shantell was looking at the glass of water on the table in front of her. Her bloodless face studying the newly returned liquid. "What happened to you back then?" She asked in a barely audible voice.

Elinor slid Jason's hand from her shoulder to her hand, pushing her chair back from the table in the same move. "Maybe someday I'll tell you." Leaving all the plates and food on the table, she led her husband to the living room, motioning for Jack to follow along.

The three of them were sitting on the long family couch when Shantell and Jon walked in. The large man's face was tight and shuddered with concealed emotion as they settled onto the loveseat across from them.

"I haven't spoken to my parents since college!" Shantell opened with.

"It's true," Jon confirmed. "After you left that last time and she learned what they had done. Shantell had a blowout with her parents about their actions and what they had done to you. They went too far, and she acknowledges that, but she also had no part in what they did."

Jack was sincerely wishing he had not returned to the house. There was too much to this conversation. He didn't know anything about his mother's college life or whatever friendship she had once shared with Kaitlyn's parents. Which left him confused and struggling to understand everything that was happening.

"Is that supposed to help?" His mother asked in a marginally warmer voice. "Her parents may have been the cause and driving force behind everything that happened, but she is still responsible for her own actions."

"I'm not saying she isn't; I was just trying to say that she has changed, regardless of what you may want to believe."

"She certainly didn't act like it the other night, or any time we've seen each other since then." She said waspishly.

Shantell looked up, meeting her eyes. "I was shocked to see you and just reacted. I never meant to reignite the old issues we've had with each other. If anything, I would rather we became friends again, like when we were younger. That is especially true if the kids are going to bond together."

She seemed sincere, and Jack wanted to believe her. There were a few red flags about the woman that he couldn't just forget, namely the way she seemed to enjoy hurting him while also healing him. Of course, that could just be a simple quirk of hers and not a larger part of her personality.

Elinor sighed and nudged her son. "She has always been a little sadistic." She whispered for his ears alone. He had no idea how she had known what he was thinking at that moment.

"I'm willing to at least try getting along with you, but know this Shantell, you only get one chance, and you are only getting that because of Jon, Kaitlyn, and our friendship as children. If you waste this chance and betray me or my family, I will take you directly to the council and make sure your '*Well*' is ripped to shreds along with all your mana channels."

Shantell swallowed, the last of the blood in her face fleeing. "I understand."

Jon shook his head, but smiled. "Thanks for that."

"Good, now that we've decided, we won't kill each other for the moment. Honey, why don't you take Jon out back and get to know him better? Jack, sorry, but can you wait out front for the girls to return?" Elinor asked them, the tension leaving her body.

"Sure, I'm alright with that." He leaped from the couch, making a break for the front door. He was more than happy to get away from them.

The last thing he heard before opening and hurrying through the door were the words. "Let's just say that Penny is special in a different but no less troublesome way than Jack and leave it at that for now." He shut the front door and sat on the grass in front of the house, thinking. After that rather scary argument, in the end, she had still told them about his sister.

Gazing up at the evening sky, streaks of orange appearing overhead, his mind drifted to thoughts of Kaitlyn. After experiencing the strength of his mother's magic, he now had a firmer idea of the younger girl's strength. It was apparent from Shantell's reaction that his mother was strong, even knowing that it brought the sheer difference in their strength clearly into view.

The new information giving him an idea of the gap that must have existed between the young woman and her school friends. It was something that would have become increasingly obvious as time went on, making it all the more impressive that she had been able to fool them for as long as she had.

A blonde-haired young woman with electric blue eyes and tall boots appeared above his head, looking down at him. A muffled giggle came from the road.

"I can almost see up your skirt," He grinned, meeting her eyes.

"Pervert!" His little sister called from her place on the driveway.

"I thought you were going out to eat and get away from here."

"We did." She held up a white fast-food bag. "I thought you were going inside?"

"Our moms are busy trying to kill each other while our dads are out back becoming friends."

She demurely swept her skirt into place as she sat down on the grass next to him. Reaching into the bag, she handed him a small burger and waved Penelope over, the open grass providing plenty of places for her to sit without being too close.

"So, what did my mom say to start the fight this time?" She asked while unwrapping her own burger.

Penelope snorted and began to cough as some ketchup went down the wrong tube.

Jack felt a moment of regret as Kaitlyn began to thump on her back, helping to dislodge it. He didn't like not being able to help his own sister.

"She wanted to know about Penelope," He told them once she had stopped coughing.

Penny winced and spoke with a rough voice. "Yeah, that would do it. Mom has gotten just a tad more protective since this all started." She coughed again and bit into her hamburger.

"Yeah, she has." He said somewhat helplessly, realizing how mature and grown-up his sister was being about all the changes. The only time she had broken down was when their father had learned the truth. Since then, she hadn't complained once.

Kaitlyn leaned back and laid down on the grass, in a position reminiscent of how they had found Jack upon their return. "What did your mother say?"

"She... got scary." He hesitated before continuing. "The air grew colder, the water on the table froze and your mom freaked out. She said something about how our mom's main element used to be fire or something. What exactly does that mean? We haven't gone over elements, main or otherwise, yet."

"No, we haven't. It didn't even occur to me that it was a topic we needed to discuss. My main element is lightning, while my mother's is light, which is traditionally used for healing. My father is an ice mage." She stopped speaking and pulled out a limp fry from the greasy bag. "Don't start thinking that main elements mean anything great. It is just the gauge for what people can use the easiest and with the least amount of magic and effort. Most magic users can use any element. It will just cost far more, depending on their affinity with it."

They continued talking about how magic worked, Penelope chiming in on occasion as the light slowly faded from the sky and they were forced back inside the quiet house.

The table had been cleared and their parents were sitting around it staring at each other in an awkward silence.

"It's getting dark," Jack informed them, stepping away from his sister and closer to Kaitlyn.

Shantell sighed and pushed away from the table. "That's fine. We were done talking anyway. With your help, I'll work on healing my daughter and then we can leave. She will need to do the rest on her own. Strengthening the connection to her well so this doesn't happen again is paramount."

Kaitlyn nodded along gloomily. This was something her mother had been saying constantly since the night before.

Jack walked back into the living-room and waited by the couch, while his sister disappeared further inside the house.

His mother appeared in the doorway a moment later with the LaCouture family behind her.

"She is going to do this quickly so they can go home before it gets too dark. However, doing the healing so quickly and roughly means it's going to hurt." She informed him as Shantell reached for his wrist. "Shantell and I will be going out later tonight to hunt and possibly eliminate whatever we can find."

Seeing his puzzled look, she continued. "Depending on how much of her energy she has to use in healing Kaitlyn, she may need to do this a second time to finish the healing process. It would be better for you if she was able to finish the process in one go."

Steeling his nerves, Jack nodded and braced for the same fiery pain he had experienced before.

Kaitlyn settled onto the couch next to him and reached for his free hand while offering the other to her mother.

"This is going to hurt," Shantell whispered to them, her eyes flicking nervously to her child. "And I'm not going to enjoy it as much as I normally would, especially since one of the people feeling the pain is my daughter.

Just know that all healing hurts when done rapidly. It only feels good when it is done slowly."

"What about me? I'm not being healed." Jack was curious. It had never really hurt when he was working with Kaitlyn or his mother.

"I'm not bonded to you and I'm not cycling the power through me and back to you. I am going to be actively taking it from your well to power the healing. With time, you will learn to relax and maybe even control the flow of energy. Until that time, it is going to hurt. Of course, it will hurt much less, I am told, once you have fully bonded with someone.

"Of course, at that point, they are the only one who can use your power and the process will no longer be forced. Now hush, I need to concentrate on this. Healing the channels in a person's body is much more difficult and energy-intensive than working with flesh and bone."

He understood what she was trying to say, with the bond he was giving the energy he generated to the person. Otherwise, it was being taken against his will. He and Kaitlyn already had the beginnings of a bond, not to mention he could already somewhat sense and kind of control the magic in his body. Maybe he could direct it to Shantell this time and reduce the pain her just taking it would have inflicted.

It didn't work.

Whether it was because it wasn't possible, or he simply didn't know what he was doing, any attempts to direct the energy failed. Likely it was a mixture of both and more. He had only been practicing for a few days, after all. Not to mention the first time he had shown any kind of control was the night before. There was no real chance for him to pull off a miracle this time, and the pain now coursing through his body ensured that wasn't going to change.

The hand holding Kaitlyn began to glow with an inner light as he felt that now familiar shift as the magic within his well was pulled from his body. She pulled heavily, forcing him to his limits in order to heal her daughter as quickly as possible.

He clenched his teeth and tried his hardest to not scream, even as blood dripped from the edges of his lips. There was no reason to scare Penny and draw her from her room.

Next to him, Kaitlyn began to whimper, her eyes shining with a color not her own. The normal electric blue glow replaced with a white light that matched the glow emanating from her mother's hand. The light began to spread from her eyes to the rest of her body, highlighting the channels her magic flowed through. The spirit-based channels had no physical form, but at that moment, everyone would have sworn they did.

The ragged edges of the channels were plain to see to the naked eye, the light-gathering around the weakened and frayed spots. At each location, the light grew in strength and pulsed as the healing began.

Kaitlyn's hand gripped his tightly, their eyes meeting in shared agony.

Dimly he was aware of the light in her channels, evening out and becoming uniform as they healed. The line of blood dribbling from the corners of his mouth increasing in size as ever more energy was forcefully pulled from his body. It was a small blessing that he didn't have to look into the cruel and malicious eyes of Kaitlyn's mother this time.

Instead, he was able to stare into the eyes of the young woman, who was quickly coming to mean more than she should to him. More than the short amount of time they had known each other allowed. He was fighting a losing battle against those feelings. He was afraid of how strong they were, and even more afraid that she might not feel the same.

He knew she at least liked him as a friend, but not if her feelings went any deeper. Realistically, they shouldn't. It hadn't even been a full week since they first met. It was too soon for anything more than a friendship level of feelings to develop.

Yet, that is exactly what had happened to him.

Kaitlyn's back arched as her body spasmed and lifted her off the cushion, her neck pressed firmly against the upper edge of the couch. Jack held tight to her hand, doing his best to keep her eyes on him even as the light behind them grew brighter.

"Almost there," Shantell muttered, sweat dripped from the tip of her nose, and splashed on her arm below.

The light spread around her body and slowly converged on her eyes as the channels healed. The ragged and frayed edges were no more.

Inhaling sharply, mother and daughter released him at the same time. The color of Kaitlyn's eyes changed back to her normal blue, glowing brightly from all the pent-up energy she had unwittingly absorbed while holding his hand.

Jack jumped off the couch as she collapsed and started to spark everywhere. It had felt so natural for them to reach for each other just then. He hadn't even considered the possible consequences.

The sparks from her fingers coalesced into an orb of plasma as she began to concentrate. Jon helped his wife to stand as they shared wide-eyed looks with Elinor and her husband.

"I can't hold this for much longer," Kaitlyn ground out, barely holding it together.

The rapid and intensive healing her mother had just done on her had ground her mind down to the metaphorical bone. She had never felt so tired before in her life. Not to mention what holding all the energy was doing to her well. The connection to the source of her power was damaged and maintaining a connection to Jack's power had helped solidify and marginally strengthen it. Now it was too much, and she had begun to lose control.

"Pour everything you have into the orb!" Elinor commanded. She stepped forward as the ball of plasma burned white-hot and grew in size.

"That's all," Kaitlyn panted, not knowing why she had been ordered to create something she couldn't control.

"We're going to carry you outside. As soon as you clear the door, toss it as high into the sky as you can." Elinor waved the men forward to pick her up.

Jack hurried over to the front door, opening it just in time for the group to burst past him.

Without a second to spare, she tossed the glowing sphere high into the sky, using the last of her energy to get it as high as possible.

High above them, it exploded out in the dusk sky, sending tendrils of electricity snaking across the sky. The clap of thunder followed within a heartbeat, and then the lights all across town went out.

Elinor sighed, her head tilting back as she looked upward. "Well sh-"

Chapter 15

Chapter 15

S hantell smoothed her hair down with a sigh. "Are you going to be able to explain that?"

Elinor crossed her arms with a small smile. "Of course not, but I also don't need to. It's the main perk of being in control of an area. I don't need to report my actions to anyone if I don't want to. As the local baron, I only need to report when something that affects the state at large happens." She stopped, a thoughtful look spreading across her face. "Depending on what we learn tonight, I may still need to contact them though, but not in regard to this."

Jon continued to cradle his daughter as the group looked up at the sky, and then towards the dark buildings around them. "Well, uh, I think it's time we started off home. It is nearly dark, after all. I'll send Shantell back with the SUV around ten-thirty or so." His deep, rumbling voice broke them out of their stupors.

"I'll pick you up in the morning," Kaitlyn called out, waving weakly goodbye as they sped away.

"How come holding that much energy didn't harm her?" Jack asked his mother as they wandered back into the house.

Penelope was standing in the doorway of the kitchen, waiting for them. "I think something just fried my laptop and phone."

Jason reached for his daughter. "Come on, let me have a look at them."

"Mom, who are Shantell's parents?" Jack asked, broaching a subject that had been bothering him. "You mentioned before that if Kaitlyn's parents were who you thought they were, then I needed to bond with her. As far as I can tell, her parents aren't anyone super special. So, it must be Shantell's parent's you were talking about at the time."

She stopped and looked up at the ceiling as the light flickered on. "It's not that simple, but you are half right. I did have a sneaking suspicion about who her parents were at the time. She looks like Shantell did at that age, after all. Don't be fooled though, Jon is not as simple as you might believe. Neither is Shantell, for that matter."

He watched as a melancholic expression flashed across her face as she remembered the past.

Blinking her eyes, she focused on her son and continued. "That entire family is trouble for us, but," She sighed, "But, they are also the best chance you have of staying safe once word of you leaks out."

"Your position won't help?" He asked as his father walked back into the room holding Penelope's phone.

"It will in the beginning, sure. However, by its very nature, it will also put you more into the spotlight. When that happens, my position will be more of a hindrance and they will be more useful." She took the phone from her husband's hand. "It's fried. How was the laptop?"

"The power brick is dead on it, but it still turns on. It will probably be fine for a couple of days, but I'm sure it was damaged as well."

Jack looked at them both. "I should probably check on my stuff as well." Thankfully, he had his computer and TV plugged into a surge-protector setup, so they were probably alright.

Penelope was lying on her bed reading a book when he walked past her room. "Is everything alright?" She asked, tilting the paperback to the side. Her eyes were wide and with only the barest hint of molten caramel in their chocolaty depths. The newest streaks of red in her hair had already faded, leaving only the older and deepest colored ones behind.

"I think so. Kaitlyn's mother was able to heal her before my power almost overloaded her. The ball of lightning she threw into the air knocked out power to most of the town." He leaned against the door frame while talking to her.

"Yeah, it fried my phone and laptop."

"Dad said it only killed the power supply and not the laptop itself." He corrected her. "Your phone is dead though."

"Humph, potato, tomato. Either way, I can't use it right now." She placed the book on the small nightstand next to her bed and sat up. "I liked Kaitlyn, by the way. You know, if that matters. She seems really nice to me, not to mention I loved the outfit she was wearing tonight! Did you see those boots? They were so tall."

He smiled. "It matters to me. She is pretty cool. The whole situation with her is just so confusing to me. I have no idea if she likes me or is just going along with what our parents want."

A sly smile crept over his younger sister's face. "Oh, she likes you. You can trust me on that. It might take a while for her to show it though, I think she has major trust issues."

"You got all that just from spending a short car ride with her?" He asked doubtfully.

"Oh, I got far more than just that from the car ride. I promised her I wouldn't say more than I already have though." She picked up the book. "Now go away. I can feel my hair changing color."

He didn't know if that was actually something she could feel, but it was true that her hair had begun to change colors. Rolling his eyes, he backed away. "Whatever, sleep tight, and don't worry about your phone and laptop. Dad and mom will get them fixed."

"It's not time for bed yet!" She called after him.

"Yes, it is," He mumbled tiredly.

Slipping into his room, he collapsed weakly onto the waiting bed. The light on his computer was blinking like a gentle heartbeat as he pulled his cell phone from his pocket. The screen refused to turn on, instead reflecting a dark lightning tree across the burned pixels in the light. The electricity in the air must have been enough to fry it while inside his pocket.

His body groaned in protest as he rolled off the bed and clambered to his feet once more. It had taken a lot to heal Kaitlyn and his body was most definitely feeling the aftereffects of having so much pulled from his well. Lifting the lid on his computer, he moved the wireless mouse and watched as the screen came to life without a problem. A quick check on the TV and he wearily left the room behind, every step taking more effort than the last.

"My phone is fried, but everything else was plugged into a surge protector and seems to be fine." He announced, placing the phone on the counter for them to see. With that done, he turned around and left, not interested in disturbing or interrupting their conversation more than he already had.

He barely had the energy to undress before collapsing onto his bed. His mother had put him through the wringer earlier in the day with her training and then, providing the energy needed to heal Kaitlyn, had finished him off. It had all left behind a deep-seated weariness that he could feel down to his bones.

Jack hoped she healed quickly so he could go back to training with her instead of his mother and her more draconian methods. While he was sure they were more effective, he preferred the one-on-one time with a certain beautiful blonde.

The last thing he heard before passing out was the annoying shrill howl of sirens running all about the town.

***

His mother dragged him from his bed early the next morning. "Come on, time to get up. Kaitlyn will be here anytime." She looked as though she had been up all night. An air of frazzled energy clung to her messy hair,

177

and her normally spotless jeans were sprinkled with dirt and splotches of what looked like blood.

"How went the hunting last night?" He asked, stopping his mother at the doorway. Looking down at his own disheveled state, realizing he had never changed his clothes before falling asleep.

She looked up at the ceiling. "I'll tell you tonight after you are done training with Kaitlyn."

"Is it alright if she stays for dinner? She wanted to practice cooking with me at some point. We might as well start tonight."

A smile ghosted across her lips. "That should be fine. Right now though, you need to get ready for school and I have some calls I need to make."

"Is it that bad?" He asked, pulling out his towel and some fresh clothes to change into after his shower.

Her face turned hard. "I don't need to notify the council just yet, if that is what you are asking. However, someone is stirring up the monsters that have settled in the area since my last purge, that is all I'll say for now."

He nodded dumbly, unsure of what to say. Stirring up monsters could be a common occurrence or something that was incredibly rare. He had no information from which to form a reply, and so instead, remained silent.

"Just get ready. We'll talk more tonight."

"Wait, mom," He called out before she could fully disappear into the hallway. "Her mom is still alive, right? You didn't take this as an opportunity to get rid of her and bury her somewhere deep in the mountains. Right?"

"Would I do something like that?" She called out behind her.

"I wonder," He muttered to himself, hurrying off for his shower.

Steam clung to his newly washed skin as he stared at his face in the mirror. His skin was pale, with a slightly unhealthy pallor to it, a mark of how much strain he had gone through the day before. He was just glad there weren't any bags under his eyes.

He pulled on a pair of faded blue jeans and a long sleeve shirt, leaving the fog-filled bathroom behind.

"Your dad is going to replace all of our phones today, so just bear not having it until then." His mother told him as he entered the kitchen once more. She was sitting at the table, a steaming mug of dark liquid in her hands.

Kaitlyn was leaning against the door frame, "Yeah, sorry about that. I just couldn't hold it in any longer. It fried all of our phones as well. We were lucky it didn't do anything to the car."

Jack rarely ate breakfast in the morning and decided to skip it, and nudged her from the room without delay.

"Don't worry about it. We were all due for upgrades anyway. Have a fun day at school!" His mother called out behind them with a laugh, a barely heard mutter finishing it off. "I'm going to sleep for the entire day."

"Did you hear anything from your mother this morning?" Jack asked, closing the front door behind them.

"No, she came crawling into the house just as I was leaving for here. She was completely exhausted. Whatever they did last night mixed with having healed me, I think was too much."

"I can imagine. I was completely wiped afterward, and I only provided the energy for it." He reached for the driver's side door and opened it for her.

"I didn't even do that, and I have no memory of ever entering the house after leaving here." Flashing him a warm smile, she climbed into the driver's seat and waited for him to walk around to the passenger's side.

"How are you feeling today?" He asked, buckling his seatbelt.

"Honestly? I'm still tired from last night, but having all my channels fixed and working properly again feels really nice. I know it was only for less than a day, but not having the option to use my magic if something happened was nerve-wracking."

"After training tonight, do you want to come over for dinner and practice cooking?" He asked, looking out the window. "I think my mom wanted to talk to you as well. Well, both of us really. It's about what they learned last night."

The car roared down the empty early morning road, managing to hit nothing but green lights all the way to school. Not that there were many. It was a two-stoplight town, after all.

The tires of the powerful vehicle squealed as she turned sharply into the school parking lot.

"Sure, what are we going to be making?" She asked curiously, throwing open her door and grabbing her backpack from the backseat.

"Well," Jack started, grabbing his bag and trailing after her. "How bad of a cook are you, really?"

180

She shrugged and turned around, walking backward towards the school entrance. "Guess we'll find out."

"We'll start off with something relatively simple in any case." He walked around her and pushed against the school doors, smashing into them when they didn't open.

"You need to pull on the door, not push." She snickered.

"Give me a break. I'm tired." He complained, pulling on the door.

"Today is going to be a slog for sure," Kaitlyn agreed with a yawn.

"We could cut out early," He offered in a hopeful tone.

She shook her head. "Nope, we already missed yesterday. I refuse to miss a second day in one week."

Jack trailed after her, surprised at her response. "You're surprisingly responsible when it comes to school."

"No, I couldn't care less about school here. It teaches nothing of value for our lives as adults who will be part of the magical community." Her steps slowed and her voice lowered so no one else could overhear them talk.

"Then why are you refusing to skip school today?"

They came to a stop in front of their lockers, ignoring the crowd of people around them in the hall.

She tapped the padlock on her locker and opened it while thinking. "I had time to think yesterday when I couldn't use my magic and it got me thinking about what you said the other day. We may live different lives than these people, but that isn't a reason to ignore them now."

The sudden change in her attitude left him stunned, as the bell rang out loudly and lockers began to slam shut.

Classes dragged on until lunchtime, when Steve found them both. "So, I noticed that neither of you came to school yesterday." He opened with, slapping his plastic lunch tray onto the table. The cardboard pizza bouncing into the air from the impact.

Jack decided to evade the insinuation. "Oh, you weren't here either, Kaitlyn?"

It didn't work.

"So, what were the two of you up to that kept you from school?" Steve bit into his pizza with relish, not minding that it had no actual taste.

Kaitlyn poked at her food suspiciously, "I was at home in bed all day."

"I wouldn't eat that," Jack pushed her tray towards his pizza hungry friend. "The pizza here is only edible by him."

"It's not my fault the rest of you filthy casuals don't have my refined palette." Steve grabbed the offered pizza.

"Whatever, I wasn't really that hungry," She lied, like Jack she had skipped breakfast that morning.

"If we hurry, we can go get some fast-food?" Jack offered.

Nodding, she led their way from the table at a brisk walk.

"What are you hungry for?" He asked as they hurried from the building.

"Anything, as long as it is not from the same place as last night."

"Didn't like it or just want to try something different?" The wheels of the car chirped violently, preventing him from saying more.

"It was alright for fast-food; I just want to try something else. Are there any decent local food joints around here?"

"There is one place outside of town. I just went there with my mother actually, it's an actual restaurant though. Oddly enough, there aren't any diners or the like around here."

"What about that?" She pointed to a sign that had been set up at the stoplight.

"Let's try it, turn left here, and then again at the hardware store." The sign was for a food truck that was there for the day.

A minute later they pulled into the hardware parking lot and they hopped out to join the line for the food-truck. It was a simple fish-and-chips truck, that also made patty-melts and reuben sandwiches. It was an odd mixture to be sure, and not one that he entirely trusted. People who cooked fish should stick with trying to make fish as palatable as possible.

"Something has been bugging me for a while now," He opened with as they stood at the back of the line. "How do you keep normal people from finding out about magic and monsters."

"It's actually not that hard, the process was taken care of far in the past." Her eyes took on a dreamy quality as she spoke. "It comes from the only known spell cast with '*Deep Magic*', and it keeps those without magical ability from properly acknowledging what they see or saw."

"Who would have the power to cast a spell-like that?" The little he knew assured him that the cost would have been enormous.

"No one now, not even people like you can generate enough magic to work a spell of that magnitude. It was the '*Fae*' who did the magic behind it all, a parting gift of sorts for a world they were leaving behind."

"What do you mean, leaving behind," He asked as more people joined them in line.

She stepped closer and lowered her voice. "Our world was moving towards using ever-larger quantities of metals and was becoming unsuitable for them to live or even visit here. The decision was made for them to abandon Earth and seal the doorways that allowed them to cross-over." She was forced to stop talking as they ordered and waited for their food to be done cooking.

She continued once they were safely back inside her car. "Anyway, as I was saying, when they left they offered to use the residual magic from the doors closing for one deep magic spell, for a price. The council at the time accepted, and though the price is unknown by any but those at the top, the spell was cast. They sank the magic deep in the earth, changing the very fabric of reality and anchoring it with the closing of the dimensional door."

Jack took a moment to process her words, the patty-melt making its way into his mouth. "So, what you're saying is that the *Fae* really existed?"

"That's what you got from that?" She asked in disgust, her own sandwich clutched between her fingers.

Chapter 16

Chapter 16

He nodded around, his mouth full of hot sandwich. "The rest is interesting, and I do have questions about it all. The thought of the Fae being real though, with the Winter and Summer Courts and Seelie versus Unseelie and everything they represent. That is the stuff of legends. Finding out that any part of that might be true is mind-blowing."

Kaitlyn cocked her head and shifted the transmission into gear, handing her sandwich to Jack to hold until they were fully underway. "I guess I never thought of it that way before," She said, at last, taking the food from him at the same time. "It was always just something that I knew to be true. There wasn't any mystery or feeling of awe associated with them."

Jack decided to let the subject rest for the moment and moved onto the questions she had been expecting him to ask. "What are the limits of the spell? Does it still work if you do magic right in front of someone? What about last night? How will people who saw that ball of electricity in the air remember it?"

She shoved the last bite sandwich into her mouth just as they pulled into the school parking lot. "It differs from person to person." She said after swallowing. "For some, it fades over the course of a few minutes. While for others, it's like waking up and suddenly finding yourself in a different spot than before.

"The real fun is in how they remember it. The spell doesn't force them to fully forget it. Part of the idea behind it was to help people be more at ease with magic and the unknown." She glanced at the clock on the dash and settled into her seat upon seeing that they still had time before they needed to be back to class.

"What do you mean?" He asked when she failed to continue the tale. The last of his sandwich disappearing into his mouth a moment later.

"Some of the most famous fantasy authors had some interactions with magic in their past." She hinted vaguely while he finished swallowing the food.

"Wait," He said as understanding dawned. "You mean some of those stories were real?"

"No, not the stories themselves, just certain details that sparked the stories. Haven't you ever wondered why so many different stories across different genres revolved around the Fae and the use of magic?" She glanced at the clock again and opened her door.

"I just assumed they were copying someone else who did it before them because it was interesting." He replied, walking beside her.

"And that is the case for some of them, I'm sure, others though have experienced the real thing and it comes through in their stories."

186

"What about the Fae? Have they been heard from since whenever this took place?" He was talking softly and quickly as they neared the school doors.

"Not that I'm aware of. They vanished entirely and haven't been heard from since the days of Merlin." She smiled after dropping one last knowledge bomb on him and opened the doors.

"Merlin was real?" He muttered in shock.

His mind was filled with even more questions during the remainder of his classes that day. Everything he heard and supposedly learned went in one ear and out the other without even bothering to stop for directions. He had more interesting subjects occupying the space needed for normal thought.

Kaitlyn waved her hand in front of his face and snapped her fingers. He blinked and jerked away as his eyes focused on her.

"What?" He asked dully, his mind slow to catch up after being stuck in his thoughts for so long.

"It's time to leave. School is over for the week." She crossed her arms across her chest and stared at him. "That means get up so we can leave!"

He shook his head, clearing it. "I think you broke my mind with the bit about Merlin." He explained, getting out of his chair.

"I noticed; I didn't think it would be that big of a reveal." She tugged him along through the crowded halls to their lockers.

"It wasn't, at least not really. It was just more of the same thing that happened with the Fae. There are so many stories that I discounted as a kid that I'm now wondering about what parts might be true in them, if any." He rested his head against the cold metal of the locker, letting it close under the pressure.

"You could always ask your mom sometime," Her locker closed with a slam, the impact jostling his head.

"I'll do it with Penny at some point. She really loves those old legends and myths. You ready to head to my house?" He asked, changing the subject.

They dodged through the crowd of teenagers and hurried over to her car.

"Do we have any homework today?" Jack asked, sliding into the passenger seat next to her.

"Nope," The word popped off her lips.

"Good, what about from yesterday?"

She tilted her head, thinking. "Uh, I'm not sure. None of the teachers mentioned us even being absent. In fact, the only one who said anything was Steve."

"Two days without homework?" He asked in disbelief. "That is weird. They love giving us homework here." He wasn't complaining about the sudden lack of extra work. He had been barely getting everything done each day lately.

"We're going to take our training slow today, make sure that there aren't any lingering issues from the other night, for either of us," Kaitlyn said, pulling into his driveway while leaving enough room for his dad's car.

"I'll ask mom where she wants us to train," He jumped out of the car with his bag in hand, making it two steps towards the door before spinning on his heel. "Sorry, I almost forgot my manners." He grinned cheekily as he opened the car door for her.

The look she gave him was one he couldn't quite decipher as he helped her from the car.

"Your mother taught you well," She commented, pausing behind as he unlocked the front door.

"No, it wasn't my mom. It was my dad who drilled that one into me."

"If he drilled it into you so well, then how come you haven't done it before?"

He stumbled and threw his hands into the air, catching them on the lintel. "There were, uh, reasons." He mumbled with a red face that had nothing to do with his sudden clumsiness. It had been a mostly unconscious action resulting from his growing feelings for her.

Inside the house, he knocked on the closed door of the bedroom that belonged to his parents. "Mom, you awake?" He called out softly, opening it a crack when she didn't answer. The bed was empty and had already been made, indicating that she had been up for a while by that point. "Mom?" He called out again, louder this time.

"I'm in the basement," She called out from below them.

Curious as to what she was doing down there, he led the way to the stairs and down into the basement. They never used the space for anything as far as he was aware and was mostly off-limits to him and his sister. It had always been filled with old items from the early days in his parent's marriage. Junk they had never seen fit to throw away, and heirlooms inherited from his dad's grandparents, who raised him.

"Mom, what are you doing down here?" He called out at the foot of the stairs, new boxes lined the sides, creating a clear area for them to walk.

"I'm clearing a space for you to train, and down here is where I have always done mine. The boxes and other junk were just a convenient excuse to keep you kids from coming down here all the time." Her voice led them down the path and into an open area that had previously been concealed from view by the boxes.

A large rune made of silver was inset into the concrete floor. Closer to the wall was a second circular rune that had been drawn by hand using chalk and seemed to refract and distort the light around it.

"Be careful when stepping into that rune. The chalk will smudge easily. I'll start carving up the concrete later and lay down a proper version of the rune in silver this weekend." Dust lined his mother's face and covered her clothes. She cracked her neck and thought about what she had said. "I guess that means tomorrow, maybe I'll do it on Sunday then. I need to get enough silver first."

"Does mom know that you can do this?" Kaitlyn asked, standing beside the older completed rune.

Elinor looked away from them, "I haven't told her, so no, but if she takes the time to truly think about it, then she'll figure it out."

"What's going on?" Jack asked, not understanding some once more. A feeling that he was quickly growing tired of and was determined to remedy the first chance he got.

"Your mother can create meditation runes." She pointed to the chalked version they would be using. "And control and energy inhibition runes." She pointed to the silver rune beside her.

Elinor smiled, "I didn't think you would recognize what that one was, though you missed the third and fourth function on it." She ran a hand through her dusty hair. "It's not like I was trying to hide it or anything. I had just forgotten how big of a deal it was."

"Only certain people are allowed to lay runes, the training needed is extensive."

"No, it's extensive if it is going to be your focus. If it is only for training purposes and certain ones for protection, then it isn't nearly as bad." His mother turned to look at them. "All nobles must learn how to create and control certain runes for their territories, it is sort of a requirement."

Kaitlyn groaned and sank to the floor, "That makes so much sense. I can't believe I never realized before now."

Jack stepped closer to the swirling lines. "What are they used for?"

"The one closest to the wall is for you two and Penelope. It helps the person sitting inside it concentrate and feel their magic as it moves through the body during meditation. It should be especially effective for helping you and her to get a better grasp on your respective controls." His mother said with a smile.

"The one in silver is for my use and has a few different functions. The two mentioned by Kaitlyn, however, are designed to push the user's limit. It pushes your magic until you can barely control it, making you fight for it constantly. While the other inhibits your magic, which again helps with control. It forces me to refine my energy usage on each spell until I am using no more than is absolutely needed. A situation Kaitlyn has become intimately familiar with from what I understand."

Kaitlyn nodded, "Mom was able to get a simple circle with that function built at our last house, it was what helped me to refine my control to such a degree." She finished sadly, remembering everything that had happened.

"Good, then I don't need to explain how to use them," Elinor said, reaching out and touching the young girl's head. "Don't worry about those people. Soon enough, they won't be able to bother you anymore."

"I know. It's just I thought they were my friends at the time." Kaitlyn climbed to her feet and shook her head. "If we are training down here, then where will you be working with Penelope?"

"We'll be using the backyard until dinner, which I have been informed you are making with Jack?" At Kaitlyn's nod, she continued. "Good, then I will get out of your way and let you get started."

"Mom," Jack called out before she could leave. "Do you have any books on magical society and history? The two of you keep talking about things that I don't understand, and it is getting old quick."

She nodded. "I'll get some books out and put them in your room for later." With that done, she left them alone, winding her way through the boxes and up the stairs.

Kaitlyn waited till they heard her feet hit the stairs before waving him towards the far circle. "Come on, I'll show you where to sit. Be careful not to smudge any of the lines."

Paying specific care to the placement of his feet, Jack stepped into the chalked rune circle and sat where she indicated. From there, it was just a matter of her sending a thin tendril of energy into the special chalk used to make the rune, activating it before they joined hands and began their training for the day.

Jack felt his body fall away as the meditation circle came into effect. Without his body getting in the way, it was easy to see the fluctuations and movements of energy as it moved through his body and entered his well. In his meditative state, he could follow the energy as it left his body and cycled through Kaitlyn's. Her well was under ever-increasing pressure from his energy, and despite its small size, there was something he found far more interesting.

The color of his energy in his mind's eye was a cool green that felt natural. While hers was an electric blue that matched her eyes. What was interesting was how his energy clung to hers, the two mixing together before separating as it came back into his body. His energy was slowly changing hers, making it more compatible with his abundant power. The color never changed, just how easily they mingled and then separated.

It was an effect he was sure she had noticed, either before or just now, the same as he had.

Together, they went through the training exercises. The deep meditation their minds and bodies were in helping them to make more progress than before. They lost themselves in the feeling of control and pressure, enjoying the flow they had never before seen or experienced so clearly. The state of concentration Kaitlyn was in kept her own powers under control, under its effects she was able to see whenever her energy grew close to her limit of control.

When they separated hours later, the runes had faded into ash as the magic burned through the chalk. The meditation circle would have to be redrawn before it could be used again.

Kaitlyn's eyes were glowing faintly, providing the sole source of illumination in the gloomy basement. The small window above their heads revealed the orange sky of late afternoon.

"We should start preparing dinner before it gets too late. I don't want you driving at night." Jack stood and looked down at her. "You aren't sparking this time or covered in sweat."

"The circle helped me stay in control. I was able to see when I was holding too much power and needed to back off on cycling the energy before continuing." She explained, beginning the process of bleeding off the small amount of excess energy that had gathered despite her efforts. The glow in her eyes fading as arcs of bright electricity began to flow from one hand to the next, creating a constant circle of snaps and crackling lightning.

The smell of burning-ozone flooded the basement as she worked the energy into a ball that floated between her hands. Her hair shot straight out as static electricity filled the air until, with a pop, the glowing orb vanished, and the strands of blonde hair fell back into place. She stood with a sigh and wiped the dust from the seat of her pants.

"Come on, I think I have the perfect recipe to start with," Jack said, his hand twitching as he repressed the urge to reach for her.

"What are you thinking?" She trailed along behind him as they wound through the path of boxes to the stairs.

"Tacos," He said simply, regretting not having taken the meat out of the freezer earlier. Working with frozen meat was a slightly different process than when it had been defrosted.

She frowned, "Tacos? How many steps can be involved in such a simple food?"

"You might be surprised; besides it can be an easy recipe to start with. Depending on the recipe you use, that is." Jack led the way up the stairs, feeling the burn in his channels. The progress he had made that day was surprising and more than a little impressive, to say the least. He was sure that with another time or two in the circle with her, he would be able to grab hold of his energy.

Kaitlyn stood to the side as he pulled out the different ingredients and spices they would need for the recipe. Laying everything out on the counter, he showed her what to do, and how the toppings needed to be cut. Next to them, the smell of sizzling meat filled the kitchen. He was using the heat from the pan to defrost the frozen meat, breaking it apart as he went.

It was only when the meat was broken apart and cooked that they moved onto the next step. Taking care to add the spices mixed with tomato sauce and water in the proper order. On the counter, they added the toppings separated in little piles of onion, lettuce, and the red peppers he enjoyed on his tacos.

They finished cooking and turned off the stove top as his mother poked her head in from the back porch. "You done?" She asked, sniffing the air.

Kaitlyn frowned, glaring at the pan of sizzling meat. "Is this really all there is to cooking?" She seemed confused and disappointed.

"Pretty much. Following a recipe eliminates any guesswork. As long as you follow that, it is usually pretty easy. Except for baking, I always seem to mess up the food whenever I try making something with dough." He handed her a taco shell and began loading his own up with meat and toppings.

The front door of the house opened, and a moment later, his father stepped into the kitchen. In one hand, he held their new phones and a small bag with the power supply for Penelope's laptop in the other. "Nice timing!" He exclaimed happily as the door to the back porch slid open and they were joined by the girls.

"Oh, before I forget," Elinor sidled up to Kaitlyn. "Would it be possible for you to give me a ride to your house when you leave? Your mother and I have to head out again tonight."

Chapter 17

Chapter 17

Kaitlyn was waiting by the front door after dinner, talking quietly with Jack while they waited for his mother to finish changing. She trailed off as Elinor stepped into the room. She was dressed in a leather outfit made for taking hits and matching bracelets with glittering emeralds adorning bracers at the top of each arm. A pair of silver athames or daggers hugged her thighs in sheathes that matched the rest of the outfit.

"Have I ever told you how much I love the way you look in this outfit?" Jason asked, coming up behind her, his arms encircling her as the two teens watched in shock.

"Only every time I put it on," Elinor smirked in delight, looking up and back at her husband. "Are you sure it fits alright? I haven't worn it since Penny was a baby."

He kissed his wife thoroughly instead of answering properly, stealing her breath away. Jack went bright red at the sudden show of his parent's affection for each other.

"Let's give them a minute," Kaitlyn whispered to him, pulling him out the door before he could say anything.

"That was, wow, I mean, obviously they..." Jack trailed off, his words making no sense.

"Your mother is a good-looking woman. I think it's nice that your dad still appreciates her after they have been together for so long," Kaitlyn said maturely.

"Careful there dear, you make it sound like we're old or something." Elinor grinned, joining them outside, her face flush.

"Oh, leave her alone mom," He kissed her cheek and stepped towards the house. "Kaitlyn, I'll see you tomorrow for training. Mom, play nice with Shantell and don't steal her toys." He wagged a finger at her like he would a child, and then retreated into the house before she could say anything.

He slammed the door shut before she could retort, though when he peeked out the window, he saw a suspicious smile on his mother's face.

"Come on dear, there are a few fun stories I can tell you about my son on the way to your house." He heard her say loud enough to ensure he heard them.

He groaned and banged his head against the door, wondering what terrible lies or, even worse, truths his mother was going to tell her? Wandering back to his room, he turned on his new phone and began the process of setting it up like his old one. On the corner of his desk were the books his mother had promised to set out for him. He planned on reading them that weekend.

Jack didn't sleep well that night. He kept imagining he heard noises outside his window. Thinking that the monsters had found where he lived and wanted to eat him. There was nothing there whenever he looked, his powerful flashlight illuminating the area. There were no tracks or other markings that indicated something was ever there. Yet each time he lay down to sleep, he imagined the noises coming back.

Eventually, he gave up, and turning on the light next to his bed, he picked up the book on magical history. For the next several hours, he was absorbed in reading about a history he had never known. One that worked alongside what he had been taught in school. It was like he was being told another part of the story, and things he had never thought to question suddenly made a little more sense.

It was his mother opening his door that shook him free of the captivating book. "Did you get any sleep at all?" She asked, leaning wearily against the door. Her leathers were smudged but undamaged, and signs of a hastily scrubbed face had left traces of blood on his chin and below her ear.

Shaking his head, he pointed to the areas on his face. "You missed some spots of blood." He closed the book and looked at his clock. It was almost time for him to be getting up in any case, even if it was the weekend. "I kept hearing noises outside my window. There was never anything there when I looked, but it still got to me. I think I gave up around midnight and just started reading the history book you left me."

She nodded along and yawned. "That's too bad. You would have liked to have that sleep tonight, I think. Shantell and I were talking, and since neither of you will have school tomorrow, we are going to bring you along when we hunt tonight. I would have liked to bring Penelope along as well, but we can't have the two of you that close yet."

"Are things bad?" He asked haltingly. "You never really told me yesterday. You just said you would tell us later, and that someone was stirring up monsters and then never did."

Elinor walked into his room and collapsed on the chair in front of his desk. "Things are getting complicated; we took out two different nests or dens last night. It depends on how you think about the monsters for the proper name to apply. What we learned though, is that they have been slowly creeping back into my territory for the last year or so.

"Those two and the one we took care of yesterday were only the tip of the iceberg. Someone or something has been preparing to make a power move in my domain. If it hadn't been for you and Kaitlyn, we might never have known in time. We may still not have enough time. Normally, and if I was anyone else, I would call in reinforcements from the other nobles and the council. For obvious reasons, I can't do that this time and I doubt they would have responded even if I did."

"And you want to bring me into that?" He questioned in disbelief. "I can somewhat understand Kaitlyn. She has magic she can use to defend herself. I don't!" He struggled to keep his voice low as he swung his legs off the bed and stood. Walking over to the closed window, he opened it and pointed out into the gloom of approaching dawn. "I was scared of that last night. How can you expect me to react better when the threat is real and not just inside my head?"

"Easily, because I know how you reacted when faced with danger already. Remember, you and Kaitlyn both told us what happened that night and how you tried to protect her." She stood and cracked her back. "Trust me, son, often times the monsters that exist inside our minds are worse than the real thing. Not always, mind you, but I have found that is usually the case. The reason they are so scary right now is because they are unknown. Tonight, we will strip away some of that mystery and remove the power they hold inside your mind."

Jack watched her leave with a complicated expression. She was his mother; he trusted her, at the same time, it simply sounded like something just waiting to go wrong. Looking back outside, he closed his window harder than he meant to and grabbed the clothes he was going to wear that day and a towel. No matter what the rest of the day held, he was up now. He might as well start getting ready for it.

He started the shower out cold, to shock his system fully awake. Just because he had been up-all-night reading didn't mean he wasn't tired. He was. He wanted to crawl into bed more than anything now that his mom was back, and the sun was coming up. That simply wasn't in the cards though, and he needed to move on. Cue the shockingly cold water.

His teeth were chattering by the time he stepped out, and the towel felt abnormally rough on his goose-pimpled skin. He had stayed under that chilly spray for longer than he cared to admit, and his fingers were clumsy as he pulled on his clothes.

Stepping out of the bathroom sometime after he had entered, he felt more normal and ready to meet the day than he had hoped for. He would just need a decent amount of caffeine to keep feeling that way throughout the day.

The kitchen was empty when he walked into it and peeking down the hall; he found the door to his parent's room closed. Undoubtedly, his mother had fallen right to sleep after talking with him. It would be up to him to make sure breakfast was ready for his dad and little sister. Looking up at the clock, he found that it was almost time for his father to be getting up as well.

Like any normal, insane adult, he seemed to like getting up early on the weekends instead of sleeping in. He didn't wake up to go golfing or doing something normal either, no he woke up to go to the shooting range and other places for training. His father was an odd man.

Jack shook his head and set about his self-given task.

Penelope was eating the breakfast he had made for her when Kaitlyn pulled into the driveway. Jack waved to his sister and hurried out the door. During the few minutes they had been close to each other in the kitchen, his sister's hair had started to change colors.

It was there at the end that he stood still and looked inside to where his well was. Doing it without Kaitlyn guiding him was a struggle, but he had done it enough times with her at that point to just barely manage. What he saw his magical energy doing was more annoying than anything else he had seen that morning. Despite their recent training efforts, his sister's energy had reached out to his and formed a bridge like connection.

With Kaitlyn, they had to be touching for his energy to transfer to her. His sister, on the other hand, just needed to be near him for it to happen. With a grunt of effort and almost a minute of concentration, he had finally succeeded in cutting the flow of energy to her.

Then Kaitlyn had arrived, and he had hurried out the front door to greet her.

Kaitlyn was watching him from the driver's seat of her car, her eyes tight with displeasure.

"What's wrong?" He asked, hesitantly openly her door for her.

"No, get in first. I like going for a drive right now before we begin today." She waited for him to get in before backing down the driveway. "Did your mom do something to my mom last night?" She demanded angrily, the wheels of the powerful car chirping against the asphalt.

"I don't think so, but I know they ran into trouble last night. Why?" He thumbed the button for the window and felt the cool breeze on his cheeks.

"My mom was covered in blood and beyond tired when she got back. I thought something might have happened." She explained stiffly.

"I think that they mostly buried the hatchet on what happened already. I could be wrong, but I don't think I am. We'll have a chance to decide for ourselves tonight in any case. My mom wants us to go with them tonight."

She jerked the steering wheel at the unexpected announcement. "She wants the two of us to go with them tonight; while they hunt monsters?" The car straddled the middle of the road for several seconds before she got it back under control.

He nodded, smiling at the shocked expression she wore. "My mom said she wants us to see them for what they are, instead of what we think they are."

She was quiet for a while longer as they wound their way through the sleepy town. "There is no way this is going to end well. Is there?"

"Not likely, no." He replied with a yawn.

***

Kaitlyn tapped Jack on the shoulder as she pulled back into his driveway a little while later. "You need to take a nap after our training, otherwise you are going to be completely out of it tonight."

She wasn't wrong. He had been yawning almost non-stop during the entire drive. He had been putting his mind through a fair bit of stress lately, so while his body was only a little tired from not sleeping the night before, his mind was utterly exhausted.

He nodded along and yawned again. His eyes drooping as he walked around the car and opened her door for her.

"Why are you so tired anyway?" She asked, having held the question in all morning.

"I couldn't sleep last night," He kept back the specific reason, not wanting to appear like a wimp who was scared of the dark. "I stayed up all night reading the history book my mom gave me."

Her eyes narrowed, part of the answer not ringing completely true, but decided to ignore it for the moment. "Did it answer your questions?" The car locked with a beep behind them.

"In part. I haven't finished all of it obviously, the book is huge."

She glanced quickly over at him. "Do you feel up to training, or should we skip today?" There was more than a hint of trepidation in her voice. He wasn't the only one who got something from their sessions, if anything, for the moment she was getting more from it than he was.

He smiled, his closing as he enjoyed the sudden breeze that blew past. "No, I think I should be fine. It might even help me get right to sleep afterward." Not that he would need it.

The house was quiet when they entered. The door to his parent's room was closed. His mother was probably still sleeping after all the excitement from the night before. Together, they crept down the stairs and made their way through the boxes.

At some point either before she left the night before or in the last hour or so, his mother had redrawn the runed circle in chalk for their training.

Kaitlyn activated the circle and grabbed his hands, the two of them falling into what had become a familiar rhythm. Reaching for the magic circulating through his body, Jack tried to affect it the same way he had earlier. The concentration it took was almost too much for his tired mind, but he was able to just barely manage it.

He wasn't able to make the magic do anything, but he could at least stop it from moving outside his control. Of course, that was only while inside the circle, deep in the depths of meditation. Without that helping him, the most he would be able to do was what he had done that morning. It was a good first step though, one that would eventually allow him to be around his sister a little more.

It needed concentration and focus, which meant it was only viable when he had enough time to do so. Still, it felt good to realize for sure that he was making progress. Not bad at all for a week's worth of work, he thought. Progress was always easy to see in the beginning.

Jack focused on the training exercise and did his best to follow the path of energy as it left his body. He was able to see Kaitlyn's well, and more than that, he was able to see the pressure it was under. The walls slowly expanded in size each day, like a muscle undergoing a workout.

He had no idea what was considered normal, but the current size was already larger than it had been in the beginning. If it maintained its current pace of growth, then soon no one would be able to make fun of its small size.

At the same time, when that happened, she would no longer need him. Not that he was overly worried about that at this point. He didn't believe she would betray him like that, especially not when they were thinking of bonding.

It was through their combined efforts that when Kaitlyn pulled back at the end, her fingers weren't sparking everywhere. His experiments and her growing ability to control and hold more energy kept her from being overloaded as she had been in the past.

The glow of her electric blue eyes was the only visible indicator that she was even actively controlling her magic.

"I'm impressed. The two of you have been making rapid progress." His mother, Elinor, congratulated them as they separated. The basement lights were on, and she was leaning against the wall watching them.

Kaitlyn started in surprise and then ducked her head, looking away from the older woman. "My control has always been good. It was the small size of my well and channels that were holding me back. My channels grew a bit in size and thickness after that last attack, and my well is slowly growing at the same time."

She brushed the hair from her face and looked at Jack. "I'm more impressed with him. He has already started to help control the flow and show that he can cut the connection when needed."

His mother shook her head at that declaration. "Make sure you don't tell anyone that, even your parents. The fewer who know what he can do, the better."

"Is it really that odd?" He asked, confused. It was just another part of controlling his abilities and making sure that nothing happened by accident to Penny or Kaitlyn.

"Yes, it really is! Don't forget what I have told you in the past. Generators are supposed to generate magic, nothing more."

"You said there were records of them being able to control it..."

"Only after they had fully formed their bond, and even then the control they showed was nothing special." His mother was growing agitated with him.

"But you said that I might be able to use magic at some point?"

Kaitlyn sat silently inside the charred remains of the chalk circle with him and didn't say anything.

"It was hypothetical! Mostly. The more power you have the harder it becomes to control and shape properly. That is why it is so important to start training when you are young! When the size of your well and the power you possess is at their smallest."

"So what does that mean for me?" Jack asked, not quite understanding why she was so worked up.

"It means that you may at some point have enough control to use magic." Kaitlyn supplied.

He shrugged, still not understanding. He had thought that was always going to be the case, they had been talking like it was from the beginning.

"Even without the stabilizing effect that the bond will have on you." She finished a moment later.

"Ohh," He said dumbly, a hint of the trouble it would mean creeping into his head.

"Yes, oh. Arggh." His mother turned and kicked the wall. "Whatever, you and I will talk about this later. Kaitlyn, we'll arrive at your house just after it gets dark. That should give us enough time to get in position before they become fully active."

Kaitlyn took the hint and leaped to her feet. "I'll see you then." She waved to Jack, a brief complicated expression flashing across her face. Then she hurried through the boxes and ran up the stairs, leaving them alone.

"You, go take a nap. We will talk about this on the way to their house."

Chapter 18

Chapter 18

J ack yawned into the car's windowpane. He had fallen asleep within seconds of his head hitting the pillow. Still, a couple of hours of naptime almost made it harder to stay awake at the moment. He needed, or at least wanted, more sleep. The feeling would pass once he was up and moving around. Sitting back down in the car was almost enough to send him right back to sleep.

Luckily, his mother was sitting behind the wheel instead of him. She was wearing the same leather-protective outfit as the night before.

"Do I need a weapon, too?" He asked as the car rolled to a stop at the light. The last rays of sunlight glittered over the distant mountains to their left, casting the area below in deep shadows.

She flicked the hilt of the dagger on her thigh and glanced over at him. "Not if Shantell and I do our job properly. The two of you will be there for learning purposes only, not to get involved in the fighting."

The wheels chirped as the light changed to green.

He sat up straight and looked over at his mother, feeling the tense, oppressive air as she lost control of her emotions. It wasn't an effect of magic or anything supernatural. The tense feeling was a pure result of her anger.

Straightening up, he thumbed the button for the window and let the cool evening air shock his mind awake.

A minute later, they rolled up to the LaCouture house. Jon was sitting on a lawn chair in the middle of the driveway, waiting for them. He sidled up to the passenger window and leaned down to look through it. His tall, heavily muscled form, making the simple movement look more impressive than it was.

"Elinor, Jack," He began by way of greeting. "The girls should be almost ready. They, and by *'they'* I mean Shantell, wanted me to wait out here and I quote stop that woman from stepping one filthy foot inside our house." He looked up towards the house and then inched even closer to the car. "Just between the three of us, there was a lot less cursing involved than I was expecting. Whatever the two of you have been doing the last few nights has really caused her to mellow out."

"She hasn't told you? I told her she could." Elinor asked in surprise.

"No offense, Ell, but I want nothing to do with the council or even the nobility and their actions. I had enough of that growing up and living with it until recently. I'm enjoying my distance while I can." His eyes flicked to Jack, sitting a few inches away from his face. "It isn't going to last as long as I had originally hoped at this point."

Jack's mother shrugged, the words not affecting her. "You're the ones who moved here." She said glibly.

He snorted and backed away, heading up to the front door of his house.

"I meant to talk to you about your magic and control before we got here, but I guess that will need to wait until tomorrow now. Sit in the back with Kaitlyn. Shantell should be up here with me." She finished as both women walked out of the house.

Obediently he climbed out, leaving the door open for Shantell, and hopped into the back seat, reaching over and opening the door for Kaitlyn as well. His mother smiled seeing his actions, pleased with what he had done.

Kaitlyn smiled at him, dropping a bag onto the bench between them while her mother slipped into the passenger seat up front. "Thanks," She whispered. Both of the LaCouture women were dressed in clothes made for fighting, designed specifically with ease of movement and protection in mind.

"Which area are we hitting tonight?" Shantell asked, buckling her seatbelt.

"Same area as last night, south of Kiowa towards that small Elbert town. I know we cleaned out the nest there last night, but my gut tells me that we missed something." She explained, the car accelerating smoothly.

Jack struggled not to ogle the blue-eyed, blonde-haired young woman sitting opposite him in the back. The dark, supple leather clothes clung to her form and incited thoughts that he struggled to control. Her clothes were well taken care of, but showed hints that led him to believe they had been worn before.

Noticing his gaze, Kaitlyn looked down and smiled, a hint of barely visible red creeping into her cheeks. "It's called a dueling outfit." She explained, shifting uncomfortably. "They are required to be worn by council-led schools for duel practice."

"What kind of high school did you go to before moving here again?" He queried. Had her old school been like the one in the books where the kids were forced to fight against each other under the guise of training?

She noticed the odd expression and troubled look in his eyes and guessed where his mind had gone. "It probably isn't exactly like what you are imagining, but also not entirely wrong, either."

"Uh, what?"

She clasped her hands together and looked out the window. "Duels are a great way to practice your control and speed in a relatively safe situation, one that at the same time is stressful. They are a major part of what allowed me to fool everyone for so long about the size of my well."

Her fingers began twisting about in complex motions only she could make sense of. "More than that though, they're great practice for what many of us will do at some point in our lives. They train us for what to do when we find ourselves in a situation much like the one we are in now."

Jack saw his mother nodding along from the driver's seat. "It isn't as common as it used to be. Back in the day, everyone fought the monsters. Now, we have been at a superficial peace for so long that most will never need to seriously even think about facing them."

Shantell turned around and faced them both. "Neither of you will have that luxury, however. As the granddaughter of council members, on both sides, Kaitlyn never had a choice. As a powerful generator and the son of a baron, you also suffer from a lack of choices in the matter. Both of you will be expected to face the beings that threaten humanity. Whether it will be on some battlefield or as overseers of a territory, like your mother is up to you and the council."

"What about you? Have you served on the front-line?" Jack asked, seeing the way his mother reacted to her words.

"No, I was deemed unfit," She said quietly, with a pointed look towards Elinor.

"Because of whatever you did to mom?" He couldn't help but dig a little deeper, twisting the proverbial knife.

Shantell glared at him but said nothing as she twisted around to face the road once more.

Kaitlyn shook her head sadly, her shadowed gaze lingering on the back of her mother's head.

Jack knew he had taken it a little too far and was quick to change the subject. "So, what can we expect to see and do tonight?"

"You will be doing nothing!" His mother was quick to say. "You are here to learn, not help. Once we have cleared out the nest, then you can look around the area if you want."

Shantell nodded. "Exactly. I'm tempted to make you wait in the car until we are done clearing it. Unfortunately, that would defeat the purpose of having you come along in the first place."

Kaitlyn rolled her eyes, the car accelerating as they left the town behind. The last rays of sunlight were behind them as they headed east.

"Why did you need to wait until night to clear out the monsters?" Jack leaned his head against the closed window, looking out at the passing fields.

"What do you mean?" Elinor asked, pressing on the brake as they neared the turnoff that would take them to the tiny town that was their destination.

"I think I asked this before, but why are we attacking them at night when they are awake, instead of during the day when they are asleep?"

"We call them nightwalkers," Shantell supplied, not answering the main question. "Since that is when most of them are awake."

He had heard them use the term before, but it hadn't stuck around until that moment.

"To answer your actual question though, it is because it is easier to find them during the night. The dens they hide in and create can be almost impossible to find during the day when they are asleep. At night, they are active and usually have lookouts guarding their homes. Besides, there are other monsters that are active during the day. Ones that aren't necessarily dangerous to us at the moment." Elinor flicked on the high beams and pressed the accelerator as they left civilization behind.

There were miles to go still to reach their target.

"Aren't there any, I don't know spells, or something, to locate these nests or dens?" Kaitlyn spoke up, leaving him nodding at the question.

Elinor sighed, "Yes, there are. They are a part of every baron's domain. However, I have ignored some of the requirements for them in recent years. When I tried to activate certain area spells the other day, I discovered that not all of them were in working condition. It is a simple matter to fix them, it just takes a small amount of time. Which we don't have right now. In a week or two, though, I'll have everything working properly again."

"Mom," Jack sighed. "I know you care for us and want to keep us safe, but it really sounds like you should be focusing just a little more on your territory."

Kaitlyn nodded, not feeling the need to say anything more on the matter.

"It's not entirely my fault!" She protested, the car swerving briefly into the other lane as she jerked on the wheel. "The condition of the territory when I first arrived was absolutely abysmal. I've been slowly fixing things since I took over years ago. Though I will admit I have put some things off for longer than I should have." She finished quietly. The reason she couldn't spare the magical energy went unsaid. At least Jack would understand.

"Didn't the council give you any help when you took over the area?" Shantell asked.

"No!" Elinor barked shortly. "Certain pig-headed council members decided it wasn't needed, despite the official reports stating otherwise." She glared at the other woman, her eyes hinting at just who those members had been. "They haven't even bothered to pay me since that first year either."

Shantell shifted in her seat uncomfortably and didn't reply, instead remaining silent for the last few minutes of the drive.

It was getting harder to see inside the ever-darkening interior of the car, but Jack could have sworn that he saw Kaitlyn look away from her mother in disgust. In the silence that followed, he could hear knuckles popping as his mother squeezed the steering wheel in a near-death grip.

A minute later the car slowed and came to a stop in the middle of the road. On the right side of the road was a small gas station and convenience store, while on the left was an old, dilapidated post-office. Farther up he could see a larger building that had the look of a school of some sort.

"This is it?" He asked when it became apparent they had arrived at their destination.

"Yup, this is the town. The nests we found last night were behind the school, buried in the trees. Ever since we left last night, I haven't been able to shake the feeling that there are even more of them somewhere behind the store or around there." Elinor turned the wheel and drove into the gravel parking lot and parked out of sight behind the store.

"You want us to go into that?" Kaitlyn asked, looking hard at the line of trees that butted up to the gravel lot.

It was a dense line with the thick, tall pine trees letting none of the failing light in. It was as dark an area as they had ever seen, and just thinking about walking into those depths was enough to trigger a sense of danger in them.

"Don't worry, you'll be with us."

Jack climbed out of the car as his mother shut off the engine and walked around the motionless vehicle, opening the door for each of them.

"Thanks, dear," Elinor said as he helped her out, her finger thumbing the trunk release before closing the door.

Buried inside the trunk was a set of backpacks and powerful flashlights, next to a thick parka coat.

"Why don't the two of you carry the bags?" Shantell spoke up, flicking on a flashlight, and shining it towards the woods.

"At least take your weapon first," Elinor rolled her eyes and unzipped one of the bags. Inside was a small 9mm handgun that Jack had never seen before. She took it out and clipped the plastic holder to her belt. "We can't use these this close to the town or other people, since we need to remain as unnoticed as possible. They're for emergency use only." She finished explaining, before handing the bag to her son.

Jack picked up his flashlight and shined it across the line of trees nearby, joining Shantell's beam in illuminating the area.

Kaitlyn picked up her own flashlight with one hand and held the backpack out to her mother with the other. "How many people actually live in this hole of a town?" She leaned back and studied the four buildings that occupied the main street running through the pit-stop of a map marker.

Shantell took the flashlight and then shrugged on the parka, despite it being a fairly warm night.

Elinor made sure her daggers were ready before answering. "You saw that school across the road from the gas station?" She waited for a beat, the lack of light preventing her from seeing their nods. "Well, that was originally built as a high school years ago, and then the town went downhill, and they combined it with the elementary school. What you may not have noticed is that the entire back half of it has been missing since 2009, when there was a tornado that destroyed it. Until recently the state didn't care enough to give them the funds to rebuild it despite the years they have been petitioning for it."

"Uh, that doesn't answer the question, mom. It just tells us how pathetic this place is." Jack swung the backpack into position and cinched it tight.

"Oh, well, I think the official number is around two-hundred and thirty people." Elinor slammed the trunk closed, the car beeping as she passed the keys to Jack.

"So, do they have the funds now?" Kaitlyn asked, holding back as the two moms headed for the thick woods.

"Yeah, they are scheduled to begin rebuilding it next year sometime," Elinor answered before motioning them to be quiet and stepping into the dark void of the pine trees.

The two teens shivered as Jack's mother gathered her magic and let it permeate the surrounding air. Holding it at the ready, cold seeped out and froze the ground at their feet and encrusted the bark.

Jack brushed against a tree as they walked into the depths, the bark shattered, and the tree listed to the side in frozen death. "What the...?" He whispered to Kaitlyn, his eyes wide with shock.

Kaitlyn stared back with equally shocked eyes. Elinor wasn't even trying to destroy the trees or freeze their surroundings. It was caused by a minuscule amount of her power seeping out, and it was causing more damage than should have been possible. The thick coat her mother was wearing suddenly made sense.

"Is that normal?" He asked, holding back from following them too closely.

"Not even close," She answered in an awestruck voice. A heartbeat later, a noise different from the howl they had heard before echoed through the woods. They were tracking a different kind of monster than the weird acidic wolfen monsters from the other day.

Elinor's hazel eyes glinted ice blue as she turned around to look at the two teens, an almost feral smile on her face. "They just woke up, stay close, and don't do anything to draw attention to yourselves."

An audible sigh burst from Shantell, who stamped her feet and kept moving.

"Uh, mom?" Kaitlyn burst out in a worried tone. She was seeing sides of her mother that she had never known existed before then.

"It's fine, let's just hurry this up." Her voice held a defeated quality that had no place on the proud, slightly sadistic woman they knew.

The chill in the air deepened, and the trees groaned, while dried branches and pine needles shattered underfoot.

Hurrying forward, they moved deeper into the woods and to the nest buried within. Minutes later, and after enduring three more hair-raising calls, they stopped outside of a clearing. The beams of their flashlights lit the open space bright, revealing the entrance to an underground cave.

Jack held back as his mom stepped outside the ring of trees and stomped. A wave of glistening ice exploded out from where her foot hit the ground, encasing the entrance and sealing it tight. A moment later the clear block trembled, as the refracted light glinted off the claws of a monster hidden within.

Shantell skated across the icy grass, the thin blades shattering in front of her feet. In her hands, a compressed orb of light formed, floating gently above them. With a grunt, she pushed the glowing sphere into the wall of ice, the refracting light pulling together to form powerful beams on the other side.

The light pierced through the closest monster, before dissipating as the ice cracked from the pressure.

"One down, a bunch more to go," Shantell yelled with more enthusiasm than she had shown the rest of the night.

Elinor stopped next to her, magic circulating through the air as they both withdrew their daggers. Jack and Kaitlyn held up their flashlights, so their mothers could hold a dagger in each hand. Carefully they slid down the slick ramp into the cave, ignoring the hole-ridden body that had been pushed to the side.

The air was still, with a thick musk that contained undertones of burnt flesh. A long dark tunnel extended a few feet in front of them before it opened up into a large, cavernous area.

Chapter 19

J ack felt his feet freeze to the ground next to Kaitlyn, both of them taking in the sight before them. At the top of the cavern, tree roots could be seen sticking out through the soil, searching for a purchase they would never find. The cave had been formed partly in the side of a small hill, while the ramp had taken them at least thirty feet below the rest of the forested area outside.

Bodies, both those barely alive and those clearly dead, littered the ground in front of them.

Both mothers cursed aloud, shocking the teenagers. "They've already moved on!" Elinor hissed, nudging a misshapen corpse at her feet. The blood was still pooling around the warm body. "We must have just missed them."

"What are they?" Jack asked in a horrified whisper, never having expected to find that much death during their excursion.

"Banes, or rather almost banes. Someone is experimenting with bringing them back. Almost all of the nests we've found have contained variations of the age-old monsters," Elinor explained as she began systematically killing all the surviving monsters with ice and then fire, burning their bodies to ash.

"These experiments are all highly illegal and very dangerous. The fact that someone has not only managed to accomplish this but also has been doing it for long enough that some of these monsters are at least a year old spells trouble for your mother. If news of this ever got out, holding onto her title as a baroness would be among the least of her problems." Shantelle explained softly while they watched her work.

"What do we do now?" Kaitlyn was crouched next to a hole-ridden body by the tunnel they had come through. "These injuries look like they came from a gun, not magic."

"Is that... normal?" Jack asked, unsure of how to properly phrase the spontaneous question.

"What do you mean?" Shantelle smirked as he squirmed under her gaze.

"I mean, you all can use magic. Wouldn't most people use that instead of guns?"

"That would indeed normally be the case," His mother finished, looking around for bodies to burn, and rejoined the group. "Unfortunately, I believe the people behind this problem are not part of the official magic community. No one with any amount of proper knowledge on the matter would ever dare to experiment on these creatures or the other monsters we found.

"I think it is more likely that we are dealing with untrained people who contain only a smidgen of magical power who stumbled on some nests years ago." She paused and looked back at the remains of the nest they had intruded upon. "At least I seriously hope that is the case. If this is the work of dark mages, then this would be a problem we are unequipped to deal with."

"Are these what we heard in the woods earlier? Whatever it was sounded alive then, and these are all dead." Kaitlyn stood and moved closer to the group and away from the dark tunnel.

"No, I don't think these are what we heard," Elinor said softly while tensing as she looked up the tunnel they had come through minutes before.

One set of eyes after another, each reflecting the light back at them like a cat, appeared at the top of the dark ramp.

"Those are what we heard," Shantelle explained with a gulp, stepping in front of them and standing firm next to the other woman.

Jack reached for his mother and Shantelle, hoping to give them what energy he could.

"No." Kaitlyn held the back of his shirt and pulled him back. "They have more than enough energy for something like this, save what you have for later when it might actually be needed."

"Why? I thought I had plenty of it to give."

"You do, but the strain on your body caused by transferring and passing that much energy to multiple people at once won't be light." She had doubts about how well it would work in the first place, but most of what she had heard about generators in the past had already been overturned by him. Which either meant that he truly was someone special, or more likely, that information concerning them had been purposefully changed for the masses.

"Give me some light, please." Elinor requested, the ground at her feet beginning to ice over.

The two teens directed their flashlights as Shantelle pulled a thin tube from a long pocket that ran down the leg of her pants. Carefully, she removed two end-caps from the cylinder before spinning it around and holding it firmly with her left hand. A sphere of bright white light appeared above her hand for a split second before she shoved her hand against the closest end of the tube.

"I can't believe you are still using that thing after all these years," Elinor sneered, as the tube condensed the light into a thin but powerful beam of light.

"You don't have to keep saying that every time I pull it out!" Shantelle snarled, keeping a firm grip on the device while carefully twisting her hips. The beam speared through one monster after another at the top of the tunnel ramp, leaving only steaming bisected corpses behind.

The ice around his mother's feet stopped growing and instead began to shrink as she sighed in defeat.

"Light is still faster than either my ice or flame," She muttered to herself softly.

"Hah," The blonde-haired mother laughed spitefully. "I win this time!"

"I just wanted to give you the chance to show your daughter you were useful. Then you had to go and ruin it by bragging."

Jack rolled his eyes as his mother shot down Shantelle in front of Kaitlyn. "Do we need to worry about more at the top, or you know whoever was controlling them?"

"What makes you think they were controlled?"

"Why else would they attack this nest right now?" He finished awkwardly, suddenly wondering if his assumption was wrong.

"Well, you are right this time. They were being controlled, but that doesn't mean they needed to be. They could have simply smelled the death emanating from this nest and come to investigate." Shantell carefully replaced the end-caps on her tool and slipped the cylinder back into the long pocket of her pants.

Elinor took the lead again and led them out of the cave and past the bodies that had been cut in half by the light. At the edges of the clearing were more of the beasts that had dared to enter the tunnel with them inside.

Jack looked away as his mother's face went cold and emotionless.

"I'll handle these ones," She growled.

Kaitlyn gasped softly and reflexively pressed against him as she too, turned her face away. A wave of heat engulfed them and then sped out all across the clearing. From the corner of his eye, he was able to see trees going up in flames and writhing bodies struggling beneath them.

The direction of their eyes did nothing to block or mute the screams of burning monsters alongside the hissing of boiling liquefied fat.

"She said they were being controlled," He said directly into Kaitlyn's ear in a bid to distract them from the nightmare-inducing noises. "That means those dark mages she mentioned are involved. Right?"

"Was that really necessary?" Shantelle asked as the flames began to die down, taking the worst of the noise with them. "You could have just frozen them all. Instead, we had to listen to those *things* scream in pain and terror." Her words were in direct opposition to the cruel enjoyment he knew she had found in their suffering.

Kaitlyn groaned and threw herself back from him. Her eyes were glowing with power and her hands were dripping with molten castoffs from the charged electricity circling her fingers. "I wasn't prepared for that," She gasped out as a thick line of energy went from her hands to the ground, with another shooting off into the trees.

Jack wanted to curse at their combined thoughtlessness. True, she had pressed against him first, but he had held her close and practically embraced her without thinking. The control Kaitlyn was working to instill in him was worth nothing if they both forgot to use it.

Unlike when she had been forced to launch the ball of electricity into the air outside their house. This time, there was no cabling or piping running underneath the ground around them. She also now possessed slightly better control over moving larger amounts of magic than she could store. It had only been a couple of days, but the results of their practice were already showing through for her.

She was able to bleed off the excess in a relatively controlled fashion.

Both mothers cursed at the sudden light show, and the constant booms of thunder as the air ignited around the lightning. It wasn't enough to be heard more than a mile distant, but it was as good as announcing their presence to anything magical in the area.

"Come on, it's time for us to go!" Elinor ordered the group, as she made sure each corpse had been turned to ash.

Nothing good would come from leaving evidence behind for a normal person to find. It was best to not be overly dependent on the grand spell. You never knew when someone might have some latent magic in them and would end up seeing through its effects.

Shantell kept a hand on her tube, ready to pull it out at a moment's notice as they ran back through the trees.

Howls lit up the night air behind them as monsters straight out of fairy tales and books began to chase them. Jack's mother fell back, taking up the rear position, where she could freely freeze everything behind them.

Trees cracked and boomed as the sap inside them flash froze and expanded, shattering their trunks. An entire swath of the forest came down on the heads of the monsters behind them. Screams soon followed as a controlled fire raged through, carbonizing every last one of them.

The locals would be left wondering why they had a section of burned forest in the morning before the grand spell came into effect and they forgot about it.

Jack's mother was pale and trembling from the concerted effort using so much of her magic took on her when she rejoined them a minute later.

"Um, do we need to be worried about other nests for the monsters you just killed?" He asked uncertainly as they neared the old gas station where the car was parked.

"No, those weren't banes. They were just normal nightwalkers who got attracted by the noise we made. I'll need to take care of them at some point, but that is more to keep my area free from trouble than rules imposed on me by the council." Elinor explained softly, resting against the side of the car. "Jack, we're done here for now. Can you drive us to the next one?"

"Sure, just tell me where to go." He thumbed the unlock button on the remote and opened the passenger door for his mother and then the trunk.

A few minutes later, they were back on the road and heading towards the town of Bennett.

"Okay, I keep hearing you mention banes. What are they?" Jack asked, glancing first at his mother and then into the rearview mirror.

"Banes are the bogeyman of monsters," Kaitlyn answered when no one else did. "They can be created from anything, human, animal, werewolf, vampire. It doesn't matter. The process of becoming one changes them and morphs them into something else. It makes them more dangerous and enhances the hunger they feel towards those of us who possess magic. They are one of the oldest species of monsters known to exist, and no one knows where they originally come from. But it's believed they were exterminated at least four different times, only for them to come back each time."

"That's more or less correct." Elinor lifted her head from the window and twisted around. "Do you want to tell them the rest, or should I?" She asked Shantell.

"I'll do it." The other mother muttered. "The reason they keep coming back is because banes were created. They're not natural. Using technology, humans can now examine strands of DNA, and to a limited extent manipulate them. Well, magic was able to manipulate it since ancient times. However, unless you were very good, it couldn't be done in a controlled manner. Anyone who tried would either explode or end up with cancerous growths all over themselves or their target."

"So, who managed to succeed, then?" Jack asked as he slowed to make a turn.

"I'm getting there. It was Merlin. He was the one who discovered that the key to making it work was fine control, a dose of Fae magic, and one or two other things. Now the bane are obviously not as old as some would have you believe, since Merlin was only alive a thousand years ago. The rest of what she said was true, though. They were an accident and have been repeatedly exterminated. Yet somehow they keep coming back, even without the Fae around."

"And you what? Think that someone is trying to use technology to fill the magical gap and bring them back this time?" He guessed. "Is that why you said before that no one with any knowledge about them would ever dare to experiment like this?"

His mother nodded and pointed to an upcoming overgrown driveway. "Turn here. I got a brief hit in this area before the spell failed. And yes, that is what I'm thinking. However, the problem then becomes that someone must have told them something about the existence of banes to give them direction. Which means they are working with someone, and judging by what happened a little bit ago, that person is a dark mage."

"I don't buy it," Shantell said, as he turned on the old overgrown driveway. "Even if these people only contain a small amount of power, and have a grudge against the community, they must know how dangerous the banes would still be to them. Anyone could tell them that! Moreover, why would a dark mage want the bane brought back? They're just as tasty a snack to them as anything else."

"Maybe they think they found a way to control them by combining technology and magic, or something." Jack offered as he swerved around a sudden pothole.

The bright white LED headlights lit up the crumbling remains of a grey farmhouse. It was missing its door and the stairs leading up to the porch had been eaten away by time, weather, and insects. To the side and further back, they could see the general outline of a burned-out barn.

"Keep going past the barn. I think that's where I remember the hit coming from. There must be an old root cellar or bomb shelter back there." Elinor braced herself as the car rocked back and forth as the sedan went off-road.

"We should have taken the SUV," Shantell muttered. "But going back to what you said, plenty of people have tried to control the banes over the years and all of them have failed. It's one of the oldest 'control the world' schemes in existence, but if they did manage to combine magic with technology to create something new..." She let the thought dangle.

Elinor cursed softly and unbuckled her seatbelt as the car came to a stop. "I'll need to look into it more before I tell the council anything either way. Someone playing around with banes will freak them out, and with good reason. I would prefer to just handle this on my own, and then tell them after the fact if at all possible."

"That would definitely be for the best." Shantell agreed.

A couple of minutes later they were all geared up and searching the abandoned grounds. Each looking for anything out of place or that went underground, a root cellar, a bomb shelter, an old well. Anything of that nature.

It ended up being an old cistern that was buried inside a small hill behind the charred remains of the barn. A rotting wooden door hanging from two rusted open hinges had been placed on the side of the hill at the opening. The concrete bottom had been cracked and left to drain years before. All around the inside of the cistern were the remains of things living inside and having made it into a nest.

"I've been meaning to ask this for a while now," Jack began, softly plugging his nose, as an unpleasant smell hit them. "You keep mentioning nests when you mention nightwalkers. Does that mean werewolves, vampires, and whatever else is out there live like this as well?"

"Nest has a different meaning in the magical community than what you are familiar with. It doesn't mean a literal nest, like with a bird, but a communal living space similar to a den." Kaitlyn explained as they sifted through the detritus on the floor. "So, in answer yes most live in nests of some form, they enjoy or need the feeling of community. However, they rarely devolve into being animals like this, and live as normalish humans most of the time."

"I found something," Shantell called out, holding up some dirtied papers.

All three rushed over to her.

The papers were smeared with crusted over filth, and no one dared to take them from the woman who could heal herself.

Jack directed his light to it and squinted. "It looks like a report of some kind. 'Model using' then there's too much filth, 'Succeeded on patient fifty-seven of group three, the rest failed.' One of the things here must have swiped it before the tech left."

His mother stepped closer to the page and began scraping at the filth with a knife. "What do think they meant by succeeded? It didn't turn into a ravening mindless monster or they actually created a bane?"

Shantell shook her head. "I... hope it doesn't mean the second one, and I doubt it does either. However, even if they did, it sounds like they haven't perfected the process yet either. We still have time."

Elinor looked up at her wanly. "Not as much as we might need, but some."

Chapter 20

Chapter 20

"Are we going to wait here for them to return?" Jack asked after they had finished looking through the smelly space.

The group rushed back out into the night and breathed in the clean Colorado countryside air.

"I haven't decided yet," His mother replied tiredly. "We still need to take them out, no matter what. Why don't you and Kaitlyn check out the farmhouse while we continue to look around or something?"

Shantell nodded and waved them away. "Go on, we won't kill each other while you're off exploring. Just be ready in case any of them come back unexpectedly."

The teens yawned and shrugged. "Okay." They said at the same time.

"Wait, Jack, do you want to carry this?" His mother asked, pointing to the gun clipped to her belt. "The rest of us have other forms of protection. You might need it." She took it off and handed it over without waiting for his opinion. "Just keep it away from bolts of electricity and I know it's been a while since you last went to the range, but don't forget the basics."

"I know the six basics; it hasn't been that long, mom." He took the gun and clip holster from her with both hands and put it on his own belt.

"Alright, just be careful."

The two teens rolled their eyes and walked away. The beams from their flashlights illuminated the rusted remains of old farm equipment as they passed. All of it had been discarded in piles behind the barn, left to rot along with everything else.

If the age of the equipment was anything to go by, then this farm had been abandoned for at least thirty or forty years. It was uncommon, but not as much as people assumed it was. It was a location that was just waiting for some developer to swoop in and buy the place up for their next project.

The house rose up in front of them, taking on a haunted quality under their flashlights.

The back door was closed, and the glittering remains of broken glass littered the ground around it. The small window in the door had been broken ages ago by some vandals or kids long past. Walking through the glass shards, Jack pushed opened the door for them.

"Shall we?"

Kaitlyn hesitated for a moment. "I know I went into that old school by myself a few times and can't really say this. But this house is creepy!" She muttered before going inside.

"Yeah, it is. Why do you think it has been abandoned all these years? Taxes, or did something happen here?"

"From what I hear adults say in the stores, the IRS is scarier than any monsters. So, I'm going to go with taxes on this one. They probably just couldn't keep up with the rising cost to use their land and had to abandon ship." She slowly swung her flashlight from room to room as they walked, the old hallway creaking under them constantly.

"Well, I certainly don't see any signs of monsters having broken into the place." Jack brushed across a couple of dusty piano keys. The light pressure breaking one of the mechanisms inside, while the second key let out a dull off-key noise. "This is definitely the kind of place that I would find creepy any other night of the week."

"And now?" Kaitlyn tentatively stepped onto their stairs going up.

"Now? I don't know. My mind is kind of fixated on what we saw and heard before. I think I'm going to need some time to process everything before I can make heads or tails of it all."

"Well, just don't let it distract you in case they decide to come back early."

"I won't, or at least I'll try not to." Jack scraped away some cobwebs from an exposed beam and frowned as he saw glints of inlaid silver. "Here, help me pull off some more of these boards. I want to get a better look at this beam."

Both of them were nursing several splinters by the time they had cleared away enough of the old boards and plaster for him to see.

"Are those runes?" Kaitlyn asked in a whisper.

"Yeah, there's a restaurant outside of town with similar markings on the pillars. Another group must have lived here at some point in the past."

Her finger traced the markings. "Back before creating runes became the specialized knowledge that it is today."

"Is there a reason that happened? Why did it suddenly go from normal knowledge to something practiced mainly by the nobles?"

Kaitlyn inhaled sharply and pulled her finger back from the wooden beam. "It's not, at least not really. There are certain runes, like the ones your mother uses, that are restricted to those trained in their use and construction. The nobles just happen to be required to learn it, at least according to your mother. As for why it was restricted..."

She hesitated and shined her light on the pillar. "This looks like it goes all the way down to the basement. I want to see if they have any more runes down there. Anyway, people do stupid things sometimes for good reasons, or at least that's what I've been told. During World War Two, there was a group who thought they could use runes to create a portal to somewhere else. An unknown third realm, similar to where the Fae live. They didn't succeed, luckily, but the attempt freaked everyone out."

"I bet. What if they had opened up a portal to hell or something?" Jack muttered, freaking out.

"No, that's already been done. Anyway, I guess I should have said fourth of maybe even fifth realm. Regardless, everyone involved was killed and then the various magical communities spent the next several years collecting slash taking all information on runes from the masses." The stairs creaked and groaned as they walked down into the cool concrete walled basement.

"And how successful have they been in taking back the information from everyone? I can only imagine that even with the fear the event caused, most wouldn't give up their secrets willingly."

Kaitlyn laughed sardonically. "That's an understatement. We're talking about their family's legacies here. Almost no one was willing to give them up without a fight. They burned them instead. A lot of runes and their information were lost in those days. Everyone assumes the families reconstructed the books with what they could remember, but it obviously wouldn't be the full thing anymore."

"That's sad. All that information just lost." Jack used his foot to scrape away some fallen debris from the ceiling. "Have the magical communities relaxed on the guidelines at all in recent years?"

"A little, but there are still enough people around who remember the event and the chaos it caused for years afterward that change has been slow coming. Places like this have instead turned into goldmines of information with potentially lost runes or connection methods hidden in their walls. Maybe not in this particular one, since I don't think this house is nearly that old, but you get the idea."

"Great, another reason for the council to come down into the area." Jack remarked dryly. He had scraped away a clean space around the main pillar in the house, revealing a small silver rune circle.

"I think we might need to get our mothers to look at these." Kaitlyn grinned impishly. "I don't recognize the symbols at all."

"That sounds reasonable." Jack waved his flashlight around the dark basement. "This is a really creepy house at night though."

"Yeah, now come on and let's be quiet about it. I want to hear what our moms are talking about."

They snuck uselessly up the creaking stairs and out the door they had left open. Dried crab grass and weeds crunched softly underfoot as they made their way back to the hill with the cistern.

"Have things with the council really gotten that bad?" They heard Jack's mom say as they stopped outside the rotten door.

"You have no idea." Shantell replied sadly. "All of the old generation are being pushed out of their positions to make way for the younger people. Which sounds fine on paper, except each and every single one of them is desperate to make their mark. They're all power-hungry, and more-or-less above our laws. My parents, and Jon's parents, have somehow managed to keep their spots on the council for now. Not that it will do us any good in this situation."

They heard a deep sigh from inside.

"We need them to bond faster. That's the only way Jack will ever be even remotely safe."

"What about your daughter?"

"Penelope is different... She's special. She has a lot of potential for sure, but she also seems to have a natural bond with Jack."

"Natural bonds are rare, even among families with generators. I can see why you said before that she was troublesome in her own way. Especially if she has the potential, you believe she does."

"She does. I've already tested. Even with us starting her training late, her well is only a little underdveloped, and her power is already decent. Her control is what's lacking for the moment, but that will be the big hurdle for her, I believe."

Jack motioned for Kaitlyn to follow him in. He had heard enough for the moment.

"Anyway, I'm telling you I saw similar ones to those in a restaurant outside of town." He bumped into the side of the wall as they entered, sending a cascade of dirt and loose debris down around them.

"I'm not debating that. I'm just saying, how can you be sure they belonged to the same group?" Kaitlyn questioned, getting into the sudden charade.

"I'm not, and I don't think they do." He protested.

"What are you two talking about?" Elinor asked as they came into view.

"We found some runes inside the house, similar to the ones from that restaurant you took me to." Jack quickly described to them what they had found.

"Show me, please?" His mother requested, with a muttered curse. "I'll have to take apart yet another house after this, I guess."

"Say what?" Shantell asked in surprise.

"What, you thought I was going to inform the council of these runes and let them inspect them? Please, this is my territory. I get to decide what happens inside it. If they don't like it, then they can change the rules, but I don't see that happening anytime soon. Do you?"

Kaitlyn's mother chuckled. "No, no, I do not."

Inside the house, they led their mother's upstairs to the first runes they had found and then down to the basement.

"I recognized the ones upstairs as warding and protection runes. They match others I have found in the area. However, I don't recognize what this one down here is meant to do. It's the first time I've run into this particular rune." Elinor snapped a few pictures of everything using her phone and pushed them back up the stairs. "I might just burn the house down and take the pillar and slab of concrete afterward."

"What have you done in the past?" Jack asked her as they walked out of the house.

"It varied from place to place. Some, albeit rarely, like at the restaurant I left alone. For others, I demanded council-provided funds to retrieve the needed portions and nothing more. Those were usually the houses that were still occupied or close to others. Then you have places like this where I can just demolish them without the council being the wiser. Which works out for the best, since we are trying to not attract their attention right now."

"Plus, you get to keep any information gained for yourself," Shantell put in from behind them.

"There is also that." Elinor agreed, not at all put out by having her actions revealed to her son. "Playing by all the rules won't get you anywhere in life. Your parents showed me that Shantell."

Kaitlyn looked sideways at Jack, who could only shrug. This was a side of his mother he had never seen before.

The two mothers bickered back and forth as they found themselves walking toward the car. "I'm telling you, I never even saw the lookout here at all!"

"Wait, where are we going?" Jack asked, interrupting them. "I thought we were waiting here for them all to return."

His mother abruptly yawned, setting off a chain reaction with the rest of them. "No, we don't need to with this one. Now that I know where it is, I can come back to it during the day when they would all be asleep and eliminate them if I need to. Right now, the question is, do we feel like driving out towards the Kansas border tonight or heading home for some sleep?"

"I think we should do the border tomorrow and leave earlier. Don't forget, it's still like a two-hour drive to get there from here." Shantell pulled out her phone and lit up the screen, showing the time. "It's a little after one in the morning right now, so we could make it with plenty of darkness, I suppose." She had been hoping it was earlier than that.

"There aren't any other nests or problem sites close by?" Kaitlyn asked as Jack unlocked the vehicle for them.

Elinor yawned again as she buckled her seatbelt. "I'm sure there might be. I just don't know about them. Without the detection spell working on this portion of my domain, things have been slower going. Like I mentioned earlier, though, I'll have everything working again in a week or two."

"So, home then?" Jack clarified, handing his mother her gun and holster before starting the vehicle.

"Yeah, let's call this an early night. I'll use the rest of the night to work on rebuilding the spells inside my domain. Can I get your help with that, Jack?" She asked, tucking the gun into the glove box.

"Sure, what do you need?"

"Just your energy. Rebuilding the spells takes a lot of it, and I've been exhausting myself trying to do everything all at once." For the first time, he was able to detect the hints of just how tired she truly was in her voice.

"Of course, mom. I'd be happy to help. Just let me know if there is anything else I can do." Honestly, he just wanted to get some sleep, but he also wasn't just going to leave her alone. Not when she had taken the time to ask for his help.

"Thanks, honey, just take us back to their house for now, then." She yawned a third time and leaned her head against the window, closing her eyes for a quick nap.

"Don't let her spend too much time on the spells tonight, Jack," Shantell told him softly once they were back on the main road and speeding towards their home. "She may be able to use your energy to fuel it, but using the control stones for her territory will still be mentally taxing."

He glanced over at his sleeping mother and then back at her before responding. "I won't, thanks. I wouldn't have expected you to be concerned about my mom at all."

"I don't hate Elinor," She replied softly. "I never did. There was a time when I was jealous and was forced to stay away from her. During that time, I did a few petty acts against her, ruining our friendship, but I never wanted to truly hurt her. What I unknowingly played a part in because of my parents—" She cut off as a sob came from the front seat.

"What did you have to be jealous of with me back then? I had nothing but our friendship growing up until you cast that aside." Elinor's hands were clenched tight, as the temperature in the care began to drop.

Shantell gave a halfhearted, hollow chuckle. "True, you grew up as the daughter of regular magic users. They weren't nobles. They didn't have excessive expectations of you growing up. I don't even remember how we became friends in the first place. Our paths never should have crossed normally."

"It was during our potential testing when we were four or five," Elinor replied. "My parents brought me, while your butler and a random servant brought you."

Jack caught Shantell nod in the rearview mirror.

"And that is exactly what eventually led to me being jealous of you. Your parents. They loved you, they paid attention to you. They did the things that mine never did with me."

Elinor snorted as the temperature dropped again inside the car. Jack reached over and turned on the heat to full blast. "My parents cared for you as well, and you know it."

"I do, but it was never enough. Like I said, I was jealous. It was almost a relief when my parents told me I couldn't hang out with you anymore. But I never wanted to hurt you, especially not in the way you were. And I still don't know why my parents suddenly went as far as they did."

"Neither do I, but it doesn't matter. The next time I meet your parents, their lives will be forfeit." Elinor ground out.

Kaitlyn, who hadn't said anything the entire time, suddenly spoke up. "But they're on the council! I admit I'm not exactly fond of them myself. They pretty much threw me aside when they found out how small my well was. The experience was eye-opening, to say the least. However, that doesn't change who they are."

Elinor fought for control, the icy layer that had been creeping up her window receding. "Shantell, you remember at dinner when you asked how I could suddenly become an ice witch when growing up my main element was fire?"

"Yes," She answered hesitantly, wondering where the other woman was going with the question.

"Do you remember what my parent's main elements were?" Jack's mother had to force the words out.

Kaitlyn's hand flew to her mouth as her eyes opened wide.

"No! Please tell me you're joking," Shantell shouted, the suddenness of her effusive reaction startling Jack.

"Didn't you ever wonder how I survived?"

"Of course, I wondered, everyone did. Who would have guessed that your parents would do something so forbidden though?"

"Um, I'm confused. What did your parents do? Hell, what did her parents do to you, and why was surviving enough to make you a noble?" Jack demanded. He was getting annoyed with the constant secrets and lack of knowledge on his part.

Chapter 21

Chapter 21

E linor looked over at her son and sighed. "I know you're getting frustrated sweetie, but some things are better left not talked about inside a car."

He rolled his eyes, keeping a steady hand on the wheel. "After everything else we have already talked about, that's what makes you worried?"

"No, she's right on this one. Some topics are best discussed where they can't be scryed or picked up by prying ears. We've been playing it entirely too fast and loose up to this point as it is."

"So, the restaurant then?" He suggested.

"Not right now, but yes, later." His mother agreed.

Conversation drifted off with that as the passengers closed their eyes, leaving Jack to stew in his thoughts alone. Up to this point, he hadn't really felt like anybody was deliberately holding anything back from him. It was just a matter of knowledge and him learning it or needing to ask the right questions.

Now suddenly, there was a family secret that he needed to wait to learn anything about and it was frustrating him.

A few minutes later, they entered the town limits, and he dropped the speed of the car down as they neared the LaCouture residence. Shantell and Kaitlyn opened their eyes as the small car jostled from side to side as he pulled into their driveway.

"Thanks for driving Jack. I'll see you in the morning sometime." Kaitlyn muttered with a yawn.

Her mother grunted in agreement. "I'll talk to you later, Elinor. We need to figure out what we're going to do with this nest and the border still."

Elinor cracked her eyes open a fraction. "Later, Shantell, rebuilding the spells for the territory will be draining. No matter how careful I am, or how much energy he gives me. I doubt either of us will be getting up before the afternoon sometime."

"Remember what I said. Make sure she doesn't go overboard." She told Jack, popping open her door. "Just be careful Elinor. We've both heard the stories of what happens to people who try and do too much too quickly with their control stones."

The door closed behind her with those parting words. Jack kept the car in the driveway until he was sure they were both safely inside the house. Only then did he begin backing up onto the road.

"Where to?"

"Hmm?" His mother looked up in confusion. "Oh, sorry, just take us home. Everything we need can be done from a secret room in the basement."

"Are you alright mom?" He asked as he turned the car towards their home. "I know that what happened with Shantell tonight brought up a lot of old memories. You never talk about your parents, and I can only assume that whatever happened wasn't pleasant."

His mother reached across and squeezed his arm. "Thanks honey, but I'll be fine. It's just not something I like to think about is all. I wasn't there when it happened to them, so I have no idea what it was like. All I have to go on is the old stories, before the act was outlawed and banned. The depictions aren't pleasant."

Silence filled the car as Jack turned onto their street and hit the brakes.

"Mom, look!" The car jumped to a standstill as he jammed the pedal to the floor.

The front of their house was swarming with cops as they inspected a broken front door.

Elinor jumped out as soon as he screeched to a stop, dodging the police that tried to stop her from getting any closer. Jack was hot on her heels but had less luck with evading the bacon force.

Still, he managed to get close enough to see that the front door had been completely demolished. Whoever had done this had really wanted to get inside their house, and it looked like they had succeeded.

Jack kicked and shoved his way free from the officers and ducked into the house. Their shouts falling on deaf ears. All he wanted to do was get inside and check on his little sister and father. They weren't outside talking to the cops. That had to mean they were still inside, right?

No such luck. They were gone. But they hadn't left without a fight. There were broken pieces of chairs, plates, and every other conceivable item. The blood coating the walls and sharper pieces of weaponized debris told the story that the intruders hadn't simply broken everything themselves.

"Who did this, mom?" Jack asked her when he found her standing in the hallway that led toward his and Penny's room.

"The people behind the nests we found tonight. They left a note for us to find. Not one that normal people could see, thankfully." She sounded tired, and more than a little defeated in that moment.

"They don't know who you are, do they? That you're the local baron. I mean, there is no way they would have done something like this to the person who controls the territory. That would be just stupid." He was grasping at straws, and he knew it.

"It would be for any other territory, yes. I've maintained such a low profile since your birth that most probably assume this is an ungoverned territory again." She sighed and looked up at the ceiling with a sad smile. "We had a good run, Jack. The four of us had a peaceful life for nearly eighteen years, less for Penny because of her age. But I will call the council and get them involved if it means getting them back safely."

He swallowed and nodded, agreeing with the decision. There were ways to speed up the bonding process if it came to that, and if Kaitlyn agreed. "Let's take care of the police first and then rebuild the spells. Maybe we can use those to locate them first." He hesitated, feeling like he was forgetting something. "What did the note they left say?"

She shook her head; her face was pale as she replied. "Later. Just know that they're both safe for now."

Jack stayed out of the way of the officers and let them do their work while he stewed in his thoughts. He might not have had a lot of respect for the profession, but he wasn't going to hinder them, either. He had simply seen too many cops who abused their authority, and let the power they wielded go to their head. The rare few who weren't bullies were an exception.

It took over an hour for the police to finish the last of their work and then leave. Honestly, he had expected it to take even longer, considering there were two kidnapped people involved. Maybe that had something to do with the grand spell, or was normal. He had no way of knowing.

Still, a little while later, his mother pulled him down into the basement with a growl. "Help me open up a path!" She ordered, indicating the mess that prevented them from easily getting to a particularly dark corner.

She had been carefully picking her way through the last few days as needed while the kids were at school. Before then, it had been mostly ignored for a long time. However, the time for secrets was over and past. It was time to get her territory into working order and find her family. Then, when that had been accomplished, there would be hell to pay.

"Mom," Jack interrupted her thought process as he shoved an old box of clothes to the side. "Are you going to tell me what the note said now?"

Elinor threw a box angrily away before responding. "It said that they had your father and Penny and that nothing would happen to them as long as

I stopped destroying the nests or investigating them. That's all. It made no mention of the LaCouture's, or me being the baron, nothing. It was short, to the point, and written in a way that a normal non-mage would look over it. It also made no mention of them being returned to us."

Jack's mind went back to what they had been discussing earlier that night. "So, are we leaning more towards dark mages now than the uneducated magic users you were originally thinking were behind this?"

She kicked a box, putting her boot through the thin cardboard and cracking into whatever was hidden inside. "I don't know. Dark mages don't typically take hostages, but you're right, the note does imply they're not uneducated. However, all of that was always just my thoughts on the matter in any case. I never had any proof they were one or the other. For all we know, they could be something else entirely."

He grunted and pushed aside one last wall of boxes and other crap they had never gotten rid of. "We need to clean up the basement." Jack complained, shining his flashlight on a doorknob that had been hidden behind everything. The door itself blended in with the walls.

"This is exactly why we never have," His mother explained. "I needed a decent way to hide this room without straight-up banning you and Penny from entering a section of the house. I think we both know how that would have ended up. Besides, a lot of this is stuff I inherited from my parents when they passed." She felt the edge of a random box. "I've never had the heart to look through a few of them till now. I suppose it might be time to change that."

Jack took a moment to look inside the box beside him, finding its contents utterly normal.

"I'm not going to leave the really odd or dangerous items just lying around where my children could have found them." His mother chuckled weakly as she unlocked the door and walked inside. "Come on, let's get to this. We had to waste enough time because of those dawdling cops as it is!"

A light flickered on as she entered, showing a room filled with runes inset into the floor, walls, and ceiling.

"This is why nobles, specifically nobles in charge of territories, need to know about runes." She said with a wave of her hand. "All of these go into the management and control of their territory and must be constructed by the mage themselves as a rite of passage.

"Even when the domain is inherited, the original control rooms are destroyed and must be recreated by the new owner. Otherwise, things don't work quite as well. Because I created this place from scratch, the runes work better for me than they would anyone else. No matter how closely related we might be."

In the middle of the room was a pedestal with a large, peculiar marble orb sitting in a fitted depression.

"It sounds like they're different from the runes you set up for Kaitlyn's and my training out there." Jack managed to say after several seconds. His mouth suddenly dry. He had no idea something like this had been underneath their house.

"The runes are special, yes, but not in the way you are probably thinking." Elinor shook her head and approached the pedestal. "It's because of this, the control stone. It knows who created them, and forms a bond with their creator. With enough magical energy, these control stones can do some truly miraculous and terrible things."

She sighed. "You will eventually have that kind of energy output, but you don't yet, though you are getting close. Regardless, your body certainly wouldn't be able to handle the strain of moving that much energy at the moment in any case. Which means we are going to have to do this the old-fashioned way, and recreate the spells I let lapse because I didn't have enough energy to maintain them on my own."

He winced. "Sorry."

"Don't be. I made my choice, and I don't regret it. Putting that spell on you was more important to me than this territory ever was. But now we have to find your father and Penelope. It's time to go to work!"

She reached for the orb and glanced at her son. "Come on, put your hands on top of mine and get ready to work."

Jack breathed in deep and placed his hands on top of his mother's. The connection wasn't as easy as the one he shared with Kaitlyn or the odd effortless familial bond he shared with Penelope. Still, it was there and within the space of a heartbeat, the magical energy from his well began to pour into her hands.

Elinor gasped as the magic suddenly began interacting with her own and clenched the control stone. Her eyes beginning to glow with an icy light. She had initiated the connection between them as she began pulling on his energy. He didn't have enough control yet to establish it on his own.

"Just bear with this. It's going to be boring for you." She told her son a moment before closing her eyes.

Recreating the spells was a different beast entirely from maintaining them. One just required her to inject a certain amount of magical energy into the control stone each month or so. A relatively easy task now that she had enough to spare. It was a different matter from before, where she had little in the way of excess to keep it powered.

Building the spells that would cover her territory required her to walk the land in her astral form. Laying down the new spells with every step she took. It was a time and effort-intensive procedure, requiring a constant stream of magic to fuel the creation of everything.

The only plus side was that in her astral form, Elinor was able to cover her territory at a greater speed than ever before. The speed of a car had nothing on her as she surged through all the dips and valleys, flying like a bird above it all.

Then she ran into a wall, where none should have been.

Elinor had been working on rebuilding everything during the last few days. However, she hadn't made much progress because of their nightly patrol activities, leaving her exhausted during the day. If it wasn't for that, she might have discovered that the Kansas baron was encroaching on her domain. Shrinking her territory, and possibly inadvertently hiding where her husband and daughter had been taken.

It was an insult and a breach of conduct that she couldn't let stand. Not right then, in any case.

She opened herself up to Jack's magic and drew on it more deeply than before. She was going to need all she could get for what she was about to do. The borders of a noble's territory were sacred and were not to be encroached upon. Every baron knew that, and yet here she was faced with someone daring to do exactly that.

It was time to show them who truly owned that land.

Her goal was to do only two things, well, kind of three... Reestablish the proper boundaries of her territory and strengthen them so they couldn't be torn down right away. That was the first thing. Number two was fixing the tracking spells that had fallen into disarray. The last item was sort of part of the first in that she was going to do the exact same thing to them that they had to her.

She was going to establish two boundaries. The proper one, and then a second one as far in as she could push without collapsing from exhaustion afterward.

Elinor took a few minutes to examine each of her boundaries and found that two more of her neighboring barons were doing the same thing. They were encroaching on her land. She ground her teeth and opened her eyes.

"Jack, I'm going to need all the energy you can give me. It seems the nobles have been encroaching on my domain while I wasn't paying attention."

He stared blankly at her. "What does the size of your domain have to do with finding dad and Penny?"

She growled and cracked her neck, fighting for an increasingly difficult to find calm. "Inside each domain, there are anchor stones, it's what the spells get tied to and decide the size of your domain. The smaller the domain, the fewer anchor stones, and the weaker your spells become. All domains are traditionally left at a certain size, so the spells never become too weak.

"In other words, while I may not have been paying attention to things, them doing this certainly didn't help. However, that's not what matters right now. What does is the strength of the spells. I might not be able to find them, or do anything, even if I can find them with what I have left. Which is why I need to expand my domain back to what it was, and maybe more. Do you understand?"

Jack gave her a hesitant nod. "Kind of. I got enough to know it's important and will help us rescue them. Which is good enough for now. You can go over everything with me more later."

"Alright, good. I just wanted to let you know I was going to be needing your help, is all. Me taking the energy will tire you out more than if you help push it into me. Besides, it's good practice."

She closed her eyes again and grabbed hold of the control stone like she wanted to break it into pieces.

Already she could feel him giving her magic to work with and she was going to use every single drop of it. Just because she had stopped actively using magic didn't mean she had stopped learning. That would have been stupid.

Elinor always knew that the day would come when she would need to fight for her son's safety against the council. It was a given as soon as she knew what he was. So, she had kept learning, studying every spell and rune she could get her hands on. Even if she couldn't use them at the time due to her lack of power, she could still train and practice.

Which she did, constantly.

Now, it was time to turn all that theory and knowledge into something real.

She slowly pushed each baron back, one anchor stone at a time, reclaiming them, and tying them back to her domain. When she reached the proper boundary, she reinforced the spells, ensuring something like this wouldn't happen again. It was a magic-intensive affair to take someone else's anchor stones. They most likely only dared to do it because she had been neglecting them.

It didn't make it right, but it was somewhat understandable.

However, that didn't mean she was going to let the matter rest, not by any stretch of the imagination. She continued to push into their territory, taking an equal number of anchor stones plus one more. It was petty, sure, but at the moment she didn't really care.

Finally, with that matter taken care of, and after making sure they couldn't be easily taken back, she began on the territory spells for tracking. Retaking her domain and then expanding it had been a delay of maybe an hour or so, thanks to her son's help.

The expansion had taken only a few extra minutes, so while it felt like forever to her. The delay hadn't been that long at all.

Dealing with the police had taken longer than this had.

Chapter 22

J ack watched as his mother concentrated on the marble control stone.
All he could do was focus on sending her the energy from his well.
So, that's what he did. He was the glorified battery source of their little
operation and little more.

Unfortunately, despite the circumstances, he couldn't pretend it didn't
hurt his ego just a little. He wanted to be able to do what his mother was
doing, and be an active participant in their rescue. As it stood currently, he
felt helpless.

It wasn't a feeling he enjoyed.

All he could do was stand there and do his best to supply his mother with
the energy she needed. Every moment he felt a little more of himself being
drained, taken by the process. At the same time, he couldn't help but think
of how different this was from when Shantell had healed him. Back then,
she had torn the energy from him, and the process had left them both
exhausted.

This time, he was giving the energy to his mother willingly, and even
helping to pass it to her. They had been working for close to half an hour
by this point, and he still had more in the tank to give. Jack had no idea

where he was on the scale compared to other magical generators, but he could suddenly understand the allure of having someone like him around.

He was like the ultimate backup battery and power source in one. He could make it so any magic user could cast their spells long past where they should have run out.

A minute later, Elinor stepped back from the stone. Her eyes glowed with an icy light, and a feral snarl had appeared on her face.

"Come, we'll need Jon and Shantell's help to get them back!" She spun on her heel and pulled her son along behind her.

"You found them already? Where are they?" Jack asked, trying to keep up with her or risk getting dragged up the stairs.

"Of course, I did. Once I got the tracking spell working again, it was easy to find them both."

"Well, where are they?"

"The old industrial area of Denver. It looks like they took over an entire section and repurposed some of the old factories and warehouses to their needs."

"And we need Kaitlyn's parents to what, storm the place?" He asked as they walked out the missing front door, stumbling as the toe of his shoe caught on something. "Wait, mom, hold up!" He pulled his arm from hers and bent over the path that led to their front door.

"What is it?"

Jack pulled out his phone and turned on the flashlight. "My foot hit one of these as we were walking just now. They look like the acid pits that were created by that monster Kaitlyn and I ran into at the old school building." He lifted the light further, revealing what had once been a smooth path, to now be a pit scarred mess.

"If it is the same, then we might have a larger problem on our hands."

"Why?"

"Because those weren't caused by any bane or other nightwalker I've ever heard of. Which means they're experimenting with regular monsters and letting them back out. What did you say it looked like again?" She handed him the keys to her car again and jogged around to her door as he thumbed the key fob and unlocked it.

"I don't know, a slavering, scruffy werewolf? Kaitlyn could probably give you more details, simply because she is more familiar with everything." The car started with the gentle purr of German engineering. "Is Denver even part of Eastern-Colorado?"

"Colorado's a big state sweetie. What someone might consider the eastern part is fluid based on location."

"So, that's a nooo?" He asked slowly, rolling to stop at the stoplight.

"Colorado has three barons currently, but it used to have five. I handle everything east of the mountains for the most part."

"Mom, like you just said, Colorado is a big state. That's a lot of territory to cover! How have you been doing it all this time?"

She raised a brow and shrugged. "In the beginning it was tough, but the control stone and the domain spells helped me weed out everyone I didn't want around. After that, well, I just did the bare minimum, so it wasn't exactly hard then either."

"Surely people must have wanted to move out here though, or drive-through and create some trouble."

"I just refused all applicants who wanted to move out here. They stopped coming after a while. As for troublemakers... There have been a few, yeah, but they weren't anything I couldn't handle, even with my diminished abilities."

He pulled into the LaCouture's driveway a few minutes later and shut off the engine while his mother hopped out and raced to the front door. Lights went on all in rapid succession as she pounded on the front door.

A moment later, a shirtless, hulking Jon yanked open the door.

Jack ran up behind his mother in time to hear her explain what had happened.

The large behemoth of a man nodded to him and then turned around to look at his wife. "We should help them." His deep, gravelly voice felt even rougher this early in the morning.

Shantell nodded once. "Agreed. You realize this is going to call the council down on you though, right?"

Elinor gave them all a grim smile. "We'll cross that bridge when we come to it, but yes, I have a feeling that will be the case. After we do this, Jack and Kaitlyn will need to work on forming their bond. If the council does show up, that might be all that saves him."

At the back, Kaitlyn agreed with a sad smile. This wasn't how she had wanted to form their bond. She had envisioned something more natural, romantic even, and certainly less forced.

Real-life sucked at times.

"We'll go get changed and meet you outside in just a minute." The door closed, leaving them outside, hopping from foot to foot impatiently while they waited.

It was frustrating. Both just wanted to get on their way and save their family members, but they couldn't do it alone.

Jon reappeared a minute later, pulling on a heavy jacket and a dark hat. "Don't worry, they're right behind me. Where are we headed towards?"

"The old industrial part of Denver, on the north side."

"Alright, I guess we're taking two cars?"

Elinor nodded. "We'll need the extra room for when we rescue them."

"Are we 'running under cover'?"

"I haven't heard that term in what feels like forever." A nostalgic smile flickered across her face. "Not right away. We might need all the energy we can muster for this one. Only put it up if you get spotted, but we are certainly going to be speeding, so have it at the ready."

The big man grinned. "You know me. I'm always looking for an excuse to use that spell."

"You haven't changed in the slightest. I was glad to see you never sold the spell to the council, at least."

He snorted. "Despite being on the council themselves, mom and dad wouldn't let me even if I had wanted to. Besides, half the rights of the spell belong to you. I couldn't make that decision on my own. It was just a stupid spell we created together in college anyway. It's fun for us, but if it ever got out, it could cause some issues."

"They never tried to make their own version of it?" Jack couldn't help but ask, not even entirely sure what the spell did.

"Oh, they have tried, but making proper new spells is hard. There's a lot of guesswork involved, and you have to know where each piece goes as you construct it inside your mind. From what I understand, they have had some limited success, but nothing approaching what we have with ours. We were just that good back then."

His mother snorted. "No, we just got lucky, and I had an unfair advantage over most people at the time."

Jon nodded, his eyes drooping sadly.

Behind him, the door to his house opened and Kaitlyn stepped out with Shantell hot on her heels.

"Looks like they're ready, let's do this." Jon tapped the roof of their car and hurried over to the Charger Kaitlyn had been driving lately, opening the doors for both ladies before going around to his own.

"Was there ever anything romantic between you and him?" Jack dared to ask his mother, as he started the car and backed out of their driveway.

"You know, for a minute I thought there could have been, and then everything happened with Shantell's parents. Not to mention, my parents dying... It was a lot at the time. When I made it back to the university, I was completely closed off emotionally. I wouldn't let anyone in. I think it was the end of my first day back that I broke down and just sat in my dorm room, crying for the entire night.

"I decided I was done with the place after that and started packing everything. Somehow, Jon found out I had come back and just showed up and started helping. That was the last time I ever saw him until the other day. After I left school, the council started training me to receive my title and domain. It was around that time that I met your father, and the rest is history."

Jack risked a glance at mother as drove, taking in the distant, haunted look he had never seen before. This was a part of her life that his mother had never told them about, and certainly a side that his mother never let show.

"How did you meet dad? I always thought you met at college, but obviously that wasn't the case. I'm guessing something must have happened that brought him into contact with the magical world or whatever."

"What makes you say that?"

"Well, you just said you were being trained at the time, besides dad remembers everything. The grand spell doesn't affect him like you said it was supposed to."

Elinor rubbed her eyes tiredly. "We should have grabbed some energy drinks before we left the house. I'm wiped. The grand spell doesn't work as well on your father because he has become immune to its effects. The spell is strong, but it isn't perfect."

Jack looked over when she didn't continue. "Well, what does that mean?"

She yawned and looked ahead as he sped up. "Our first encounter was indeed during one of my training exercises by the council. The other young noble I was training with had gone to goof off somewhere, and left me alone, a big no-no even back then. You never, never leave your partner by themselves.

"Thankfully, I was able to take care of everything on my own. Then when I turned around to leave, I found Jason standing there, with a video camera like a big dumb goober and a weird look on his face. He thought I was that vampire slayer chick come to life after that."

Jack glanced over at his mother. "Buffy? No, not in that outfit. Selene from the Underworld movies maybe..."

"I was wearing something different back then. The all-leather outfit was something your father actually got me. Anyway, that's how we met the first time. I destroyed his camera and went on my way, slightly curious about why he had been there, but nothing more. I figured he'd forget about me and wasn't worried. Then a few days later I ran into him again, with another camera.

"I found out later that the second time he had also been wearing a concealed one. Even back then, the grand spell didn't work as well on him. My guess has always been that he had a lot of run-ins with magic growing up and it slowly made him immune to its effects."

Jack nodded. "So, what, with the concealed camera, he was able to record you and hunt you down or something?"

"No, nothing like that. Well, actually, sort of. He was able to get a decent recording of the nightwalker I was hunting before it disappeared. It was enough to keep the grand spell at bay and for him to remember what happened the last time we had met. The next time I saw him was a month later, just waiting outside the gates of the council building, where I was learning about runes. He had tracked me down to ask me out on a date, and the rest is history."

"It can't have been that simple!" He protested.

"Oh, it wasn't, but I'm stubborn when I want to be, and Jason was worth it. I knew that back then, and I know it now."

"Ugh, I think I just got a sugar rush," Jack muttered, feeling his heart grow warm. His parents could be so sappy at times, it was heartwarming, not that he would let them know that.

"You're just jealous things aren't going as well with Kaitlyn."

"Yes, mom. That's exactly it," He replied dryly. "I'm jealous that I'm not already engaged and married to the girl I've known for a week and a half."

"And how are things going with her? Even if you speed, we still have twenty to thirty minutes ahead of us. We might as well talk, and cover a few of those subjects we keep seeming to gloss over because of time."

"Things are good, I think... We're still getting to know each other," His fingers drummed the steering wheel in thought.

The yellow streetlights flashed by as the conversation stalled for a moment.

"Honestly, we haven't really talked a lot about ourselves yet. I don't know the world she comes from, and she doesn't seem to understand ours. It made things tense that first day at school, for sure. Everything we do is really just focused on magic, and building our bond around that. I mean, I do like her, but I guess that might be more because of her looks than anything else. Couldn't it?"

Elinor nodded. "That is a very mature response, Jack. However, I do think Kaitlyn is a good girl, so I wouldn't worry too much about it."

"I wasn't originally. Now that we might be forming our bond sooner... I have to admit, I am kind of freaking out about the entire thing." His hands gripped the steering wheel tighter as he glanced into the rear-view mirror to make sure Jon was still behind them. "In my head, the bond is still just this concept. I don't know, or understand, how it is going to change everything."

"Well, like I said, we have some time, so why don't we talk? Ask your questions and I'll answer them the best I can. Then, we can also talk about what being able to control your magic while being a generator would truly mean for you."

He swallowed at her serious tone. "Alright."

***

The short drive had been enlightening in many ways, and he wished they had made the time to have this conversation sooner. However, the time for talking was over. They had reached their destination. Or at least as close as they were going to get with the cars.

Jack pulled into a nearby parking lot and turned off the car with shaky hands. His face suddenly pale as he tried to grin at his mother, the result looking sick. "We'll need to continue this conversation later. Right now, let's just focus on getting dad and Penny back."

She nodded. "Let's find you some gear to wear."

They were standing by the trunk when the LaCouture's arrived.

"How are we going to do this?" Shantell asked, her eyes roving around the area.

"As quietly as we can, until we can't, and then as quickly as we can. I don't care about collateral damage. When I walked through the area earlier, it was all deserted or looked like it was a part of their operation. As far as I'm concerned, once my husband and daughter are safe, we can send the rest of this place straight to hell."

Jack felt a shiver run down his spine as his mother's voice took on a cold, emotionless tone. There would be no mercy for those who threatened her family. He was seeing a side of her that he had never imagined had even existed before this.

A brisk wind blew past, kicking up the dust and trash in the area and whipping it around the parking lot before moving on.

This night had been an exhausting, terrifying, and eye-opening experience on so many levels. And it wasn't even over yet. He just hoped that they managed to pull this off without a problem.

They had to.

His mother handed him the same gun and holster from before, along with a spare magazine. "I don't expect you to use this, but it's better to be safe than sorry." After everyone had flashlights, and the doors to the cars were locked, Elinor pulled them all to the edge of the parking lot. "That building right there is the one I detected them both in earlier."

She pointed to a refurbished warehouse surrounded by new fencing. A row of semis and their trailers had been backed up to the loading dock, and they could distantly see people scurrying about even at that late hour.

Jon scowled at the sight of all the other people they risked getting involved with what they were about to do. "Were you able to tell how many of those people are nightwalkers or magic users, at least?"

Elinor shook her head. "I didn't want to push myself or Jack that far by reconstructing that many spells tonight."

Shantell snorted. "And by that, you mean you found them and then forgot about everything else."

His mother turned away. "Maybe, but what I said is still true. I had to take back parts of my domain before I even began."

Kaitlyn's father groaned. "Please, tell me you didn't retaliate against them?"

"Of course I did! I needed to make sure that Jason and Penny hadn't been brought outside my area because of them."

"That is definitely going to call the council down on you!" He hissed.

She shrugged, unconcerned. "The only thing I'm worried about when it comes to the council is Jack and Penny. My daughter should be fine as long as she isn't close to Jack. It's him we really have to worry about.

"Besides, they did it first. I made sure to record proof inside the control stone. I'll make each of them pay through the nose to get those pieces of their territory back. Even if I hadn't, I never particularly cared about being a baron. I simply enjoyed the peace and quiet it gave me out here."

"Fine, whatever. I'll talk to my parents about it later, after this is all over. Let's focus for now. It's going to be hard to locate them once we get inside."

Elinor stared at him and shook her head, pointing to herself. "Mother, remember? Once we get close enough, I can do a blood-to-blood calling spelling. It's old school, but it'll work to locate at least Penny. Hopefully, Jason is with her. If not, well, we have Jack's blood to work with as well."

"Fine, let's go. Stealth is key for as long as possible. Kaitlyn, I want you guarding Jack. Once we have them both rescued, I want you to supercharge yourself and blackout the facility, just like you did the town the other day. Understood?"

Each of them nodded at the instructions.

It was time to go rescue Jack and Elinor's family.

Chapter 23

Chapter 23

Jack ran behind Jon as they raced for the fencing around the busy warehouse. They only had a little over an hour's worth of night left before dawn would start to creep in over the horizon. They needed to get in and out fast if they wanted that blackout to do any good.

"We're *'running under cover'*," Elinor said from behind them, the words suddenly having an odd connotation it didn't the first time he had heard them say it in the driveway.

The air rippled around them as they neared the fence, obscuring them from view. The spell was meant for eyes, but it also had a small effect on weaker detection spells.

Jon formed his hand into a fist, and after taking a moment to gather his magic there, punched out. A blast of freezing cold air hit the metal links of the fence. Ice crystals formed on each of them as they froze together and began to creak.

He nudged them with a boot, shattering them all in an instant, and leaving them with a way inside the fence.

The group crunched over the frozen metal remains and ran towards the large warehouse that Elinor had indicated. That would be where she would need to take a minute to cast the blood-to-blood calling spell. As long as Penny was somewhere close by, they would be able to find her.

Shantell raised the same magnifying tube Jack had seen her use before and gave the front a quick twist. It narrowed the beam down to a laser-like focus, something that would be hopefully less noticeable in the urban environment.

"There aren't any wards or other perimeter spells around the area. I made sure of that when I first located them." Elinor told them all as they reached the side of the warehouse. "Shantell can cut our way in through the side, or we can use the door. It's up to you."

"Either works for me," Shantell said.

They looked at Jon, who took a moment to study the area. "We're in the dark here and without anyone around to see what we are doing. Let's make a small hole so we can see what's on the other side, and we'll go from there."

She brought her tool up to her hip and after everyone turned away, quickly cut an eyehole into the side.

Elinor spun around as soon as she finished and crouched in front of it. "It looks like we have about three or four feet of room between the wall and some crates. I can't see anything else."

"Do we risk it?" Jon asked.

"Hold on, let me cast the spell first and make sure they are inside this warehouse before we go any further." She took a moment to work through the old, complicated spell, her eyes closed in concentration. "I can feel her, toward the middle of the warehouse, and down a little. Not a lot though, there must be a basement. Penny is here for sure. Jack, give me some of your blood, please?"

He extended his hand to her and watched as his mother pricked his finger with one of her silver athames. She let the blood drip onto the blade for a moment before pulling it back and holding her hand over its surface. Elinor began the spell a second time.

"Jason is down there as well, but it doesn't look like they're together. His signature is pointing farther in." She said with relief, looking up at everyone. She pressed her eye to the hole for another look and then nodded. "This seems to be a good spot. We are in an out-of-the-way location out here, and if the same is true for in there, then even better. Shantell, if you please?"

The woman in question gave a sharp nod and pointed her magnifying tube at the wall a second time. She knew how to make a door.

A moment later, a section of the wall fell away, revealing the inside of the warehouse. They stepped through and hid behind the crates right on the other side.

"Remember, let's try and keep this as quiet as we can until we've rescued them both." Elinor reminded them all one last time now that they were inside. "And thank you all for being so willing to come and help, especially you, Shantell."

The other mother looked away, unwilling to say anything at the moment.

Jon peeked around the corner of the crate and motioned them forward. "They have cameras pointed at the stairs, and I imagine at each of the entrances as well. Making our own was the right call. Kaitlyn, once we get close, it'll be up to you to make sure they no longer work. I want something quiet, but powerful enough to ruin them if they happen to be shielded for sure protection."

She nodded nervously, her face pale. "Just point them out to me, and I'll do my best."

"I didn't see anyone patrolling this area. They might be all down by the loading docks with the trailers at the moment." He gave them each a moment to breathe. "Let's do this. The first camera I saw is about twenty feet above our heads and there may be more. Keep your eyes open and call them out if you see them. The only stairs I saw were going up. There was no sign of the ones going down."

With that said, he led them out from behind the crates and into the open.

Kaitlyn was right behind her father, a spark held at the ready for any camera that was spotted. The first one he had seen above the stairs was destroyed the moment she got close enough to accurately hit it.

Above them, they could hear the buzzing of the lights and the distant chatter of the workers as they loaded the trucks. Elinor didn't even want to think about what the group behind the monsters they had been seeing was shipping out. If they had enough time later, she would need to find out as they left.

It was her responsibility as a baron.

A second camera began to smoke as Kaitlyn zapped it into oblivion. She had been ignoring the ones above the doors for the moment since they were nowhere near them.

"I don't see any stairs going down," Jack muttered as they drew ever closer to the voices by the loading area.

"They must be here somewhere!" His mother hissed in return, the stress of the situation beginning to get to her. Trying to do all of this quietly was worse on the nerves than just waltzing in and attacking the place. Unfortunately, that option wasn't available, not if she wanted her husband and daughter to remain safe.

"There!" Shantell pointed to a barely visible railing behind some crates by the wall. From their current angle, the metal looked as though it simply plunged into the concrete flooring. "That railing doesn't extend up towards the ceiling at all. It must be going down instead."

It was also uncomfortably close to the offices where they could hear everyone talking at the moment. If there was ever a time they were going to get noticed, this was it.

"Everyone get close together. I'll put us back under cover while we make for the stairs. Kaitlyn, if you would please handle any cameras we come across the spell wasn't designed to handle electronic watchers."

The air around them rippled as it obscured them from view. They were safe for the moment.

Keeping close together they hurried for the stairs, maintaining a solemn silence as they ran. A thin bolt of electricity ran from Kaitlyn's finger to a camera above the now visible stairs leading down to the basement.

A loud curse came from the office nearby. "Another bloody camera just went out! It's the one just outside too, take a look at it and see what's going on, would you?"

They all stilled feet from the stairs and held their breath as a warehouse security guard appeared. The man looked up at the smoking camera for a brief moment, before shaking his head.

"Stupid old building. Sure, the new owners will pump money into the place with fancy equipment, but they won't even upgrade the wiring." He went back inside the office and closed the door. "It's just a power surge knocking them out, they'll need to be replaced. Those weirdos down below are probably playing with some expensive toy down in the basement that draws a ton of power or something."

Elinor cracked her knuckles and took a step towards the stairs. If she could take a shot at the people who had been messing with her territory and had dared to take her family while she was here, then all the better. There were some things you just didn't do.

Messing with banes was one, toying with her domain was another, and lastly, you never messed with her family. Not if you wanted to live a long happy life anyway.

"Come on, it seems we have a party to crash downstairs." She growled.

The metal stairs thunked with every step they took, announcing their presence to anyone listening below. It didn't matter how carefully you stepped on the things, they refused to be quiet.

Elinor kept up the cover spell until they reached the bottom and entered an entirely different sort of basement than they had been expecting. The first room was more modern and evil lair-looking than basement of a warehouse.

And if what the guard upstairs had said was true, the entire place was extremely vulnerable to Kaitlyn and her brand of magic. She promptly overloaded the keypad on the door and let them into the area hidden beneath several feet of concrete.

"Why would someone build something like this below a functioning warehouse?" Jack asked, more than a little intimidated by the gleaming white walls of the hallway they had found themselves in.

"That is a very good question." His mother muttered as they walked past a window that showed a room with expensive lab equipment inside. "It looks like they set up a research lab under the place. I mean sure having the warehouse right there has some certain advantages. But I can't imagine they outnumber the many, many disadvantages that such a setup brings with it."

"What about magic or runes?" Jack suggested as they continued on down the empty hall.

"Spells would be a terrible choice for a long-term solution. Runes would be much better, however, that would mean they have someone with the knowledge to use them backing them." Shantell answered as his mother directed them towards where she felt her daughter.

"It's more likely they just put up with the occasional problem. Actually, that might even be why they are loading the trucks now instead of during the day when it could disrupt their work." Elinor continued distractedly, feeling that they were getting closer to Penny.

"Why haven't we seen anyone down here yet? No guards, scientists, or random bad people? I haven't even seen an obvious security camera." Jack pointed out when they stopped in front of a solid metal door.

"Well, hopefully, we've been quiet enough that no one even knows we are here yet. That said, it's more likely we just haven't seen their hidden cameras." His mother said pessimistically as she swung the metal door open.

The area behind the metal door changed from the sterile environment of the lab to something more in line with what they had been expecting. The concrete walls were unpainted, and the bright LED lights had been replaced with old-school hanging bulbs. Each one swung softly in a forgotten breeze as they cast the area in a yellowish hue that made everything look sickly.

Small empty rooms with cots made up the bulk of the hall, except for at the very end, which is where they found a softly crying Penny. There was a single open-barred cell, and she had been thrown inside it, still wearing her pajamas.

"Penelope, sweetie, are you alright?" Elinor asked her daughter as Shantell went to work on the lock.

Penny stayed away from the bright laser burning through part of the door and ran up to her mother and brother. "How did you find us?" She hugged them both desperately through the bars, her body trembling with a mixture of fright and exhaustion.

"Magic," She waggled her fingers at her daughter as Shantell finished and the door popped open. "Now come on, we need to get your dad as well before everyone comes back from wherever they are."

Penny scurried on out of the cell, as though she was afraid it would suddenly lock with her inside again. She sniffed and wiped away her tears, reaching for her brother's hand.

"Jack, I need another few more drops of blood so we can locate your father."

He extended his free hand to his mother and let her prick it with the silver blade again.

Elinor took a moment to perform the spell. "This says he's on the move now. His location is completely different from before."

"Could they be moving him?" Jon wondered in his rumbling voice.

"Maybe, but why? Were they questioning him this entire time, or do they know we're here? Do you know anything about where they took him, Penny?"

Her daughter shook her head. "I never even got to see dad. I knew he was in the van with me because I could hear his voice, but they covered my eyes as soon as they burst into my room."

"What the-" Elinor ground her teeth together in a desperate effort to stop herself from cursing in front of her daughter. She was too young to see her doing that. "What is going on with this place?"

"I'm not sure, but mom? We should probably hurry before something happens to dad, or we overstay our welcome and get discovered." The *if we haven't been already*, went unsaid.

They hurried back down the bleak hallway of rooms and burst out into the gleaming white of the lab area.

Elinor once more took the lead as she used the spell to track down her husband.

"How big is this warehouse?" Kaitlyn asked a minute later. "We must have already passed beyond the boundaries of what we saw above us."

"We have," Her father replied simply, his face set in a cold stony mask.

They had passed any number of off-shooting corridors and windowed rooms with expensive equipment during their short run. This was not a small operation or place, but a serious problem that Elinor had unknowingly allowed to fester in her domain for too long.

Finally, she took them down one last junction, slowing as they heard the sound of fists hitting flesh beyond. There was a pained grunt followed by another fleshy smack and then the sound of a body hitting the floor.

Shantell looked at Elinor before raising her tube of magnifying lenses. Depending on who walked out that door, they would be ready.

There was some muffled cursing followed by a couple of grunts and a dawning look of understanding on Elinor's face. She motioned for Shantell to hold on and went to open the door. Inside that room was her husband, only he was silly enough to use some of those made-up words when he was angry.

She quietly inched the door open, revealing her husband in all his mostly naked glory, along with the equally naked man on the ground. "Having fun, are we?"

Jason dropped the pants he had just stolen from the man and spun around. "Don't do that!" He hissed when he saw it was his wife. "You nearly gave me a heart attack. I wasn't sure when you'd arrive, or if you even would. You mentioned some of the domain spells weren't working right anymore."

He collapsed onto the floor, in an exhausted puddle slowly working to finish pulling on the stolen pants. "Have you found Penny yet?"

"We got her first." She waited until he was semi-decent and threw the door open for everyone else to see him. "How did you escape?"

Jason looked at the hallway they were standing in, and the unconscious body he was stealing clothes from. "I was still working on the escaping part when you all arrived." He gingerly touched at the red marks all over his bare upper body. "However, it seems that the people who took us were more interested in answers than anything else. After they took us from the house, they brought me down here and began to question me."

"Why didn't they just use magic?" Shantell wondered, silently holding out a hand offering to heal him.

"Mental magics don't work on him," Elinor replied with a nod. "Even the Grand Spell has limited effect on him." She finished proudly.

Jon took in the smaller, lean man in approval. This was proof that not all normal people were worthless. Especially if he had built up some sort of immunity to the Grand Spell itself.

Penny waited until her father had been healed before releasing Jack's hand and giving the man a hug.

"That still doesn't explain how you got away?" Jack wanted him to finish the story.

"Sure, it does. Ever since I met your mother, I knew something like this would happen eventually, so I've been training. It's why I took you, kids, to the gun range and made sure you knew how to handle one. We may have been hiding the existence of magic from you but we both knew that couldn't last forever."

He patted Penelope's increasingly red hair. "I just had to wait for them to lower their guard and then attacked. No one expects their magic to not work against an ordinary person like me after all."

Jon nodded in agreement. It was true, no one would have been expecting their magic to fail against someone ordinary.

"Can we leave now?" Jack asked, anxious to leave this place behind.

Jason pushed his daughter back to Jack, and pulled on the rest of the ill-fitting clothes, including some slightly too-large boots. "I'm ready, let's go."

"Does anyone remember how to get back?" Elinor asked a moment later, as they stood at the first of many confusing corridor junctions.

"Um, mom?" Penny asked in a small, scared voice. She raised her hand so they could see the small flame that had engulfed the tip of one of her fingers. It wasn't painful for her, but it certainly was scary. Like her mother, she was also extremely well suited for the fire element and her own flames would never hurt her.

"Have you been holding onto Jack this entire time?" Shantell was looking at the girl's fire engine red hair, making the answer obvious.

As they watched, the flame slowly crept down her finger concealing more of it behind the dancing heat show.

Jason, however, seemed only mildly concerned. He had seen his wife do similar things in the past.

The one who was actually taking it the worst was Jack simply because this was the first time, he had seen it.

His sister smiled up at him. "Don't worry, it doesn't hurt." The fire had grown to engulf her entire hand in the few moments since she notified everyone of its presence.

Chapter 24

Chapter 24

Elinor reached out and separated her daughter from her son. "Okay, and this is a perfect example of why I didn't want the two of you touching or getting too close at home. Kaitlyn shoots electricity and fries the town, whereas Penny could burn down our house."

Jon and Shantell kept a nervous eye out as the mother began quietly talking to her daughter.

"Sweetie, do you remember what I've been teaching you about control, and the breathing exercises? All of that?"

Penny nodded.

"Good, I want you to forget all of that for the moment."

Shantell spun around, while Jon quirked a curious brow.

"I want you to instead run along behind us with your father, dragging your hand along the wall for as long as the flame lasts. Understood?"

"Alright, mom. But won't that set this place on fire?"

"Yes, dear, it most certainly will. That's what they get for daring to kidnap you and your father. But, um, don't do something like this again without me or your father's permission." She finished lamely, after seeing her husband's expression.

Jason grabbed hold of Penelope's non-flaming hand and pulled her to the back of their little group.

"Is that something you used to be able to do as well when you were younger?" Jack asked his mother as they picked a direction and began moving again.

"Not just when I was younger. I still can. Ice might be my dominant element now, but my fire is as strong as ever." She cursed suddenly as they all heard some new voices. "We have incoming."

"I'm telling you; I can feel something giving off powerful magic this way." A distant voice could be heard saying from up ahead and around a corner.

Everyone looked first at Penelope and the small flame in her hand to Jack and nodded. In their haste to rescue Jason and Penny, they had forgotten that the untrained generator in their midst had no control over himself. He was constantly putting out energy and acting like a beacon.

It was no wonder someone had noticed their presence. It was a miracle that it hadn't happened sooner. Wherever everyone who was normally down here had gone, they must just now be returning.

Which meant they would need to deal with them, and the growing fire at their backs. It had seemed like a good idea at the time, but now it could be what ended up killing them if they weren't careful.

Not that Elinor was all that worried about that happening. Between her, Jon, and Shantell, they should have more than enough power and ability to get everyone out. However, on the off chance, they did run into something truly troubling, then they also had Kaitlyn and Jack they could use. It wasn't ideal, but the two could bring some truly destructive power to bear if they were serious.

But she was getting ahead of herself. Right now, they only had a couple of scrubs to deal with first. Maybe they would even be nice enough to tell them where the exit was while they were at it.

Jon and Elinor hopped forward, ready to disable anyone that came into view. Closer to everyone else, Shantell held up her magnifying tube at the ready for anyone they missed or were unable to contain in time.

"Huh, you might be on to something. I'm starting to feel something now too! Are you sure it's a spell?" A second voice asked just as three distracted people walked around the corner.

A controlled burst of ice magic from both mages closest to them was chopped down at the back of their necks. Jon's victim crumbled to the floor in death while Elinor's merely had his spinal cord frozen. The third person had a clean little hole burned above his left eye, courtesy of Shantell.

They had needed one alive for directions, while the rest were destined to die. As the Baron of this territory, Elinor had the undisputed right to pass judgment on any and all magic users therein. As long as they were of a lower status, of course.

Even though the council had been ignoring their duties to her, that didn't mean she was going to ignore her own when they were right in front of her. Not anymore, at least.

She slapped the one still alive, shocking his mind back into action. "I'm going to ask a couple of questions and you are going to answer them. Do you understand?"

His eyes took in his dead companions, and he quickly nodded.

"Good. Now, what are you all trying to create down here?"

"I-I don't know. I'm not one of the scientists, I'm just a t-tech. All I know is they're do-doing s-something with the m-monsters they've brought in. Ni-nightwalkers of every kind have been brought in over the last few months." He was stuttering constantly as he tried to get the words out.

"And how did they come to this agreement with the local baron?"

"There is no local ba-baron here. There hasn't been for years. The others on the sides have been famously fighting over the territory for a while now."

Elinor glanced at Jon and Shantell in confirmation, who only shrugged. "We have no idea. We knew this place was quiet and saw very little action. However, we saw no references to the baron when we were investigating it."

She turned back to the scared man on the ground. Her mind was spinning through possibilities she wasn't liking. "How do we get out of here?"

They had spent too much time down beneath the warehouse already. It was past time for them to make their escape and end this farce. Plus, it sounded like she was going to have more than the expected trouble when the other barons notified the council. She was going to have to call for a truth spell to be used as judgment if they tried going too far.

He stuttered out some instructions and they went on their way, leaving the paralyzed man in their wake. He wouldn't survive long regardless, not with the fire Penelope had started.

Elinor stopped abruptly to look at her daughter and the man behind them. That was right, if they left the man alive, then his death would be on her. She couldn't let her daughter deal with that, not yet. Undoubtedly, that day would come, but she could put it off for now and she would.

She ran back to the man and knelt beside him. "Sorry, but I can't have your blood on my daughter's hands." She whispered moments before freezing his heart. There was a time to use structured spells and a time for instinctive magic.

Fighting was always easier with instinctive magic.

Jack nodded at his mother as she rejoined them and took up the lead once more. He had a good idea of why she had just done that and thought that it was a good choice. It was obvious that things were different now than they had been before. Mentally, that was obvious. Emotionally, he thought he was handling it well.

However, he hadn't had to kill anything yet, nor was he as young as his sister. Their backgrounds hadn't prepared them for any of this. Something that he wasn't sure he should thank his mother for or curse her for doing. It was such a double-edged sword; they had gotten to enjoy a few normal years. Yet it had come at the cost of preparing them for what was out there.

It was a conundrum.

The fire alarm started ringing a corridor later. The magical fire burned hot and put out very little smoke. It had taken time for it to finally reach the tipping point and set off its hidden sensors.

Penny started dragging her finger along the wall again, extinguishing the remaining flame she had built up in the process.

They raced through the corridors, following the directions the man had given them. At last, they reached an area they recognized from earlier, and ran even faster to the room they knew would lead them up.

The room was packed with *nightwalkers* of every kind, with a few magic users at the back for good measure. There were more types of beings than Jack had been expecting, that was for sure. The long-limbed creepy SOBs with elongated fangs clinging to the walls and ceiling were easily identifiable as vampires.

The shifters were harder to make out because of their sheer variety. However, he did spot the acid drooler who seemed to be stalking them.

Other than them were the walking statues that he was guessing were gargoyles. There was even a fellow with black eyes at the back that looked like he was possessed. And those were only the ones he recognized. There were several more that he didn't.

Jack discreetly took a few quick photos with his phone and sent them to the cloud before turning it off and pulling out the battery. He wasn't sure if that would be enough to protect it from Kaitlyn, but he could hope. Either way, the photos could only help his mother's case when the council showed up later. If he was wrong, then they would simply delete the photos and pretend they never existed.

Elinor pushed Jon to the side and stepped to the fore, ensuring everyone's attention was on her. "I'm sure someone among you lot can speak. So, tell me what this is about."

The shifter with the caustic drool problem spoke up, spitting with each word. "The food speaks. All of you are such delicious meals. Except for the normal one, and the snack." His eyes trailed to Jack. "But there is one among you better than the others."

Everyone on both sides backed away from him with a hiss as they were splashed.

"Yes, we all know you idiots think with your stomach and nothing more. That doesn't explain your actions tonight, or in trying to revive the Banes!"

The nightwalkers all grinned at the name.

"You were getting in on our way. It was just business." A magic user at the back answered.

"Well, you took up residence in my domain without permission. I think it was justified." Elinor returned without hesitation, not impressed by their numbers in the slightest.

She had been through far worse than a few untrained nightwalkers and barely competent magic users. This group wouldn't even be enough to slow her down if she got serious.

"Penelope, I want you to close your eyes. Can you do that for me?" Jason asked his daughter, turning her head around to face him. She didn't need to see whatever happened next.

Penny nodded quickly and buried her face in his stomach.

The group of nightwalkers in the room took a step back from her. "There is no baron for this territory. The last one caused a purge and was booted from the position." The speaker was a woman standing with the other shifters. She had a forked tongue and slit-like eyes.

Shantell smirked. "The council would never remove a baron from their position for such a silly reason. The entire point of having them is to adjudicate and manage their lands. They are the judges of everything that happens inside their domains. The ultimate voice. She was well within her right to kick you all out and then take more extreme measures when you refused to leave."

There were a few muttered and scattered cursing's among the group. "Then why haven't we heard anything from her again before now?"

"Simple, I was busy raising my family, and as long as you stayed out of my way and didn't cause any trouble, I didn't care." Elinor half-lied, unwilling to tell them the truth. "However, you then went and started to cause trouble again. Then to make matters worse, you started hunting my son and his girlfriend." The temperature in the room plunged as a layer of ice instantly formed on the floor.

"And now, as if that wasn't bad enough, you decided it was smart to go and kidnap my husband and daughter. Apparently, I have been too lenient with all of you for the last few years. The only answer is to go about and do another purge. First, though, I want to know about the BANES!"

A chilling mist engulfed everyone as she shouted. When it dissipated a moment later, three of the shifters had been turned into ice statues. She may have only frozen three of them solid, but her ice had immobilized each of them. It had climbed up to above their knees and frozen them in place.

None of them except possibly the strongest among the group were going anywhere. It was an incredible display of power, to Jack at least, and even Kaitlyn seemed shaken by it. It had been quick and brutal in its efficiency.

Elinor looked past each of the nightwalkers to the shivering magic users at the back. "I asked you a question. Who is trying to bring back the banes, and why?" Her voice was almost deathly quiet in the sudden chill.

"We don't know his actual name, just that he likes to be called Oberon. Some joke about being king of the forgotten fairies."

Elinor stilled, the temperature dropping impossibly lower. Jack stepped back, along with Kaitlyn and the rest of their group. His mother was controlling her element almost inhumanly well, with little of the cold being felt by those behind her. That is until the sudden drop just then.

The ice could be seen creeping up the bodies of the various nightwalkers as they desperately hacked at it. The cold slowed their movements as their bodies began to shut down.

"What did you say he likes to be called?"

"Obe-Oberon?" A different magic user at the back stuttered out.

"That's what I thought you said," Elinor growled through clenched teeth. She took in a deep breath and let it out slowly. "Now, what about the second part of my question? Why is he trying to bring back the banes?"

"We don't know. All we've been told is that this isn't the only site doing research into the subject for him."

"Shut up weakling," The monster that had been hunting Jack and Kaitlyn hissed. Its acid spit dribbled from its mouth and froze before it could even hit the ground.

"I wouldn't talk if I was you. You might bite your disgusting tongue." She stepped closer and touched a piece of its singed fur. "It's too bad they didn't manage to finish you off that night with the fire. It's a mistake I won't make."

A ring of ice extended out from where she had touched its fur. Within moments, it had become another ice-encased beast, unable to react as she ended its life.

"One final question, well, two." Elinor stepped around the half-frozen nightwalkers and approached the magic users. She stopped briefly by the possessed fellow before deciding to ignore him. Demons had their own agendas, and it was best to not mix with them. "When was the last time you saw Oberon, and where can I find him?"

"Nev-never, I've never m-met him," The cold was really getting to the one who had been speaking. "He do-doesn't come out here. Something ab-about an old acquaintance in the a-area."

She growled. "So, the rat bastard did know I lived out here, and he still let them set up a facility! What is he playing at?"

The gargoyles, beings of living stone, turned to face her as she retreated to the far side of the room. "Please, do not shatter us. There are so few of us remaining." It pleaded. They could survive the cold and the heat from the coming fire. But they couldn't be put back together again.

"You should have thought of that before getting into bed with someone like Oberon then!" She hissed back.

Shantell nodded. "Typical for a gargoyle, always wanting to participate, but never wanting to pay the price." Her eyes flicked to the possessed man at the back, obviously including him in her statement as well.

"Come on, everyone, I think it's time for us to leave." Elinor wasn't going to do anything more in view of Penelope.

Jack was mature enough to understand the actions she took. Her daughter, on the other hand, would already be having nightmares from everything that had happened. The last thing she wanted was for Penelope to be afraid of her. It was better for her to never see what she was about to do.

Elinor waited for them to pass before pausing beside the possessed man. "Last I checked, I had a deal in place with Amaymon, to keep your kind out of my territory. When you get back to hell, tell him I want to speak with him, and if you don't, I'll reach out to him on my own soon. Is that understood?"

The possessed man slowly nodded. "Yes, mistress of ice and fire."

"So, you've heard of me. That makes me wonder why you would come here then?"

"My prince was... concerned."

Her eyes sharpened, and she gave a quick nod. "I'll be looking forward to that conversation then. It's been a while since he and I have talked. It'll be good to catch up again."

Abruptly, the possession ended, and the man slumped over, dead. Anything that had a prince from hell worried was more than qualified to do the same to her.

She flash froze the rest of the inhabitants inside the room and climbed the steps after everyone.

The main floor of the warehouse was quiet. The trucks had all left and the security personnel had been put to sleep by the magic users before they went down a few minutes earlier.

Jack raised a brow at his mother as she joined them.

"We're good. Can someone please grab all the shipping manifest from the office, along with anything else that looks useful? As soon as that's done, Kaitlyn, I want you and Jack to light this place up. Fry all the electronics in the area. I want that fire below to go undisturbed so it can consume as much as possible."

Jon jogged into the office with his wife and began grabbing everything they thought looked interesting. Their arms quickly filled, and they were forced to snag a couple of bags from the guards to use instead.

Chapter 25

Chapter 25

"How much time do we have before more nightwalkers begin to show up?" Jason asked, pulling the gun belt from a sleeping guard.

"With any luck we won't need that, but it's close enough to daylight that more should be showing up any second. The area below was huge, with enough space for far more than the group we just met to live down there."

"What are we going to do with the guards?" Jack asked, rolling over the sleeping man after his father had finished taking his belt.

Elinor bit the inside of her cheek and sighed. "Do we know how many of them were even working tonight?"

Jack and Kaitlyn shrugged.

"Fine, we'll just gather up the ones we see and dump them out the warehouse doors. That will keep them safe when the fire spreads. They're not magic users or anything of the sort, they're simply normal people working a job. No reason to kill them for it."

Jack grabbed the man's arms and dragged him over to the large doors at the dock nearby. A moment later, his father grabbed the other sleeping guard and followed suit.

Jon and Shantell came out of the office with bulging backpacks. "There's one more guard in there as well." They were both dragging a sleeping guard behind them.

"So, we have five guards so far. Is that about right for an active warehouse this size, or should there be more?" Elinor wondered as they stacked the sleeping bodies next to the door.

"Honestly, it's probably about right. Normally I would say it's too many even, but with what was going on here..." Jason shrugged and opened the door, taking a peek outside. "I don't see anyone, but dawn is coming quick. We need to hurry!"

"Jon, if you wouldn't mind helping him? Shantell, please take Penelope and the bags to the cars. We don't want anything sensitive to get damaged by what Kaitlyn in about to do."

Jack handed his phone to his sister and nudged her towards the other woman. "Go on, we'll be right behind you."

Shantell took a firm hold of the younger girl's hand. "Be careful and hurry up."

"Okay, I'm going to go start some fires and then meet you back here in just a minute. Jack, start charging Kaitlyn up. I want something similar to what you did at our house the other day, but keep it inside the building this time. Understood? I don't want it spreading to all of Denver."

They nodded.

"Good." She ran off without another word.

Jack breathed out, some of the tension escaping from his body. "I can't believe we did it. We actually found and rescued them. It wasn't even that hard."

Kaitlyn chuckled and took hold of his hand. "Jack, your mother is terrifying. Using elemental magic to fight instead of spells is common. They're faster and they pack a decent punch. What your mother showed us down there goes far beyond ordinary. She froze that entire room in an instant! I think my dad could have only managed to do the same to one or two people max, and I've always thought he was strong."

They could see flickers of flame as they climbed ever higher from wherever his mother was at the time.

"I'm glad. She's going to need to be strong if things get as bad as she thinks they will. There is no way I'm going to be much help to her outside of as a power battery."

The young woman beside him gasped. "Yeah, and you do that very well." Her eyes had begun to glow with a deep blue light, and errant sparks were falling from her fingers. "I'll be ready to launch something as soon as your mother returns."

Elinor returned a minute later, dragging a sleeping guard behind her. "I found this one taking a nap behind the crates." She grunted and dropped his arm at Jack's feet. "Can you take him the rest of the way out? I'll show Kaitlyn where to aim for maximum penetration down below, and then we'll be right out."

"Sure, just be quick. The fire you started is spreading fast." He grabbed the sleeping man by the boots and began dragging him across the floor.

Outside, the night sky had begun to show the first signs of lightening with the oncoming dawn. He dumped the man with the rest of the guards and walked over to the others.

"Mom's just showing her where to put her lightning orb to wipe out everything here, and then they'll be out." He said before they could ask.

Jon looked at the warehouse and then to Shantell with a shake of his head. "Your parents have no idea what they unleashed. She is even scarier and stronger now than she used to be."

His wife nodded. "I know, and she wasn't even at full power tonight."

"Elinor always knew something might happen with the kids being discovered. She never stopped learning and pushing herself. Even when she didn't have enough power to cast the spells, she still made sure to learn them and rework them." Jason sighed bitterly. "I thought a part of her just still wanted revenge more than to be prepared in case something happened. It turns out she was preparing to fight a one person war for our kids."

Penny hugged her father. "Mommy had her reasons, daddy."

"I know, sweetie, but it still hurts." He kissed the top of her head and ran his hand through her hair.

"Should we get under cover or something in case more nightwalkers show up?" Jack asked, changing the subject as he glanced around nervously.

"We need to wait until Elinor and Kaitlyn come back, otherwise the spell will keep them from finding us as well." Jon told him, keeping his eyes on the warehouse doors.

Jack nodded, not willing to admit that he hadn't been talking about the spell.

A charge went through the air as all the lights abruptly died. A transformer nearby blew and began to spark as it overloaded. Kaitlyn had done it. She had managed to contain it enough that only a couple of blocks lost power instead of an entire portion of Denver.

The last two of their group ran out of the warehouse a moment later.

"Well, that should have fried anything electronic down below, as well as anything that might have seen us. I suggest we leave now, before anything arrives and finds us here. Jon, Shantell, Kaitlyn, thanks for your help with this. I... we won't forget this. As the local baron, I officially welcome you to the neighborhood.

"Let's all go home for some rest, and then why don't you all come over for dinner again tonight? I think we have some more things that we need to discuss. Specifically, items related to our past that the kids might as well be told about now."

"I think that sounds like a very good idea. It's long past time for the two of you to talk everything out properly." Jon agreed. He cracked his neck and handed the two backpacks with the all the papers and other information over to Jack. "In the meantime, I think we'll head home and crash for a few hours. I'm tired."

Elinor and Shantell looked at each other and nodded.

"Thanks for coming when we needed you," Jack said to Kaitlyn as they reached the cars and separated.

"I'm just glad we could help this time, though honestly, it seems like your mom could have handled most of it on her own." She waved and climbed into the rear seat of the car.

Jason stopped his wife short of the car. "How are we going to do this? Can Penny handle being in such a close proximity to Jack for the entire drive home?"

Elinor fisted her hands in frustration and stomped over to the LaCouture car. "Do you mind dropping Jack off at our house first? I didn't think of what might happen with him and Penny in such a small car until Jason mentioned it just now."

"Yeah, absolutely." Jon replied without hesitation.

Jack handed his mother her gun and got in the backseat of the car beside Kaitlyn. "Thanks for doing this, all of it."

"It's fine. I'm glad we were here actually. Maybe all of us also hearing what they had to say about Oberon will help your mother's case." Shantell said from the driver's seat. Jon was concentrating on the camouflage spell that would keep them undetected.

"Is this Oberon fellow really that much of a problem?" Kaitlyn asked, leaning away from the window. "I've never heard him mentioned before now."

"You wouldn't have. He is the type of man they keep out of all but the deepest and darkest history books, for fear of another getting ideas from his actions. We all thought he was dead. That your mother had killed him. She even brought back his body, and several members of the council identified it as him."

"Wait! Let me get this straight. Your council sent a girl, my mother, who was probably still in college at the time, against this guy? Were they insane? Why would they do that?" Jack sputtered before remembering why. "Your parents sent her on a sure-death mission, didn't they? Why? You two might have been fighting by that point, but that seems a little extreme!"

"A lot. It was a lot extreme." Shantell whispered, the rumble of the car falling away as he strained to hear her. "And I don't know why they did it. Not for sure anyway. My problems with your mother were born out of jealousy, envy, and even a small amount of inferiority. Certainly, nothing that would have caused them to do what they did."

"You never asked?"

"Of course, I asked!" She snapped. "But I could never get a straight answer from them. It changed each time. Eventually, I gave up and just stopped asking. I had already cut them out of my life by then, and I long since lost touch with your mother, so it no longer mattered as much. I tried not to even see them when they would come and visit Kaitlyn."

"I still don't understand how the rest of the council could go along with something like this. I mean, they obviously gave her the barony when she succeeded, but even then, it doesn't sound like they have exactly treated her well since."

"That was because of my parents," Jon spoke up, his expression clearing as he let the spell drop with a sigh of relief. "They knew I was friends with your mother and wanted to help her out when she succeeded.

Unfortunately, that was as far as their influence managed to go. Shantell's family has been on the council almost since its inception, whereas mine is somewhat more recent."

"So what, they simply pushed the issue through, forcing everyone to accept an untrained young woman for the mission?"

"Pretty much, yeah."

"That's messed up." Jack scratched his head, feeling the salty sweat crystals flake away. "And now, after everything she went through back then, somehow, this Oberon is back from the dead. I'm sure your council is going to love that."

"Exactly, which is why it's a good thing we were there tonight to hear them say that. I'm afraid what your mother did with the territory boundaries, combined with this, is going to be the start of an epic storm." Shantell took the offramp, while barely slowing.

"It doesn't sound like it's one that could have been avoided for very long, in any case. This was just one of that guy's sites. Whatever he's planning is big. If mom hadn't found out about it, surely someone else would have."

"I'm not completely convinced all of this has been an accident, Jack. Some of it, sure, but I find it suspicious that Oberon decided to even put an operation in your mother's domain at all. I think he wanted her to be the one who discovered him." Jon rumbled from the front passenger seat. "I couldn't say what his end goal is or anything, but I think there is a larger plan of his at play here."

"My life has turned into a movie." Jack groaned, slumping down into the backseat. "The bad guy has just deliberately revealed himself to his hated nemesis so she can begin preparing for their next battle."

Kaitlyn giggled at his dramatization.

Shantell laughed as she slowed at a stoplight. "It's as good of an explanation when it comes to him as any, I'm afraid."

From there, the conversation turned to decidedly less weighty topics for the remainder of the short drive. With dawn nearing, they had to slow down but were already fairly close to home.

"I can't believe it's still only Sunday," Jack complained, as they pulled up to his house with the missing front door.

"Yeah, it's been a busy week for sure," Kaitlyn replied, thinking back to how just a week earlier she had almost killed the boy next to her.

"Busy, that's one word for it. Anyway, thanks for the ride home. I'll see you all at dinner later tonight." He hopped out and waved goodbye as they drove off.

The inside of the house was a mess of broken glass and pieces of wood from the destroyed door strewn about. Despite feeling the lack of sleep pulling at his mind, Jack set about with the broom, sweeping up as much of the mess as he could in the next few minutes.

By the time the rest of the family drove up, he had managed to clear a serviceable path for Penny's bare feet.

"Thanks, Jack." His mother said tiredly as they walked in. "Go get some sleep. I'm going to need your help later fixing more of the issues with the domain. So much needs to be done before the council gets word of this, and before Oberon makes any more moves."

"Are you going to call or get in touch with the council about Oberon and the banes?" Jack asked as his father help steer a sleepy Penelope to her room.

"I haven't decided yet. By any reasonable rights I should, but with the domain in its current state and my history with the man... Not to mention you and your sister and my overall current hatred of the council, I can't make up my mind."

Jack set the broom and dustpan to the side and gave his mother a hug. "Well, whatever you decide, we'll be right here with you. Give me some time to sleep and then I'll be able to give you all the magical go-go juice you need to get this place back up and running properly."

Elinor rolled her eyes. "Even if you could give me enough, I don't think I would be able to handle the stress of creating that many spells while funneling all that energy. It will take a few sessions at least to finish rebuilding everything. Maybe more if I do everything that I have in mind. That's a discussion for later though, off to bed with you."

He nodded and slipped into his room, feeling his feet beginning to drag. The last thing he managed to do before falling asleep was reassemble his phone and plug it into charge.

***

Jack sat up with a groan and reached for his phone to check the time. It was a little after two in the afternoon. That meant he had gotten around nine hours of sleep, maybe a little more. He couldn't remember the exact time they had gotten home.

Either way, his pounding head didn't like the fact he had been asleep during the day.

Stripping carefully down, he grabbed some clean clothes and wrapped himself in a towel before shuffling off to the shower. Every move he made sent a fresh wave of agony piercing through his head. All he could think about was getting underneath the cool water from the shower.

He felt only slightly more human when he emerged a few minutes later and headed for the kitchen, desperate for water. Not all headaches or migraines could be drowned out with good hydration, but it never hurt to try. Besides, that's where they kept all the medicine as well.

Not to mention the food. His stomach reminded him that it was hungry, while his head rebelled at the thought of eating anything.

A few pills and a gallon or two of water later had Jack curled up on the cool wood floor in the kitchen. It took several minutes, but he slowly began to feel more human.

Penny was staring at him from the hall doorway when he opened his eyes. "Are you feeling alright?" She asked.

"Just a headache. Besides, I should be asking you that. After everything that happened, you handled it like a champ."

She shook her head. "Mom said I was mostly in shock the entire time. Once we were alone and in the car, I broke down crying. I actually ended up sneaking into their bed after we got back. I would have gone into yours, but well..."

He nodded and took in the sight of her red hair. "It's a good thing you like it like that because I don't think it's ever going back to the way it was before at this rate."

"No, it probably won't. Even after I get control of my power, mom thinks the color will mostly stick around."

"Do you want to talk about what happened last night at all?" He asked after a moment's hesitation. "Any of it? The kidnapping, the rescue, what mom did, what dad did?"

Her lower lip trembled, and she had to blink rapidly to keep tears from falling. "I understand what mom and dad did. They did all of that for me. To keep me safe, I understand that. But what about what I did with my fire? Did I kill or hurt anyone?"

Jack sat up and scooted back against the lower cupboards beneath the counter. "Do you think you hurt or killed someone with what you did?"

"I... I don't know, but it's making me sick to my stomach just thinking about it right now." She whispered, clutching her waist.

"There are two answers I can give you," Jack began, trying to approach her question with the seriousness it deserved. "First off, no, I don't think you hurt or killed anyone. The place was nearly empty when we were looking for you and dad. Anyone that we did find they took care of. And two, they were bad people, Penny, you have to remember that. Who knows what else they have done in the past?"

"Okay, that's enough of that conversation for now. He's right, but that's still enough. We'll talk about it more later during training tomorrow." Their mother said, coming up behind Penelope. "Jack, let's go downstairs and get started. Penny, would you mind going with your father and helping him get a new front door and everything else that was broken, replaced?"

Chapter 26

Chapter 26

J ack followed his mother down to the domain control room in the basement. "Have you decided which spells you are going to focus on first?"

His mother nodded. "I need to finish locking down the domain seals first so nothing like what happened before occurs again. I never finished what I was doing earlier. Then I'll set up the boundary spells and begin constructing the tracking and other spells. I'll be using your energy to supercharge each of those, of course."

She unlocked and opened the door. "Those are just the basic items. There are several special spells that I've come across or tweaked over the years that I want to integrate as well. I have kept a list of them and their effects."

"No wonder you were saying this wasn't going to be done in one or two sessions."

"Yup, now let's get started." She approached the pedestal and the control stone sitting on top of it. "I'll also be putting protections down on our, and the LaCouture's houses. I won't let something like this happen again, not to us anyway."

Jack put his hand on her shoulder and closed his eyes. He waited until he could feel his mother pulling on his energy and then focused on streamlining the process.

All he could offer her was his energy, so he could at least do it as efficiently as possible. She had let all of this fall into ruin trying to protect him, and he had to admit it felt good knowing she cared that much. Jack had never doubted his parent's love for him, but the renewed knowledge was nice.

Elinor dug deep into the spells she had studied over the years. The ones she had tweaked to better fit her own purposes. She needed them now. Sure, she wasn't really supposed to use unsanctioned spells as part of her domain, but she was beyond caring. Normally, the council rarely checked the spells, anyway, as evidenced by the fact that they had never once checked hers before now. However, she couldn't count on that continuing.

All she could do is tie this domain to herself as tightly as possible, and the first step to doing that was finishing what she had started last night. She made a quick pass at the extended boundaries and strengthened them where needed.

The other barons had obviously discovered what she had done. She could tell where they had started to pick away at her spells. With that completed, she moved on to the anchor stones.

She had reinforced the spells on her anchor stones before. Now what she was doing was just a little more. It was like adding a key to the door, a key that only she held. Others could still brute force it open, but it would take longer.

Elinor had other plans for the anchor stones, but those would have to wait until later. They were not exactly quick, and even with Jack's help, they would be draining. But if they worked out like she thought and hoped they would, then it would be worth it.

It would depend on how the council reacted to everything. If they tried to force her hand, then she would be left with no choice. She might not care about being a baron, but having an area to control was too precious to pass up. This was the one place she could at least somewhat guarantee her family's safety.

She would not let them take that from her without a fight.

Moving on, she began the process of laying down the spells properly this time. She redid the locating and tracking spells next, fixing the little imperfections that had been introduced in her haste before. She had wanted to get that out of the way before she moved on to the next item on her list.

The boundary spells.

Those spells could let her do a lot, especially if she were to use some of the spells she had tweaked over the years. The problem was they typically required more power than a lot of the other spells. She hadn't used them before for that exact reason.

Now, however, Elinor thought she had solved, or at least decreased, the cost for a couple of them. They would undoubtedly need to be tweaked more, as she saw them in action, but it would be a good start. There was only so much theory work she could do. After a certain point, she simply needed to see them in action before making more changes.

She could use her own time to test those ones out later. For now, it was more important to set up a restriction spell. It was one of the most powerful spells all barons used, and the most draining. She had spent a lot of time working on it over the years, hoping to decrease how much magic it drew upon. It would halt the movement of magical ingredients and infected monsters from crossing over and leaving her domain.

There were one, well, kind sort of two final items she needed to do before being done for this round. She needed to lay down the protection spells on the houses. They needed protection, so something like this never happened again. Plus, it would be nice to not have to go to that restaurant every time they wanted to talk about something private.

She just hoped Shantell and Jon hadn't said anything they weren't supposed to while out in the open. She was past caring at this point, but it never hurt to be careful. The odds of someone scrying them at that exact moment were slim. But again, when it came to her kids, she wanted to be as careful as possible.

A few minutes later Elinor slowly withdrew from the control stone, feeling as though she was reaching her limits. The rest would have to wait until later.

"How long was that?" She rasped; her mouth dry.

Jack checked his watch as he stepped back and let his other arm drop to his side. It hurt after holding it up for so long. "About an hour and a half."

"Good, I got a lot done this time. How are you holding up?" His mother asked, locking the room behind them.

"My arm is sore, but outside of that, I think I'm fine. I've still got more in the tank." He wasn't joking either. After sleeping most of the day away, he had plenty of energy to give her.

"How much did I use?"

Jack scratched the bottom of his chin in thought as he climbed the stairs behind his mother. "Maybe, a little over half my total?"

She shook her head. "Kaitlyn is going to be an absolute monster when the two of you bond. Even with you doing what you can to help the process along, your control just isn't there yet. There is still a lot of energy being wasted. With her, after you bond, that waste will be gone."

His mother turned to face him. "If what we did earlier took half of the overall energy within your well, then doing the same thing with her would only require maybe a fifth of that energy. Possibly even less, I don't know and don't forget now that it's been unlocked. Your well will only continue to grow in size."

"I thought it stopped growing after puberty for people?"

"For regular magic users, yes, that is the case because they unlocked them when they are younger. For a generator though, from what I understand, the rules are a bit different..." She covered her eyes.

"Mom, just tell me." Jack could feel his headache coming back.

"A generator's well doesn't even start growing until it's unlocked. What you have now is the same size it was as a baby."

"How long will it grow for?" He asked with a swallow.

"It varies from between two and four years usually." She finished in a whisper.

"Oh, my-" Jack cut himself off with a curse. "I thought it was big now, but in a few years, it's going to be a veritable ocean."

"And now you know yet another reason why they don't like letting generator's bond. When you have potentially that much energy at stake, who cares about wastage? You could do what we did today a thousand times over and still have more left in the tank."

"Is my well bigger or smaller than most other generators?" Jack had a feeling of unease already bubbling up inside him.

"The books don't say for certain, but I did manage to find a reference in one that mentioned a generator awakening with a well slightly larger than normal. It was about three times the size of an experienced magic user. Yours is well beyond that. I can't say if that is normal though, or if it was mentioned because it was odd."

Jack thumped his head against the wall and winced as his headache flared. "Yeah, I was afraid you were going to say that."

"It's called a well for a reason, Jack, not the lake within, but the well within. You have a lake. I mean, when you think about it, Shantell, letting you go so easily makes a certain amount of sense now, right?" His mother laughed hollowly. "She didn't know about me yet. So, all she knew is that you were a walking gold mine. Attaching her daughter to you and keeping you happy would guarantee their future."

"Mom, that's revisionist history. I don't know about Shantell, but I doubt Kaitlyn or her dad would go along with that."

"You underestimate how much you're worth to people now." She sighed. "Regardless, I hope you're right. Now let's get dinner started before it's too late."

"What did you have in mind for dinner anyway?"

"Tikka Masala. I started marinating the chicken pieces earlier. It's a fairly easy recipe, and it makes a lot."

Jack swallowed hungrily. He had no idea where his mother had gotten her recipe from, but it was easily better than most of the restaurants they had been to. The only problem he could see was, his family liked spicy food. What about Kaitlyn's?

"Does Shantell like spicy food?"

Elinor shrugged with a slight smile. "It's not that spicy, and I guess we'll find out. Now go take another shower. Your head seems to be bothering you. The cold water will help it."

His mother was right. The cold water did help his head; it also froze the rest of him. Still, by the time he climbed out of the shower, he was feeling decidedly better.

Penelope and his dad had returned by then and were in the middle of installing the new front door.

"Do you need any help?" He asked them.

"No, we got this," Jason replied, putting one last screw into the hinge. "And there, all done." He grinned. "Installing it was easy. Picking it out was the hard part. This one is a heavier-duty model than our last one. The frame is still the weak point, but your mother's magic is protecting the house now, so..."

Penny nodded.

Their father stepped back. "Penny, why don't you go help your mother set the table for everyone? Jack can help me switch the doorknob and lock over. There are a couple of things I want to talk to him about."

"Alright," She hurried off, grabbing one of the bags at their feet as she did so.

"What's up, dad?" Jack grabbed a screwdriver and began unscrewing the lock on the destroyed door.

"Your mother and I were talking things over earlier, obviously you know I go out training every weekend now. We were wondering if you were interested in joining me? Unlike Kaitlyn or your sister, you aren't going to have magic at your disposal to defend you." He held up a hand. "At the very least, not right away, if at all. I know it's something you want, but it may not happen."

"Is it really that hard?" Jack asked softly.

"I don't know, and your mother has been impressed with the level of control you've already shown. But Jack, the amount of energy you have is going to actively hinder your efforts to learn anything. You might try to make a dribble of water and flood the entire town, or not even be able to do that. Look, it's a concern, but we're not going to force you one way or the other." Jason hugged his son and swiped the lock from him.

"I... let me think about it."

"Of course, now help me finish with these before our guests arrive."

A little while later, the phone in his pocket vibrated with an incoming text message from Kaitlyn. They were on their way over.

***

Shantell pushed back from the table and reached under her chair. She came back up with a thick book in her hands that had been hidden in a backpack.

"Are you sure you want to do this, Elinor? Jon and I explained a little bit of what happened to Jack and Kaitlyn in the car on the way home. But this is different. You're talking about telling them everything. Even the things we don't know."

"No, I'm not sure. However, if Oberon is back, then they need to know what is coming and what he's already done." Elinor filled her wine glass to the brim and cracked her neck. She had decided earlier that this dinner and discussion were going to need something stronger than lemonade and water.

Shantell sighed and gently placed the book onto the table, pushing her empty plate to the side. "Very well then, at least now they'll have visual aids for part of it."

The book was actually an album full of pictures of Shantell and Elinor when they were younger.

"I didn't realize you had kept those..." Elinor shook her head. "I wasn't going to start quite that far back, but I suppose I can." She took a hefty drink from her glass and motioned for Shantell to flip the book back to the beginning. "Shantell and I met when we were around four years old. It was at a test for our future potential."

She went through the same events she had mentioned to Jack and Kaitlyn in the car the night before. Only this time in more detail.

"Anyway, we remained close all through our younger years, and even into our teen years for a while. Then things began to change, we started to slowly drift apart. Shantell's parents wanted her to associate with people in their own stratum. Which my family was decidedly not. My parents were spell researchers, brilliant ones, but we didn't belong to any particular class in regards to money or power."

Shantell took a sip from her own glass of wine and took up the tale. "I was under a lot of pressure at the time from my parents to conform to what they considered proper behavior for our station. Unfortunately, that meant I couldn't remain friends with Elinor any longer." She stared at her glass and ran her finger along the rim.

"To make a long story short, I wasn't happy about it, but they were my parents. Their word was law, and they would have found out if I tried sneaking around behind their backs. All I could do in my mind at the time was to take my frustration out on her instead."

Elinor flipped the album to the back, stopping on a page that had the two of them standing with a much younger Jon.

"And that's how we continued up until we reached college, our relationship slowly getting worse." Jack's mother drained her glass with a sigh. "Then at college, out from underneath her parent's thumb, Shantell approached me. She wanted to fix our friendship, to become as close as we once were.

"I was skeptical at first, but I also wanted to believe her. She was my oldest friend, after all, no matter how much she had hurt me. I wanted her words to be true." A tear fell from her eye and after trailing down her cheek, hit the tablecloth.

"They were true." Shantell closed her eyes and swallowed. "I wanted nothing more at that time than to rekindle our friendship. But my parents apparently had other ideas still. It was around this time that they had you sent away."

Elinor laughed wetly. "Is that what they told you? That I was sent away? I was kidnapped from my dorm room in the middle of the night and given an ultimatum. One that was enforced by the might and power of the council. That's the reason they had to give me the barony when I succeeded, especially after Jon's parent's interceded on my behalf."

"Why you? Why did the council approve of them taking you?" Kaitlyn asked, trying to keep them on track. "I mean, we've all seen how powerful you are now, but you couldn't have been that strong back then as well. Right?"

"I was strong, but nowhere near what I am now." Elinor stood and retrieved another bottle of wine. "I didn't realize we were going to go through these so quickly."

No one else but her and Shantell were currently drinking.

"It wasn't just me that they took." She mumbled, staring at the bottle.

It was Jon's turn to nod and said. "They took over a dozen people for the mission. Each and every one of them was promised the same thing. Riches and power if they succeeded. Death if they didn't. None of them had a choice in the matter. It made my parents sick."

Jason took the bottle of wine from his wife and handed her a different one that they had opened earlier to breathe. He took the corkscrew and popped the top enough to let the bottle release the gas' inside. It was probably a waste to open the third bottle like this, but it was better to be prepared than not.

"So, what? They just took untrained civilians to fight Oberon? Instead of depending on the guards or border teams, or any of the other organizations that fight monsters for a living?" Kaitlyn was positively appalled by the actions the council had taken.

"They were still using them for all the attacks going on at the front, but we were meant to be used as another kind of force. I think they had plans to use us as some kind of infiltration unit."

"Against nightwalkers or Oberon?" Jack asked.

Elinor tapped the side of her nose. "And that right there was where everything went wrong. Well, really, everything went wrong far before that. But the first time the rest of them knew something had actually gone wrong was when they realized Oberon was surrounded by nightwalkers. The chances of us being able to sneak in on a group of literal monsters were absolutely zero."

She filled her glass to the brim and took a long swallow. No one dared to say anything. From here on out, this was her story. Elinor was already beyond what Jon knew, and far past what Shantell had been privy to.

"Now where was I?"

Chapter 27

Chapter 27

"You were talking about not being able to sneak in on Oberon," Jack replied softly.

"Right, so I was." Elinor's eye held an intoxicated glaze to them. "That was the mission, but unlike the idiots on the council, no offense, Jon, our group knew better. Unlike all of them, we hadn't forgotten who our enemy was. So, we came up with an alternate plan of sorts.

"It wasn't really any better than the one they had come up with, but we at least liked it more. We felt it had a higher chance of success, if not our survival. That was never a real option. We all understood that by then. The council had lied to everyone for one reason or another when they brought them there. This was nothing but a suicide mission from the start. One with little chance of ever succeeding."

"But you pulled it off," Penny whispered, standing to give her mother a hug.

"Thanks, sweetie, and yes, we pulled it off. By a minor miracle, and my parent's intervention with a forbidden spell. A few of us managed to get inside and find Oberon."

"You mentioned the spell before, the other night," Jack said. "What was it?"

Jon looked at his wife and daughter, and then at Elinor. "It's a power transference spell. Think of it as something similar to a permanent bloodline version of what you can do. Except with some added benefits and caveats. It enhances your elemental affinities, taking them from the donor's and grafting them onto the receiver. In this case, the donors were her parents, and the receiver was your mother."

Kaitlyn, who had already figured out which spell had been used early, just sat there quietly. For Jack and Penelope, however, the news was a bit of a shock.

"How can a spell like that exist? It would be so easy to abuse it." Jack shook his head. "No, forget about that for the moment. How did they manage to get the spell to work without her there? I would assume something like that requires the participants to be right in front of each other."

"It does, and we don't know," Elinor replied, gazing deeply into her glass of wine.

Jack winced; he had forgotten they were talking about her parents. "Sorry, mom."

"It's... fine. It happened a long time ago. Besides, you're right, the spell is easily abused. That's why it's forbidden. It can only be used among blood relatives, who aren't on their deathbed. There are also a few other restrictions, along with the receiver needing to be there." Elinor reached for her glass.

Jason stopped her and shook his head. He kissed her fingers before bringing her hand to his lap.

With a sigh, she continued. "My parents were brilliant spell researchers, and they must have come up with a way around the need to have me there. All I know is we had just gotten captured and were about to be turned into dinner when I felt it happen. The sudden shift in my affinities, the change in my overall power. It was exactly what we needed to escape, and I knew what it meant. I went a little insane at the time."

The table was quiet as Elinor collected herself. Remembered tears from her parent's sacrifice trickling freely down her cheeks.

"When I came to a while later, everything had been frozen. My remaining companions were gone. They had somehow managed to escape in time, but everything inside the base was dead. It took me a while, but I managed to find the ice sculpture that was Oberon and break him into a thousand pieces. I brought back his head and pendant as proof.

"Then I went to bury my parents before going back to school for a few days. No one but you knows what they did, and I never saw anyone from the team again."

Jason hugged his wife as she finished her emotional tale.

Jack let his mother mourn in peace for a minute before speaking up. "That means that the people on the council confirmed his identity and his death. Are there spells to bring people back from the dead or to let you escape death?"

"No, nothing that I've ever heard of anyway," Shantell said emphatically. "Not even the darkest spells they mentioned in college had that sort of ability. I've never even heard so much as a whisper of one anywhere else, either."

Jon nodded silently and glanced at Elinor. "It's obvious you've done more research into spells and their construction over the years than either of us. What do you think? Is it possible?"

Elinor sniffled and grabbed a napkin from the table, wiping at her red eyes and then her nose. "I'm hesitant to say it's impossible, but I've never come across a spell or anything that even mentioned it as a possibility. At the very least, the cost to perform such a spell would have been enormous."

"What are we thinking, then? A clone, doppelgänger, some kind of shapeshifter that has his memories... a son?" Kaitlyn rattled off a few options quickly.

"A son or daughter would be the most likely," Elinor replied slowly with a shiver. "Though I pity the poor woman who bore him a child. The problem with that particular solution, however, is we need to assume that either this new Oberon is on the council or he has someone who is."

Jon cursed and leaned back in his chair, his head flopping back with a groan. "She's right, that's the only way they could have learned who killed his, her, their? Ugh, whatever, father. Even Shantell and I had no idea what Elinor had done. She never said. If we as children of council members had no clue, then no one else would either."

"You did say that a lot of the old council was being pushed out for younger members." Jack pointed out.

"That they have and knowing what we know now. I would say the timing is even somewhat suspicious."

Shantell let out her own groan. "Great, now we're suspicious of two-thirds of the council. I was so excited when some of the old fossils were replaced, too."

A ringtone blaring an ominous death march suddenly startled everyone.

Elinor reached into her pocket with a slightly trembling hand. "Speak of the devil. The council is calling me." She held a finger up to her lips and then accepted the call. "Hello?"

Everyone in the room could hear some distant yelling from the tiny speaker.

Elinor, meanwhile, was distinctly unimpressed with them and was barely listening. "Yes, I did indeed take some territory from those whimpering fools." She rolled her eyes and pulled the phone away from her ear. "If you're not even going to ask why I did it, then this phone call is over." She ended the call and placed the phone on the table.

"Was that smart?" Jon asked.

She took a second to respond, her eyes never leaving the phone. "Probably not, but as a baron, I have a specific contact within the council who contacts me. All communication goes through her. She's a right git, and I hate her guts, but she has never missed an opportunity to remind me that she has power over me. That wasn't her on the other end just now. In fact, I haven't heard from her in a while. If she was replaced, I would have assumed she would have called to introduce her replacement."

"She never did." Shantell finished for her.

"No, she didn't. Regardless, the idiot on the other end didn't seem interested in what actually happened, only in assigning blame."

"Well, we all knew you taking that land from them would cause trouble."

"I'm a little tempted to grab even more just to really piss them off now." Elinor leaned against her husband.

"I think that would be a bad idea." Jason cautioned her. "The initial amount can be attributed to their stupidity, but not if you did it a second time."

She sighed. "I know. It would have been fun though." Her phone rang again with the same ominous ringtone as before. "Hello? Where's Judy?"

"Listen, you foul-mouthed little brat! I am a BARONESS the same as those idiots. It is your job to listen to both sides of the story before making any judgements. So, no, I will not be giving them the territory back, because you have not asked me why I did this in the first place! Secondly, Judy never introduced you as my handler on the council, which you should know means I am under no obligation to listen to you or do as you say." She hung up a second time.

"You don't have to listen to him because you weren't introduced?" Penny was confused.

"Only your specific council member is allowed to contact you in this fashion. It creates a chain of command. Without it literally, anyone on the council would be able to order me about. However, Judy never introduced her replacement, so I can't be sure he is legitimate." Elinor cackled happily. "It always pays to read the fine print for these sorts of things."

"What now then?" Jack asked.

"Now, I imagine they'll start investigating the real events and maybe even reach out to Jon and me," Shantell informed him. "What are you going to do about Oberon now? If Judy is gone, that means your main contact inside the council is as well."

Jason held his wife tight as she thought through their options. "What about Jon's parents? Can you talk to them? You said they were good people."

"I did..." She agreed slowly. "Jon?"

"I can certainly ask-" He cut off as he reached into his pocket and retrieved a vibrating cellphone. "I think they know something happened. It's my parents." He hit the answer button. "Mom, dad? You're on speaker."

"Jon, dear," The dulcet sweet tones of an older woman came through the phone's small speaker. "I'm here with your father and the rest of the council. You told me the other day that Elinor Rage had agreed to let you move into her domain. Is that correct?"

He waved away Elinor's raised brows. "Yes, that's correct. Why?"

Shantell leaned over to whisper. "We only told them after we got your actual permission."

"It seems that all of the barons surrounding her domain are accusing her of stealing land from their territories all at once." There was noise in the background as one of the council members spoke up.

"All of them?" Elinor shook her head and held up three fingers. Jon shrugged. "That must be very embarrassing for them. After all, she just demonstrated that none of them were able to sufficiently guard and protect their lands. And if she did it to them all at the same time, then they have either been slacking, or she is far more powerful than them. Either way, I think the question you should be asking is why she would go and do something like that."

"Oh, we intend to. However, would you mind going over and asking her yourself?"

"Mother, you know things between me, and Elinor are rocky right now, frankly I'm surprised she agreed to let us move here at all. Besides, I can't speak to her about council business, you know that. Just have the woman in charge of her call her. What was her name? Janith, or Jabba, or something. I swear it was 'J' something." Jon was clearly having fun with the conversation.

"We can't. She is no longer a member of the council, and she left without passing on her responsibilities."

"Hmm, sounds like some of the newer members goofed when they forced everyone out so quickly. Knowing her, I doubt she would be willing to accept their excuses, either. They really should have followed proper procedure when they tried taking over the council." Sensing that he had pushed as far as he could, Jon quickly wrapped things up. "Well, I'll reach out to her when I can, but no promises. Call me again tomorrow sometime so we can catch up, mom. It's been a while since we talked, anyway I'll talk to you later. Bye."

He hung up and placed the phone onto the table.

"Well, that should give us a couple more days, at least to figure things out. I can use that time to get some things done. Starting with finishing up my domain properly. Then getting that house torn down in Bennett for the runes and going through all the information we brought back from the warehouse." Elinor looked stressed at the thought of how much she had to do in such a short amount of time.

"What about telling them that Oberon is back?" Kaitlyn inquired, as everyone began standing, apparently agreeing that dinner was over. "Don't we need to tell them as soon as possible?"

"We do, but we can't just tell the wrong people. That would be a bad move, I think," Elinor replied with a shake of her head. "No, we have to wait until, at least tomorrow when your grandmother calls again, or even later."

"She's right honey," Shantell agreed. "If we had just told the council tonight, they wouldn't have listened. They were focused on the territory dispute, and they would have thought she was trying to distract them. Nothing more."

"But that's insane! It's their job to listen to what their barons have to say." Kaitlyn finished losing steam.

"In theory, yes, and if it had been anyone else, I'm sure that would have been the case," Elinor assured her with a tired smile. "Except certain people on the council don't like me. Remember?"

"That is so messed up. That's not how it's supposed to work!"

"Maybe not, but it's what we have. This is politics. It's an ugly business for everyone involved." Jon rumbled in his deep voice while straightening his jacket.

Jack held the door open for everyone as they walked outside and into the approaching darkness.

Kaitlyn and Penny stepped to the side as their parents huddled together by the car doors. Jack joined the girls a moment later, staying away from his sister. Even during dinner, her hair had begun to edge towards a darker red than before.

"You going to be here in the morning?" He asked Kaitlyn.

She looked confused for a moment, before realization set in. "Right, tomorrow is Monday. I guess that means we have school." She chuckled and nodded her head. "Yeah, I'll be here. So much has happened. I completely forgot about it."

"I understand. After what happened, it will be hard to simply go back to class like nothing has changed."

"You know we're going to have to increase our training sessions starting tomorrow, right?" Kaitlyn asked while bunching Penny's hair into different shapes on the side of her head. "If the council shows up, then our bond needs to be almost complete."

"Yeah, I know. I just don't like the idea of this turning into some kind of transaction and nothing more." He stifled a snicker as the girl began weaving static electricity into the mix to keep the red hair upright.

Penny glared at her brother. "Why are you laughing? What's she doing?"

Jack took a picture and tossed the phone to his sister, who laughed.

"Ooh, give me horns, argh! Now make me a bloody unicorn, please?" Penny was at just the right age to enjoy having someone do silly things with her hair instead of getting embarrassed.

The parents had finished up their discussion by then and were enjoying watching the kids.

Finally, Jon looked at the darkening sky and then at his watch. "Come on Kaitlyn, we need to be getting home."

It would still be some time again before Elinor's domain could be considered safe, even with the new spells in place. Some things simply took time. There was a reason she took matters into her own hands when she had first moved here with Jason years before.

Kaitlyn retracted all the static electricity from the younger girl's hair. "I'll see you both tomorrow, then."

Everyone waved and then went back inside the house as the other family left. A feeling of weariness settled over them. Only Penny and Jack had any energy to spare while their parents had reached the end of their respective ropes.

"Why don't the two of you go to bed now? Penny and I can clean up and do the dishes. We'll talk more about what needs to happen next in the morning." Jack offered, locking the new front door behind them.

Jason and Elinor hesitated and then nodded. "Fine, but we do need to talk and decide on some things as a family tomorrow. This business with the council affects us all, and that's without them learning about either of you. If that happens, then all bets are off, especially if Oberon really does have a mole in the council."

Elinor continued where her husband stopped. "I'm sorry kids, I know you didn't ask for any of this."

Penny ran over and hugged both of them.

"No, we didn't," Jack began. "But I think this is better than not knowing things like the nightwalkers are out there. Besides, it's not your fault either. You tried to keep us out of this." He hugged them both tightly as well and then stepped back. "Now, go get some sleep and start thinking about what we're going to do next. We'll clean up this mess and make sure everything is locked up before going to bed."

They said their goodnights and tiredly shuffled off to bed, leaving Jack and Penny alone.

"Do you really think everything is going to turn out okay?" Penny asked him as he began spraying off the dishes before putting them in the dishwasher.

"I hope so," He gave a small shake of his head. "However, it's hard to say for sure. I know nothing about the council and how they work. Mom and dad and the others do though, and they seem to think we'll be fine."

That was enough to mollify her for the moment. He wasn't sure if he believed it himself, but it was a nice hope, regardless.

Together, they made sure everything was put away before starting the dishwasher. Then they went around and made sure all the doors were locked.

Jack risked a quick kiss against the top of Penelope's head outside her room as they separated. "Night, sis."

She gave him a quick hug and then ran into her room.

As Jack hurried to his room through the dark hallway, he swore he could see the shadows creeping closer. It was the first time he could remember being scared in his own house, and he didn't like it.

Sleep was a long time coming that night.

Chapter 28

Chapter 28

Kaitlyn was already sitting in the kitchen talking to his mother when Jack shambled out early the next morning. Even his shower had done little to wake him up, and his feet were dragging.

"What's wrong with you?" His mother wondered. "Are you feeling alright?"

"I'm fine," He mumbled, grabbing an energy drink from the fridge. "Just didn't sleep that well last night."

"You want anything to eat?"

He shook his head. "I don't think so. Thanks though, mom."

"No problem, sweetie, and don't be afraid to give me a call if you need to come home early or anything." Elinor was looking at her own busy day, but her family was important to her. It always had been and always would be.

Kaitlyn pushed back from the table and slid a notebook to his mother. "My mom wanted me to give this to you. I'm not sure what it is, but she thought it might help." With that done, she pushed Jack from the room.

"You seemed eager to leave," He said, opening the driver's side door for her.

"After realizing how powerful your mother is, I'm having a hard time talking to her. I'll just need a couple of days to readjust my thinking again, is all."

"Well, at least you're aware all it'll take is a little time to adjust. In the stories, people never seem to get that."

She snorted. "Only because of my mom and dad. You should have seen me before I talked to them. After we rescued your sister and dad, it really opened my eyes to how strong she is. When we got home Sunday morning, I was so close to freaking out and never talking to anyone in your family again."

Jack quirked his head at that. "Was what she did underneath the warehouse really that terrifying?" He thought back to what his mother had done and how the others had reacted.

"What she did in that room was... beyond anything I have ever seen done by anyone. Including those on the council. But no, it wasn't that, or rather just that. It was how efficient and calmly she did it. I could tell that she wasn't straining herself at all. My dad couldn't have done what she did, and that wasn't even her using all her strength."

Jack reached out and rested his hand on Kaitlyn's arm, risking the quick touch as she began to shout.

She took in a heaving breath and slowed the car to a stop in the middle of the road.

He didn't say anything and just let her breathe, calming herself in her own way. The sound of a car honking behind them woke her from her inner gymnastics a minute later.

"Sorry," She muttered simply, as the car lurched forward.

"It's fine," He replied. "I can't say, as I understand just how powerful my mom is, but I'm glad to know she is. I have a feeling she is going to need to be for whatever is coming."

She snorted. "That is the understatement of the century. You really lucked out with her as a parent. I doubt anyone else would have been able to keep that seal on you like she did. No one else would have had the power reserves to do so."

She pulled into the school parking lot and turned off the car with a sigh.

Jack stared at the building before them, an odd feeling welling up inside him. "I think I'm beginning to understand what you meant when you said we lived in a different world than everyone else here. After everything that happened, it's going to be hard to pretend to still be normal. At the same time though, I don't think I'm ready to simply ditch this life just yet."

He may have had only one real friend at school, but the place helped to ground him. It was normal and brought the rest of his life into focus as a result.

Kaitlyn shook her head. "That's not what I meant back then. Not at all. What you're experiencing is something different. Besides, I'm beginning to see the appeal of living a normal life."

"You are?" He hopped out of the car and around to her door.

"Well, it's a lot more freeing than my old school. I always had to be on my guard and act a certain way. I don't have to worry about that here. If nothing else, I like that."

"I can appreciate how a place like this would be freeing," Jack said after a moment as they walked side-by-side towards the school.

Classes passed in a boring blur as the duo tried to stay focused with middling success. Steve provided some entertainment during lunch period, but they only shared a single class period on Mondays.

Despite how grounding going to school was, there was simply too much other stuff going on for them to care at the moment. They wanted to know what was happening with the council, the domain, and most of all, Oberon. As soon as the last bell rang, Kaitlyn and Jack raced from their seats and out of the classroom.

The powerful engine of the car roared as Kaitlyn pressed the pedal to the floor. Only to hit the brakes a second later as another car took the turn ahead of them.

She growled and tapped the steering wheel.

"Calm down, we'll get there when we get there." He said, trying to be the voice of reason.

It was the wrong thing to say.

She turned to glare at him, her eyes flashing. "Never tell a woman to calm down!"

He leaned away and held up his hands. 'Okay, chill. We both just want to get to my house as soon as possible."

Kaitlyn's hands gripped the steering wheel so hard her knuckles popped. She gave a stiff nod and silently glared at the car in front of them, which was doing exactly the speed limit. It was an action that she seemed to be taking as a personal attack on her person.

Thankfully, they didn't have to follow the car for too long as they turned in a different direction at the stoplight.

She had calmed somewhat by the time they neared his house, though the lack of conversation had been stifling. Her parent's SUV was already parked out in front of the house when they arrived.

Kaitlyn pulled into the driveway and let out a sigh. "Sorry, I'm not sure why I reacted like that back there, but you didn't deserve that."

"Come on, let's head inside and see what they're all up to." He flashed her a smile to let her know they were alright and then opened his door.

Jack hurried around the car with his schoolbag in hand and opened her door as usual. Her attitude had bothered him initially, but their silent time in the car had given him enough time to think things over. At first, he had steamed and been emotional. Then, after a couple of minutes, he had calmed and found himself able to think more clearly.

It had been a freeing experience to realize that was all that she was doing. It hadn't been some personal attack; it was just an emotional response. That was as far as he had gotten before they reached the house. Still, he thought it was progress, or at least he hoped it was.

There would be future arguments, there always were. He knew that from watching his parents and arguing with his sister. It was all a matter of how you handled the aftermath that changed how happy you and the people around you were.

Inside they found his mother holding a tense discussion with the LaCouture's.

"Jack, Kaitlyn! Good, you've arrived," Shantell enthused seeing them walk in. "Jack, maybe you can convince your mother to allow the council inside her domain."

"Um... We were just going downstairs to practice. You three can keep arguing about whatever this is, feel free to ignore us." He tried pushing Kaitlyn towards the hallway. Jack was intent on not getting involved in whatever mess they had found themselves in this time.

"Why aren't you allowing them inside?" Kaitlyn asked, refusing to budge.

He threw up his arms in defeat and looked at his mother.

"Because I am under no obligation to let them in." She replied simply. "Now that I can restrict access, I am going to."

"But they're the council!" Jon growled, pulling at his hair. "Do you have any idea what this is going to look like to them?"

Elinor shrugged. "I don't particularly care anymore. They allowed Oberon to not only come back but also let their own power diminish. Tell me why I should let any of them inside my domain? We have phones. We can even do video calls if we really want to. What purpose does letting them come here serve?"

"Mom, don't you think you are just trying to cause problems for the sake of causing problems?" It was something she used to say to him when he was younger, and now he had the chance to turn it around on her.

The temperature of the living room grew icy as his mother glared at him. "I should have named you Brutus." She muttered.

"This isn't Rome, and you aren't Caesar."

Elinor stood in a huff and began pacing. "Fine, I will allow Jon's parents to enter, but only them. No guards or anyone else. Jack come; I'll need your help to keep everything powered while I modify the boundary spells on the fly like this. Jon, why don't you give them a call and let them know they'll be able to enter soon. Kaitlyn, you might as well come down. You two can begin practice after I'm done with him."

"What's the real reason you aren't letting the council in?" Jack asked his mother once they were ensconced inside the runed control room in the basement.

"That was mostly the truth. I'm sending a message to the council. I'm not their dog. They have been ignoring me for years, so now I'm ignoring them. If I thought I could take it even further and declare independence, I would. However, I doubt that would go over well for any of us."

"Won't this just draw more attention to the family? Isn't that the opposite of what you wanted?"

"Originally, yes, then Oberon appeared. After talking it over with your father last night, we realized that him coming back might actually be exactly what we needed. He, or whoever is masquerading as him, is going to stir things up just like last time."

"Which will take everyone's eyes off of you and whatever you are doing now." He was beginning to understand.

"Exactly, so yes, it will draw more attention initially, but only until Oberon makes his move."

"And what if he doesn't? What if he revealed himself to you just so you would cry wolf while he remained underground?"

"Then we would be screwed, but that won't happen. Don't forget, we have all the shipping manifests and other information from the warehouse. We know where they were taking whatever they were making there."

"Yeah, but he, she, whoever, this new Oberon is, must have thought you might take those, right?" Jack's head was beginning to hurt.

"Who can say, but I have to start somewhere, otherwise I'll just end up spinning in endless circles." Elinor placed her hand on the control orb, putting an end to their conversation.

Jack was familiar enough with what he needed to do and put his own hands on her shoulders. Then he waited for her to begin and did what he could to help the energy along.

The process of changing the spells at the boundary only took a couple of minutes, like she had said, but the energy draw was enormous. Still, it was only a short time later that Elinor pulled her hands off the control orb and cracked her neck.

"Thanks, Jack. I couldn't have done that nearly so quick and easily without you."

He snorted and stretched. Holding his arms in one position was surprisingly tiring. "If I wasn't here, you wouldn't be having to go through all this."

"That's not what I meant, and you know it. I wouldn't change you or Penny for anything. The two of you and your father are my world." She reached out and stroked his cheek. "Now go out there and begin your meditations with Kaitlyn. I'll be out in just a moment; I want to check on a few things real quick."

He nodded and hugged her. "I love you, mom. I don't say that enough, but I do. You're the best."

Outside the room, Kaitlyn was waiting patiently for him beside a newly drawn, runed meditation circle. "You know, in spite of everything that happened and how busy this weekend was. A small part of me still expected to find that she had found time to dig this out and inlay it properly at some point."

"She's good, even more than I originally thought apparently, but no one is that good." He nudged her inside the chalk lines. "Are you ready?"

"Are you? You just finished giving your mother a lot of energy."

"That just means there will be less pressure on you now." He shot back, sitting down on the cold concrete floor.

"That's true. Maybe I should ask her to do some big projects before all our sessions." She joked, settling down across from him.

"You nervous about seeing your grandparents?" Jack asked, holding off from reaching for her outstretched hands.

"Why would I be? They aren't coming for me. Besides, my dad's parents are alright. They're a little weird because of the generation gap, I think, but they're nice enough. They are at least interested in getting to know me, even if they're not sure how to go about it. It's mom's parents who are the pieces of work."

He nodded. That had been mostly the impression he was getting from the various conversations.

"Anyway, let's do this. We're wasting time."

Jack put his hands in hers and closed his eyes to focus. Kaitlyn sent a spark of magic into the circle and began their training session.

The runes had faded and burned away into ash once more when they separated a couple of hours later.

Kaitlyn's eyes had the familiar glow of electric blue energy, barely visible underneath the basement lights. She exhaled slowly and flexed her fingers, tiny arcs of electricity jumping from one finger to the next. Each flicker caused a different popping noise before they vanished.

"How are you feeling?"

"Good, the circle combined with you having a little less energy than before both helped, I think." Droplets of sweat plastered pieces of hair to her face as the hot basement grew even warmer from the electricity in the air.

"Well, either way, I think we're making progress." Under the meditative influence of the rune circle, Jack was able to catch glimpses of their magic mingling together. In the beginning, it had been a slow process. Now it was quicker.

"You are for sure. I can feel your control getting a little better each time we do this." She shook her head in amazement. "It's only been a little over a week and already you have made more progress than I thought you would."

He stood and brushed the ash from his hands. "I had a decent amount of motivation to get better. I didn't want to get blasted into another wall." He helped her up and together they went upstairs while continuing to joke.

All the previous awkwardness from earlier in the day had already been forgotten.

Penny was sitting at the counter with her eyes closed while their mother bustled about the kitchen. She looked up as they entered and held a finger to her lips. Pointing to the living room, she shuffled them out to where they wouldn't disturb Penelope.

"Is she doing her own training?" Jack asked, peeking around her. He had never seen his little sister doing her exercises before.

"Yes, and she needs quiet. I had to send your father out back to play in his little shed because he kept wanting to talk to us." She smiled at the thought of the man she had loved for nearly nineteen years.

"When did my mom and dad go home?" Kaitlyn wondered.

"It was shortly after I came back up. They made the call to the council and then left to prepare a spare room at your house for Jon's parents to stay in."

"My grandparents are coming tonight?" She was a little panicked at how quickly everything was happening.

"No, they were still in Massachusetts when Jon made the call. They made emergency reservations on the next available flight taking off for DIA, but it won't be here until tomorrow sometime."

"So, no brooms?" Jack was actually a little surprised by that one.

"Modern methods of travel are faster. They're fun for personal use and the occasional rescue mission in the forest, otherwise, no one really uses them anymore. Besides, they leave you open to the elements, and you get cold. Not to mention you can get spotted easily." Elinor took a quick moment to fill him in.

"Ah, that explains why the council wants your *'Running Under Cover'* spell so much."

"It's just one of many reasons, but it does help to contribute towards their desire, yes."

Kaitlyn brushed the drying strands of salty hair from her face with a sigh. "I guess I better get home then and help. Tomorrow could be a big day for us all. Depending on how they take the information, a lot could change."

Elinor scratched at her eyebrow with a nod. "I've met them a couple of times in the past, and they seemed reasonable at the time. Hopefully, that is still true tomorrow." She quietly clapped her hands. "Anyway, I have to finish making dinner and keep an eye on Penny. I'm sure I'll be seeing you tomorrow, Kaitlyn. Get home safely."

Jack showed her out and walked her to her car. "Will I see you in the morning or will you be skipping school tomorrow, you think?"

"No, I'll be here. If I stayed at home, I would only go crazy thinking over everything. It's better if I at least keep myself busy with some mundane schoolwork." Kaitlyn looked him over in the fading light with a grin. "Besides, I could do worse for company. I'll see you in the morning." She finished with a wink.

Chapter 29

"What did your parents say last night when you got home?" Jack asked as he slid into the passenger seat of Kaitlyn's car early the next morning.

"About my grandparents?" She focused on the screen in the dash and her mirrors as she backed out of the driveway.

"Yeah."

She chuckled. "They were... a little stressed out. This is going to be an official visit and not one under the best of circumstances."

Jack nodded. "I can understand that. Mom isn't too worried about the whole border situation since they started it and seems to think your grandparents will already know that. She's more worried about them learning about me and reporting my existence to the council and not taking Oberon's reappearance seriously."

"There is still another way we could use to form our bond quickly," Kaitlyn said softly.

Jack felt his breath hitch, as he became uncomfortably aware of the girl sitting a mere foot or so to his side. "I know, but I would rather not go down that path if we didn't need to." He ran a hand down his face and groaned. "Listen, can I be honest here for a minute with no judgment?"

"I suppose?" She answered hesitantly.

"That is so reassuring." He muttered sarcastically. Regardless, he still decided to continue with what he wanted to say. "Okay, so here goes. I like you, Kaitlyn. I think you're gorgeous, smart, strong-willed, and incredibly nice to those you like. You are exactly the type of woman I would like to get to know better and try dating. I would enjoy seeing if something develops between us-"

Jack rubbed his sweaty palms across the legs of his jeans. This had to be the most embarrassing and difficult thing he had ever done. "However, we have only known each other for a little over a week and a half at this point. All of that is superficial stuff for the most part. So, while I won't lie and say I'm not interested, I also won't throw away something more for a mere transaction. And that is all this would become if we did that now. It would set the tone and pace for everything going forward."

"You've given this a bit of thought, it seems." Her voice was carefully neutral, and her eyes were glued to the road.

He sighed and shrugged, angling one of the vents towards his face. "Ever since the bond was mentioned and what it meant for my life going forward, I've been thinking about little else. I don't want to have a transactional-based bond; I wanted a partnership. Thankfully, you were the one that got thrust into my life and not someone else. It has made the adjustment easier."

A smile had crept over her face by the time they pulled into the parking lot. "Honestly, I don't want that either, but if it comes down to it. What then?"

Jack was silent for a moment as she shut off the car. "I guess we'll find out then. I'd rather not think about it all before then. It all seems a little too doom and gloom if I do."

A knock on the passenger window startled them both. Steve was leaning against the side of the car, wearing a hot-pink shirt and faded blue jeans.

"What is he wearing? That shirt is hideous." Kaitlyn gasped in horror.

"Yeah, that's Steve for you. I'm more surprised that you are still surprised by him." Jack said, grabbing his bag.

"Who wouldn't be surprised seeing a shirt that color this early in the morning?" She popped open her door and slid out. "Steve, your shirt is... impressive." She finished with a strained smile.

"I know. Isn't it great?" He twirled and smoothed the sides of the ugly shirt as though he was showing it off.

"No, it really isn't. That thing is hideous. Which teacher are you trying to piss off this time?" Jack lightly plucked at the silky material. "Where did you even find this thing?"

"Online, of course. By the end of the day, this shirt is going to be an absolute wreck, with fuzzy little pills all over it. For now, though, it looks epic! And for your information, it's not just a singular teacher, but multiples this time. My homeroom teacher, AP Math, and the English teacher all annoyed me the other day. So now they get to look at this during our time together."

"So, what this shirt is a low-key form of rebellion or something?" Kaitlyn asked, trying to understand his thought process.

He grinned and nodded. "*Have you seen this color?* It's absolutely hideous. I almost went blind just putting it on this morning."

"Steve," Jack put his hand on his friend's shoulder and shook his head. "You have issues, and that truly is the ugliest shirt you have found to date." He sighed and pulled back. "But I can't help but feel it would have been better if you had worn it with some lime-green pants or something."

Kaitlyn gagged at the imagery. "There is something wrong with the two of you."

"I couldn't risk it; the power would have been too great if I wore pants that color with this shirt. I would have become unstoppable, and my reign of terror would have begun today." Steve stopped to scratch at his chin. "Actually, you know what? That doesn't sound so bad. I'll be the supervillain, and the two of you can be my right-hand lackey's."

"How about you do the supervillain thing, and we'll cheer you on from here?" Jack began walking towards the school doors.

"What are the two of you up to tonight? I assume you're doing something together." Steve asked, falling into step beside them.

"My grandparents are flying in at some point today, so we'll be hanging out with them," Kaitlyn answered.

"Wow, you're meeting her grandparents already. Talk about moving fast."

356

Jack held the door to the school open and smirked at him. "Didn't I tell you that my mom knew her parents and grandparents? Hmm, it must have slipped my mind."

"Dude, that's not cool!" Steve yelled.

Kaitlyn laughed and brushed past both of them. "Don't feel bad. Jack and I had never met each other until the other day. Our mothers had a falling out of sorts when they were our age."

Steve's eyes lit up, sensing some juicy gossip as he prepared to channel the nosy neighbor hidden deep within himself.

"Ah ah, none of that!" Jack pointed a finger at him. "I know that look. No trying to dig out the story from us. We just barely found out most of it last night ourselves. It's a family thing."

The hot pink monstrosity stared at them both for a second before nodding and shrugging. "Okay." For Steve, sometimes things were as simple as that.

The rest of the school day passed in a blur of annoying teachers calling for homework they hadn't assigned. It was only when the students all told them they had never been assigned any that they realized it had been a trap.

One that they kept falling for.

"I think the teachers here are all sadists!" Kaitlyn growled, her backpack bulging with papers. "Did they all get together and plan when to dump the most homework on us as humanly possible?"

"Are you going to be okay doing all of this work? I know we have the rest of the week to finish it all, but do you know all the material?" Jack asked as he opened the car door for her.

He was used to the petty revenge the teachers took on the students at their school. That was the way it had always been here, while he was attending, at least. It sucked, but it was predictable.

"I'll be better than Steve," She smirked. He had managed to get detention for the next week because of his shirt. "Besides, I'm sure you'll be able to walk me through anything I struggle with or don't understand."

"I suppose that's something I can do." He told her with a slight grin, relaxing into the comfortable passenger seat. "Do you think your grandparents have arrived yet?"

"Probably. I've been trying not to think about it too much."

"Yeah, they're going to be able to *'smell'* me right away, aren't they?" Jack couldn't forget how the mages had found them in the warehouse basement because of him.

"It's not a smell, but yes, they'll be able to sense you as soon as you get close enough. Your control isn't good enough to isolate or stop the energy you're always putting out."

The rest of the drive home was quiet, as they were both worried about how the two council members would react. A bland silver rental car sat outside his house when they arrived, just behind Kaitlyn's parent's SUV. She pulled in behind Elinor's car and parked.

Jack hesitated before opening his door and solemnly walking around to hers. "Let's do this. There's no point in putting it off longer than we need to."

They walked into the house and found everybody gathered in the living room.

"Hi mom," Jack said, walking over to her.

She was sitting across from an older version of Jon and a stylish woman with hair just beginning to gray, clutching a string of black pearls. Sitting on the couch in between them were Jon and Shantell, who looked relaxed.

"Hello, dear. Everyone just arrived a minute ago. I'm just getting reacquainted with Jonathan and Janet here. It's been a few years since I've seen them, after all." Elinor pulled Jack behind her.

The older version of Jon straightened a stiff leg, his eyes locked on Jack. "I've told you before to call me Jonah, Elinor, and you know you have a standing invitation to come visit us. Though I'm beginning to understand why you didn't. After how everything ended, I doubt you believed anyone was trustworthy."

Janet blew a strand of hair from her face and leaned forward. "Is this why you called us here? You thought we might show you leniency for hiding the boy?"

"He is not simply a boy; he is my son! And you would do well to remember that!" Jack's mother growled in a deathly calm voice. "I called you two out here because I believed you two to be the most even-minded and least corrupt among the current council members. This entire thing is a sham, and if you have done your duty, then you know that already."

Kaitlyn edged over to stand behind her parents.

Jonah pointed a finger at a leather cache case by his feet. "Yes, we reviewed all the files on the flight, and briefly spoke with the other Barons on the phone when we landed. Still, Elinor, you called out two council members for this dispute, not mediators, but actual council members! What were you thinking?"

"I was thinking that I no longer care what the council thinks. You guys haven't paid me or for the upkeep of my domain in years. I was in the right with what I did, yet some idiot refused to even listen. I recorded what they did and have proof.

"I was thinking that I was within my rights to demand a truth spell be used against the other barons! I was thinking that someone needed to be here so we could have a sensitive conversation." Elinor sat back and covered her eyes.

Shantell coughed. "Kaitlyn, Jack, why don't the two of you head downstairs? Go practice or do some homework while we talk. This is going to take a while."

Elinor nodded. "That's a good idea. They don't need to be here for all of this meaningless talk. They already know it all anyway."

Janet opened her mouth to say something but held back at the last moment.

"All right, we'll just do our usual practice then." Jack agreed with a shrug, looking at Kaitlyn for confirmation.

She led the way from the room and stomped down the basement stairs while he quickly stashed his backpack.

"Well, what did you think of that?" He asked after joining her down in the basement.

Kaitlyn glared up at him from her spot in the meditation circle. "They kicked us out just before anything good could be revealed."

He rolled his eyes and settled down across from her. "Obviously, I know that I was up there with you. I mean, how did you think they took my existence?"

She chewed the inside of her cheek. "I don't know. Your mother kind of just steamrolled over them and refocused the conversation, so naturally, it's hard to say."

"Yeah, you caught that?" He shook his head in wonder. "It was impressive. One second, they were talking about me, and then the next, they were focused on the border dispute. It was all done so naturally."

"Whatever. We came down here to train, so let's get to it." She held out her hands expectantly. "They'll tell us more when we're finished."

Jack grabbed hold of her hands and the two set about solidifying their bond while also subtly practicing their control.

Penny came down and interrupted them after they had been working for a little over an hour. "Mom wants the two of you to come back up now. Kaitlyn's grandparents want to speak with you both."

Jonah and Janet were in the same position as before, though they now had glasses of water sitting on the coffee table in front of them.

"We thought you might want to be up here before we started the official proceedings." They said as the entirety of the two families trickled into the living room. "After speaking with Baroness Rage, reviewing the reports, speaking with the other barons affected, and seeing the proof she had wisely collected, we have come to a decision. The baroness was entirely within her rights to retaliate, even if proper protocol dictated that she should have contacted the council first.

"However, considering her council contact is no longer available, that was not a viable option. Due to this rather egregious set of circumstances, her actions were justified, and no, there will be no punishment meted towards her. The other barons involved will not get off so lightly. Furthermore, it will be up to her whether she wishes to sell the territory back or keep it permanently as her own."

Elinor crossed her arms thoughtfully. "I was originally going to sell them back for a huge markup and use the funds to repair parts of my domain. However, now that you're here, maybe you can do something about the eighteen years' worth of back checks for both me and the domain upkeep? I'll decide what to do after that."

The married council members shared a look and slowly nodded. "We will look into that tonight after dinner, but we can offer no guarantee as to the outcome."

Jack's mother inhaled sharply, the grip she had on her hands tightening. "You had better be able to offer one. Every other baron has that guarantee. I want to know why I don't?"

The two sighed and subtly shrugged. "Moving on, we've been apprised of the situation concerning Oberon, as well as your potential bonding."

"It's not a potential bonding, dad." Jon corrected his father. "They are actively working towards it and are extremely compatible."

"That's not what he meant, and you know it. If anyone learns of his existence, he will be taken by force, and we are obligated to report him." Janet told them tiredly.

"Are you though? Are you really?" Elinor hadn't moved an inch at the threat. "I'm not going to be allowing anyone else inside my domain anytime soon. So, who is going to know if you don't tell them? And as for Oberon... I'm staying out of that particular fight this time; my domain is a neutral zone.

"The last time I went up against him, it cost me everything, and the council didn't even keep up their entire end of the deal. Let the rest of my party from back then get some more glory or train up some new disposable kids. Just make sure the council stays away from me and my family. Is that clear?"

Janet shook her head. "They'll never go for it, Elinor, you know that. All you will manage to do is divide the council and make them fight two different enemies at once with an attitude like that."

"What's there to fight about? I'm not asking to secede my domain from the council, though strictly speaking I am within my rights after this debacle, them not paying for anything, and Judy leaving without notifying me. Mainly those last two, I'm almost positive make this area eligible for such an action. All I'm asking is to be left alone, just like I have been for the last few years."

"Yes, but now you have reminded them of how powerful you are," Jonah interjected tiredly. "You were left alone because you had been mostly forgotten about, and a few of us there knew you wanted to be left alone. It's a different matter now. There are fewer members of the council who remember you from back then. The newer faces who don't know you, and the young ones who are taking over, will all want to use you."

"I don't have the stomach or desire to deal with any of these politics." Elinor groused, the temperature in the room dropping a couple of degrees.

"We know," Shantell muttered.

"What options do you see us having, or that the council might accept going forward, then?" Jack's father, Jason, asked, coming in from the kitchen. He had just finished changing from his work clothes and was dressed in a pair of jeans and a t-shirt that showed off his lean, muscled form. All that exercise and training he did was certainly not wasted, and it had come in handy down in the warehouse basement.

Remembering how useless he had been, Jack was determined to remind his father about the training he had mentioned while they were replacing the front door.

The older couple on the couch shared a look and then shrugged helplessly. "Honestly, it's impossible to say with these new kids. With the old guard, they may have taken your offer on the grounds that you forgot you were owed any money. However, these younger members are all desperate to make a name for themselves, to create some kind of ephemeral legacy."

Janet snorted at her husband's words. "A legacy takes time to create. I have no idea why they all want to rush it so badly. That said, if one of them is a mole for Oberon, like you believe, that could help your case. Or it could hinder you. It really depends. Does this Oberon want revenge, or you simply out of the way?"

"All we can do is tell them what you want, and offer our own suggestions while reporting everything that we have learned today," Jonah informed them.

"And what will you tell them about Jack and the bond he is forming with your granddaughter?" Elinor asked, reaching for her husband's hand.

Chapter 30

"You play dirty Baroness Rage. Has anyone ever told you that?" Janet grumbled, reaching for her water.

"It's come up before, yes." She replied dryly.

"Are you sure that you eliminated all the people who might have recognized what he was that night?" Jonah questioned, looking at a message on his phone.

"There was a demon there, but its master and I have an agreement. It won't say anything when it comes back to life. Everyone else we took care of."

He grunted and showed the screen to his wife before turning it off. "Then news of him got out some other way. That was the rest of the council asking if you truly did have a son who was an unregistered *'potere generantis'*."

"Sorry, Elinor, Jason, but they already know about him. It looks like someone told them this morning after we had already left."

Elinor cursed. "How will this change things, then?"

"We won't know until we speak with the rest of the council. Some may see reason, while others may believe he is too great a prize to pass up.

In which case, even your reputation won't protect him. Finishing the bonding process between the two would be best... How far along are they?" Janet finished hopefully.

"They only started last week," The words caused an obvious deflation in the older woman. "However, they are extremely compatible and have been making quick progress."

"Lead with that next time! I'm getting old. My heart can't take that kind of abuse."

"Please, you're never going to die, you old bat. Besides, you don't look a day over fifty." Elinor retorted. "Kaitlyn, how far along do you think the two of you are?"

"Uh, I'm not sure, maybe a third of the way there... a little less?" She answered uncertainly.

"So, in the best-case scenario, you need another two weeks?" Shantell asked her.

She nodded hesitantly. "Three would be best, but yeah, something along those lines, I think. I'm just judging off how our energy is mixing. In case you've forgotten, there wasn't any information on this process available. We're both just fumbling around in the dark here. We could be doing things in an extremely inefficient manner, or even all wrong."

"Does it feel right at least?" Elinor prodded.

"I guess it's happening naturally alongside our practice sessions."

Janet sucked in a breath. "You weren't kidding before when you said they were compatible. If all they are doing is practicing and still forming their bond, that might be an understatement."

Shantell grinned. "We told you-"

The sound of a muffled ringtone cut her off as Elinor scrambled to pull her phone from her pocket. "Everyone quiet!" She waved their protests down and accepted the call. "Amaymon, I was expecting you to reach out to me a day ago. What happened?"

She pressed the phone tight against her ear; her face growing steadily more red with every passing second. "Are you sure that's the route they want to go down?" She nodded. "No, I appreciate the heads up. Say hello to Lily and the kids for me. Yeah, I'll talk to you later. Bye."

"How's Lily doing?" Shantell asked, skirting around the main topic of the phone call.

"You could call her, you know? Phone reception isn't that bad down there."

"True, but I only knew her through you. It never felt right to call her after everything that happened."

Elinor spun the phone between her fingers and sighed. "You should have called her. She's lonely down there. Anyway, we can talk about that later. Right now, we have a bigger problem that we need to deal with. The demons have decided to not side with anyone in this coming fight with Oberon."

"I sense a *'But'* coming. There usually is with them," Jonah said wryly.

"Yup, and it's mainly so they can play both sides of the field this time. Apparently, they didn't like not being able to do what they wanted last time. It was too restrictive to their chaotic natures."

"Wait, aunt Lily and Uncle Amar are demons?" Jack knew they weren't actually related, but it's what the duo had always wanted to be called when they came to visit. Which wasn't often. The last time had been a couple of years ago by that point.

"Yes, and your seal nearly unraveled during their last visit. I haven't been able to risk inviting them back ever since. They aren't mages. There was a little more wiggle room for other beings to be around you, especially when you were younger.

"Of course, that began to change as you grew older, and the seal weakened with age despite my efforts. It would have failed at some point, no matter what." She cracked her neck and sighed. "It's probably for the best it happened now."

"Huh, I always wondered why they never visited again."

"Does that mean Aunt Lily can't come to visit us now?" Penny asked, holding onto her father. Her memories of the woman were a little hazy, but they were still there.

"I'm not sure. Amaymon said he'll keep his people as uninvolved in what's coming as possible. If orders come from higher up though, that won't be possible."

Jonah sighed and stood, offering his wife a helping hand. "This visit has given us more to think about than we originally anticipated. We'll need some time to decide how to proceed in regard to Jack and our

370

granddaughter. We'll let them know of our decision regarding the territory dispute, and about Oberon's reappearance."

Janet took his hand and stood beside him. "Just know that his existence changes everything. Now that they know about Jack, the odds of them accepting your terms to be left alone as a neutral zone have all but vanished. I would start thinking about what else you might want. I'm sorry Elinor, I know this isn't how you wanted things to turn out."

"Know they aren't, but it doesn't change that I'm not opening the borders of my domain anytime soon. The council needs to prepare for war with Oberon and whatever else is coming, not worry about taking my son from me."

"Some of the old council might have agreed with you on that…" Jonah said, walking to the front door. "But that's not how the council is run anymore."

"I guess Oberon will win this time then because I'm not going to get lucky a second time. That's all that happened that first time, I got lucky and caught him unawares." Elinor opened the door and led them out. "Take care, and I'll see you tomorrow."

A few minutes later the house was empty save for the normal members of their family.

"Does it seem like they weren't really taking the Oberon threat seriously to anyone else?" Jack wondered. "I mean you made him out to be this big bad guy and they brushed it aside like he was the villain of the week."

"It's odd for sure, I don't know if they're not taking me seriously or just plain don't believe me." Elinor clapped her hands. "Either way, that's enough of that, I've done what I can. Everything else is on them. It's time to eat."

"Are you going to train Penny after dinner, mom?" Jack asked as they crowded into the kitchen.

"That was the plan, why, did you need something?"

"No, I was just checking to see if you were going to need more help downstairs later is all. They loaded us down with homework again today. We got off light last week, and now they're making up for it."

"There is something else that both of you need to start finding time for," Their father said, his fork twirling around the pasta noodle. "You both know that I have been training for a while now."

They nodded; each of them had seen the results of his efforts just the other day.

"Well, I mentioned to Jack that I wanted to start training him each weekend, to get him a little more prepared. Then I talked things over with your mother, and we decided that you both needed to start training. You need to know how to defend yourselves in case something like this happens again.

"Penny might have the option of using her magic in the future, but as we saw magical fire will keep burning for a long time. If she ever makes a mistake, then an entire building could go up in flames. Then there is Jack, who we still have no idea what will happen when he bonds. He may have access to magic, he may not. We just don't know."

"Am I really that dangerous?" Penny asked in a small voice, her fork dropping onto the plate.

"Your fire is sweetie, just like mine is. However, with great enough control it's no longer a problem unless you want it to be."

Jack lazily spun his fork on a single tine. "I'm guessing you're mentioning this because you came up with a different plan than before. When were you thinking of having us do these sessions?"

"I can start your training tomorrow night after I get home from work. I'll need to pick up some equipment on my way home. I'll decide if we're going to with something more freestyle or structured like taekwondo then. All three of you will start going with me to the shooting range again on Saturdays as well."

"That's... going to keep us really busy." Jack finished lamely. He guessed he wouldn't be finishing any videogames for the foreseeable future.

"I know, sorry, but this is how things are going to have to be if we want the two of you to be prepared. We should have started you both in self-defense classes years ago but didn't." Jason cracked his neck. "I don't expect you to turn into world champions or something overnight. I just want you to be able to protect yourselves if something happens. That's all."

"Yeah, I think we get that, dad."

Elinor changed the topic of conversation after that, lifting the atmosphere around the table considerably.

***

Jack absently twirled his pencil around his thumb and fingers while he studied. He was making decent headway on the first of the subjects when a call from Kaitlyn came in.

"Hey, you decided you needed help with homework after all?" He joked.

"What, oh, maybe, I'm not sure yet. I've been working on the math section which I can do just fine. No, I wanted to talk to you about something I just overheard."

He pressed the phone closer to his ear and quickly glanced at the closed door. "Okay, what's going on?"

"The council doesn't believe that Oberon is back. They think it's all a ploy."

He inhaled sharply. "A ploy that's backed up by your family, as well as the demons?"

"Yup, and Jack?"

"Yeah?"

"They just declared war on your mother for hiding you. They're coming to get you and take the territory away from her."

He cursed. "I've got to tell my mom."

"Don't worry about it. My mom is talking to her right now."

"How did this happen? What changed between this morning when they learned of me and now?"

"My grandparents reported in." She told him softly. "They first told them their decision, and I don't know what else was said after that. When they were done with the call though, their faces were pale, and they had been relieved of their positions on the council."

"I'm sorry, that must have been a big blow to them."

"They're going to ask your mother for permission to move here after they go back and gather up all their stuff. With you helping your mom, they don't see a way for the council to succeed in taking this domain from her."

"Yeah, but I can only keep helping her for another couple of weeks until our bond is completed. I won't be able to help her after that, right?"

"You might still be able to send her energy." She began slowly, elongating the words. "However, no one but me will be able to take it from you anymore... I don't know. Again, half of what we know from the rumors and books seems to be wrong. According to what my mom originally told me once our bonding process got started the amount of energy you could pass to other people would grow smaller. Has that happened to you at all?"

Jack thought back to when he had helped his mother each time and shook his head, his brows furrowed. "Not that I can determine anyway. But that does present another problem going forward. I still can't control my energy enough to start sending it to anyone on my own yet. I've been depending on you and my mom to start pulling on it before I start doing anything. If she can't even touch it, then I won't even be able to do that."

"We'll figure things out in the morning Jack. I just wanted to give you an update and tell you what was coming our way. Mom and dad have already decided to stand here with your mom, and your family. We'll be staying, so we can figure things out together."

A chill ran through him at that. He hadn't even considered the possibility that they might leave. It had never come up in any of their conversations before.

"Right, well, I guess I'll see you in the morning. Night, Kaitlyn." He hung up as she returned the farewell.

He dropped the phone onto his desk and leaned back in his chair. A ripple of stress ran through him, causing his skin to perk up in goosebumps all over.

"Mom!" He called out. "We have a problem." He wasn't going to wait until it was too late to help her reinforce all the domain spells this time.

Epilogue

"**A**re you sure you want to ignore the baroness for now? Her strength is greater than we had anticipated."

"That's exactly why we are going to leave her alone. The reports that her power had diminished were greatly exaggerated and outright false. Going up against Elinor Rage would only harm us right now. Instead, we will move ahead with the plan, and cut her off from everyone. Let her worry about all the problems we've ensured she has closer to home and fighting her own people instead of us."

"I understand. We'll keep her occupied so she can't even think about worrying what you might be up to, my master. What about her son? Our reports indicate that he is quite the powerful *'potere generantis'*. It could be a mistake to leave him alone."

"It's already too late for us in regards to the boy. Do you really think she hasn't already bound him or come up with another way to keep him from us at this point? He is just an excuse for you to use, nothing more. A wasted opportunity for sure, but not one we will focus on. Is that understood?"

"Yes, as you will it, my Oberon."

"Good, now let us prepare for the next stage of my plan. Has everything been installed at the newest lab?"

Book 1 - End

Afterword

Thank you for reading the first book in my new Urban Fantasy series 'The Well Within', and I hope you enjoyed it.

Please consider leaving a review or a rating for the book, feedback is imperative for an indie author. You can follow this link to be redirected to The Well Within Amazon product page to leave a quick review or rating. So please, take the time to click on that hopefully fifth star and type out a few words about how much you liked/enjoyed the book!

If you don't want to review it, then please think about leaving a comment or even just a quick message. Remember, positive feedback is always welcome. The more good reviews I get on a book the more likely I am to continue writing that series. That holds especially true when it comes to new series such as this one, if I don't see a positive result from the readers then the priority for the next book gets placed later in my queue.

Amazon doesn't update readers when an author comes out with a new book unless you follow that author on the store. Make sure you click this link and then click on the follow button. Then Amazon will update you a few weeks after my next book comes out.

If you want to get notified of my books the day that they come out, please sign up for the mailing list below. You'll know as soon as I release new books, including my upcoming new series.

Click here to sign up.

Other places you can keep up to date on me and my works:

My Website

My Patreon Page

My Author Page on Facebook

There are a few more places where you can find me, and several other genre authors, hanging out. Here are my favorite LitRPG/GameLit community Facebook groups.

https://www.facebook.com/groups/UniverseofGods - Universe of Gods – My Group

Acknowledgements

I would like to thank my alpha readers, my family, who spend endless hours reading and re-reading everything I write, as well as seeking out any plot holes and typos. It has taken me a long time to get to the point in my life where I can actually sit down and write like I have wanted to for so very long, to all the people that have encouraged me over the years and helped make this possible, I thank you!

About the Author

Joshua Kern was born in a little town situated somewhere in Ohio and raised in an even smaller town some place in Colorado. He attended University for a time, where he discovered that while he enjoyed Electrical Engineering and Computer Science his true passion lay in writing. He lives primarily in Colorado but has been known to move around as the need arises. When not writing, Joshua enjoys riding motorcycles, reading anything he can get his hands on, and anime.

Other Books by Joshua Kern

Refton & Thomas

Forgotten Spies

Forgotten Child

The Game of Gods

Arc 1 – Human

The Beginning

The Death of Champions

Arc 2 – Demi-God

Fragments

A Tower Novella

Pieces of Divinity

Arc 3 – God

The Dungeon Alaria

Arc 1 – Integration

The Dungeon Alaria

The Creator's Daughter

Arc 2 – ??

The Nameless Chronicles

Portals of Albion

Portals of Change

The Well Within

The Well Within

Stand Alone

The Ridden

Duologies & Box Sets

The Game of Gods: Arc 1 Duology Box Set

The Dungeon Alaria: The World of Alaria Arc 1 Duology Box Set